THE
TERMINALS

THE
TERMINALS

Royce Scott Buckingham

THOMAS DUNNE BOOKS
St. Martin's Griffin ∧∧ New York

THOMAS DUNNE BOOKS.
An imprint of St. Martin's Press.

THE TERMINALS. Copyright © 2014 by Royce Scott Buckingham. All rights reserved. Printed in the United States of America. For information, address St. Martin's Press, 175 Fifth Avenue, New York, N.Y. 10010.

www.thomasdunnebooks.com
www.stmartins.com

Designed by Molly Rose Murphy

The Library of Congress Cataloging-in-Publication Data is available upon request.

ISBN 978-1-250-01155-8 (hardcover)
ISBN 978-1-250-02105-2 (e-book)

St. Martin's Griffin books may be purchased for educational, business, or promotional use. For information on bulk purchases, please contact Macmillan Corporate and Premium Sales Department at 1-800-221-7945, extension 5442, or write specialmarkets@macmillan.com.

First Edition: October 2014

10 9 8 7 6 5 4 3 2 1

This novel is dedicated to my steadfast beta reader and thirteen-year-old son, Aspen Buckingham, who is very nearly the target audience for The Terminals. *Thanks, bud, for all the advice.*

Thank you also to my incredible wife, Cara, and to Aiden, my intuitive nine-year-old, who brainstorms concepts with us at the kitchen table.

Shout out to Kaylee, Katelyn, Captain Eric, Dr. Dave, and the many others who read portions of the book and subjected themselves to vigorous cross-examination during the writing process.

THE
TERMINALS

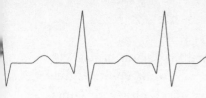

PROLOGUE

With her enhancements, she was faster and stronger than them, but she was also outnumbered and had no weapon.

Siena broke cover and fled, hurdling rotten logs and dodging treacherous thickets. Even during the day it was dark beneath the lush, dripping tree canopy, which filtered out 80 percent of the sun, but her unnaturally wide pupils darted back and forth, spotting every root threatening to trip her up, every thorn waiting to tear her flesh. Her bare teenage feet danced around them, finding flat, spongy ground again and again.

She glanced about for a loose stick she could use as a club, her long auburn hair flying right and left. There was no time to stop and break off a dead limb—she could hear the faint thump and rustle of their tennis shoes less than twenty yards back.

She hit a thinner patch of forest and saw a hint of daylight above. Grabbing a low-hanging branch, she swung up into a tree and climbed for the sky. The ground was quickly obscured behind her, and, for a moment, she thought she was clever. But she surprised a small orange monkey and sent it screeching through the limbs. They'd know exactly where she was now—thirty feet in the air directly above them.

Siena left the safety of the trunk and tiptoed out onto a thick branch. It bent under her weight as it thinned, but her balance was exquisite, not merely as good as a ballerina's, but better. It wouldn't be for long, though. Running away meant no more TS-8. Her extraordinary abilities would fade to normal, like those of her pursuers, who had only just begun the enhancement process. But it was a price she was willing to pay for even a slim chance to live.

A dart whispered up from below and struck the thin branch inches from her foot, injecting the tree with an inky fluid she knew all too well. They were coming up, and they would almost certainly stick her with the next throw. The thin branch dipped like a precarious diving board. She pushed down with her legs, and when the limber branch rebounded upward, she jumped.

Vertical orientation was crucial when canopy jumping—the way the monkeys did it. She flew toward the next tree. Its limbs overlapped those of the tree she'd left, but they were too thin at their tips to support her. She needed to break through to the thicker inner branches. It was a great distance to cover without a run, perhaps twenty-five feet, impossible for an unenhanced person. But she *was* enhanced. She crashed through the thinner branches. They drew long red lines down her forehead and cheeks as they bent against her face. The scratches might have horrified a normal girl her age—a girl going to formals or having her sorority photo taken— but Siena ignored them, bursting through the canopy toward the thicker wood near the trunk. She tilted her head to dodge the point of a branch that might have stabbed her right eye, and stayed focused, reaching for two different limbs. Her palms slapped wood, closed around it, and then she bobbed, suspended, as the branches groaned against her weight thirty feet above the earth.

There was no time to celebrate the jump. She was still darting distance from her former tree. She yanked herself atop the limbs and climbed, bursting through the canopy's upper leaves into the light. When she looked back, she saw two dark shapes rising in the tree behind her, silhouetted against the light. The evening sun hung low in the sky behind them. She turned and tiptoed along another branch away from it, hurrying east, and when she reached its springy end she jumped again.

She flew through the tops of the trees, learning more with each leap, rapidly becoming adept. She was beating them. But helicopter blades thumped in the distance. Her heart sank. Her head start wouldn't matter. As soon as the pilot spotted her, the chopper would come for her too, and it was faster, much faster. Siena frowned—it wasn't any safer atop the canopy than on the ground.

The ocean came into view ahead, a wrinkled blue blanket thrown over the world beyond the lush carpet of forest. She made for it, climbing to a height that allowed her to see up and down the coast. The rocks of the fifty-foot seaside cliffs jutted beyond the tree line to the north. She skittered out on a branch and jumped down toward them, landing and jumping again, using her descent to add speed. A look back confirmed that the others were still following. They'd gone to the ground and were running. She had to lose them, she thought, or take them out. She preferred the second option, but her odds against multiple armed opponents were fifty-fifty at best. She could hear the helicopter approaching now. The pilot had seen her, or they'd radioed to the chopper. Now she was being tracked from the air.

There were more than two behind her on the ground. The pair in the tree were merely the vanguard. Her mind clicked through her advantages. Speed, strength, dexterity. Too few against too many. Knowledge of the forest was an important one, however. She'd been here for nearly a year. The new recruits hadn't. She hopped from branch to branch, fought down through leaves to the ground, and was running again. The helicopter wouldn't be able to see her. The other kids would have to chase her down.

Siena heard twigs snapping behind her. They were clumsy, but closing in. Her feet were bloody. If she'd had shoes, she might have simply outrun them. Instead, she made for the cliff. There was a place she knew, a secret spot she'd found during training.

She could hear panting now. The two were close, one very close. She saw a familiar tree, and then recognized a patch of white-speckled shrubbery. And when the cliff edge suddenly appeared beyond it, she was ready.

Her momentum carried her over, but she kept her legs beneath her and spun 180 degrees, hands darting out to grab foliage and arrest her descent just as she drew even with a small cave in the cliffside. She swung, and her momentum threw her inside, where she skidded hard across the cavern floor into the solid rock wall. It hurt, but she didn't cry out. Instead, she bit her lip and waited, breathless.

Footsteps rapidly approached above, followed by a cry of surprise.

The boy who plummeted past Siena looked about nineteen, like her. Like boys she used to date in her other life, her life *before*. He clutched a dart in his fist as though it were a lifeline. It wasn't. She saw a sudden, horrible realization in his eyes as they met hers for a split second on the way by, and then he continued down, his limbs flailing in the air. He abandoned the dart and grabbed at the cliffside foliage, but his hands slid past or yanked it loose without gaining purchase. He tried to get his feet beneath him, but his orientation remained horizontal. Falling sideways, his head slammed against a rock outcropping with the hollow cracking sound of a coconut bursting on pavement. Siena didn't watch him fall the rest of the way. She didn't need to. It was already over.

The others would come and see, she realized. If they searched the area they would find her. She quickly removed her backpack and threw it down after the crumpled pile of male flesh on the beach that had been a teen boy only moments earlier.

The next set of footsteps arrived above her as the waves began to wash her pack of supplies and the boy's body out to sea. They were heavier, booted footsteps, according to her sharp ears. Adult footsteps. They stopped, and there was silence for a time, and then a radio crackled to life. The male voice that belonged to the footsteps reported the scene below.

"This is personal trainer," said the voice. "Siena's term has finally expired. And I regret to report that Peter has graduated early. . . ."

Siena hugged her knees in her hideaway as the ocean finished its indifferent cleanup work, leaving the beach empty.

"Looks like we're gonna need another kid."

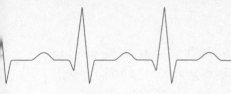

CAM'S PLAYLIST

1. HELLO MISTER GRIMM 🔊
by The Fallen Angels

2. ROADKILL
by Suicide Squirrel

3. SOUL ON A STICK
by Dog Breath

*"Hello, I've got some news for you.
It's not all good, but it's all true."*

God just screwed me over, Cameron Cody thought.

Cam lay in the adjustable hospital bed wearing earbuds with his music playing low and slow, like the tragic theme song of a nineteen-year-old who was supposed to be the Western Washington University soccer team's starting right wing this year. "Wingman," they called him.

He rolled over and glanced at his heart-rate monitor. It beeped steadily. *Still alive*, he thought. *For now.*

He felt wrong in the bed, like he wasn't supposed to be there. He was supposed to be heading out to parties on Garden Street in a few weeks, getting a tux for homecoming a month later, and making the dean's list by the end of the quarter. More important, he was supposed to be renting the ultimate party house with Kristi Banks and five other friends this term. *Kristi friggin' Banks.* Heck, he was just supposed to get a girlfriend at all. He was supposed to finish college, interview for jobs, and then make his own way in the world.

He was not supposed to be dying.

The stamped metal label on the molded plastic rail beside him read DURA-CARE PNEUMATIC BED. He'd named his bed Numo. Numo boasted 124 different positions—more than the kama sutra—all of which Cam had tried in the first hour via the touch screen controls. He found Numo disturbingly comfortable.

No wonder people come here to expire, he thought. *They make it easy. They give a guy a few months to live, this killer bed, all you can eat, Covert Ops with a wireless controller, some medication to take the edge off, then bingo! Next contestant, please.*

Corridor 3C outside his door, on the other hand, felt sterile. The blank white walls made it seem freakishly wide, and it echoed like a canyon. It smelled like bleach every morning too. When he left his room, he felt like he was entering a whitewashed institutional version of the afterlife. Corridor 3C was the hospital's "death wing," a name the staff used when they didn't think patients were listening.

The noise outside of his door was his mom and dad crying. They also thought he couldn't hear them. But he could. It was embarrassing. Like his buttless gown. With flowers on it.

Cam groaned. *Somebody please tell me I don't have to die in this.*

The sad thing was, when he thought about it, he was already dead. Get good grades? To prepare for what? Improve his dribbling? It's not like he'd be perky come playoff time. And women? He'd spent his younger years being everyone's nonthreatening, nice-guy buddy, and helping his more aggressive friends get the girls. And now that he'd finally put on twenty pounds and figured out how to wear his wispy blond hair so he didn't look like a bowl-cut dork—the secret was spray gel—some freaky disease nobody had ever heard of was going to kill him.

But there's Kristi, he thought. She was perhaps the one upside to the whole dying deal. When he'd first told her, she'd felt sorry for him, and she'd lain on the couch and hugged him for the entire late show. Now maybe they'd kiss. A lot.

Just then there was a polite, almost apologetic knock on his door. *Kristi*. Right on time. He pulled the covers up over his drafty flowered gown.

"Yo!" Cam answered. It was too loud, he decided, and obnoxious. "I mean, come in, please," he tried instead.

The door opened, and Kristi Banks peeked her blond head in. "Is this a good time?" she asked.

Unless you want to come back when I'm dead, Cam thought.

Kristi slid inside, but clung to the door. She wore a snug Western T-shirt and jeans with heels. Her fluffy, golden hair cascaded over her shoulders and flowed around her curves like a happy river winding through the hills. Cam couldn't help but stare. He heard a rapid beeping and quickly threw a blanket over his tattletale heart-rate monitor.

"Sure," Cam replied. "Thanks for coming."

"Becky said I should," Kristi explained. "I mean, I wanted to, but I wasn't sure if it was okay."

"It's A-okay."

She hesitated, cringing at the sight of all the medical apparatus. Tubes and wires were strung around him like Christmas lights.

"I know I look like a marionette," Cam said. "But I'm not contagious."

Kristi managed a weak smile. "Of course not." She walked to the edge of the bed, where she did *not* kiss him a lot, or even a little. She was so close that Cam could smell the artificially scented apple shampoo she used on her amazing hair.

"How do you feel?" she asked.

"Strangely fine. Even my regular doctor thought I was healthy. Then this specialist did a CAT scan and found a tumor in my head. But honestly, I feel like riding out to the Whatcom Falls Park and going for a swim in my underwear. Can you drive?"

"You're not too sick?"

"Well, I *am* going to die, if that's what you mean. But my symptoms won't get bad for a while. I'm just here for more testing today with the tumor doc. I should be up and around tomorrow."

Kristi nodded carefully. "Will you be up and around the entire term?"

It seemed an odd question. Then Cam realized what she was getting at. Kristi stood waiting, tapping her long, fake fingernails on Numo's metal rail. Cam felt the skinny nice guy awaken inside him. He tried to fight it, but couldn't.

"If you need to find another roommate, I understand," he said finally.

Kristi looked mildly surprised, but didn't argue. "Really? Because Ben Richards needs a place."

Cam saw her eyes dance when she mentioned Ben's name. He winced. "It's totally okay," Cam added, "seriously."

"You're so nice." She almost hugged him, but wires hung between them. She just patted his shoulder instead. There were a few more uncomfortable questions from her, a few more awkward jokes from him, but still no kisses.

"Well, I should go and let you rest," Kristi said. She patted him on the elbow this time, another completely uninteresting location. Then she edged toward the door, fingering her pink cell phone in her pants.

"I've been lying in bed all morning. I'm not tired."

"But you probably need some time to think."

Cam thought Kristi probably needed some time to think about who she could call that wouldn't be dying in a hospital bed on homecoming night. Ben Richards, perhaps.

"I'm glad I came," she said.

Cam forced a smile. "Me too."

She ducked out, and Cam could hear her fingernails clicking on her phone as she fled down corridor 3C.

The door had hardly closed shut when Cam's sister shoved it

back open. Trish was five years older than him, too old to be his friend and too young to have a mothering instinct. The result was that she found him annoying. She hadn't gone to college—not the type. She lived on the freeway side of town in one of two hundred apartments that looked exactly the same, and she sold clothes at the Ready-to-Wear store by the mall.

Trish stood beside Cam's bed in approximately the same spot Kristi had.

"Sorry if I was ever bitchy to you," she said.

She was not specific—the apology seemed designed to cover all the mean things she'd ever done or said to him in one fell swoop. Despite its brevity, it was clear to Cam she'd been working on her speech. It was just the right mix of noncommittal regret and profane defiance to let him know that their parents had put her up to it. She said it quickly, and then waited for him to accept it.

"Okay, thanks," Cam said, though it didn't seem fair to let her off the hook so easily for a lifetime of resenting him. He knew, however, that she'd immediately complain to their parents if he didn't, and he wasn't about to spend an hour of his dwindling life "working out" the issue, with their folks playing emotional referee.

At least she's efficient at cutting through the mandatory touchy-feely stuff, Cam thought.

Having delivered her speech, Trish stood chewing her gum loudly. She blew a small bubble, which popped and left a pink spot on her lip. The spot bounced up and down as she talked.

"Things have sucked since we found out," she said.

"Uh-huh," Cam agreed.

"Mom and Dad have been a total mess. They break down crying every time I need to talk to them about something important."

"That's really inconvenient."

"Don't worry about it. It's not your fault you got sick."

"Yeah, I didn't mean to."

"You're funny. I'm gonna miss you."

"I'm not going to die for, like, another twelve months."

"Yeah, well, I'll miss you after that, I mean."

There was no hug or even a pat on the shoulder. Cam didn't take offense. They hadn't had physical contact with one another since she'd hit puberty and instituted the "no touching" rule, not even when passing the butter at dinner. Cam's skinny nice-guy persona was still lurking, urging him not to make a big deal out of it. Trish seemed to be waiting for him to say he would miss her too, but he didn't think he would when he died, and he hated to lie.

"Thanks for coming to see me," he said.

"No problem." She smiled as softly as was possible for her. "I was on my way to work anyway."

The visitors kept coming.

Some guys from the soccer team dropped by with his jersey. Number nineteen. His age. It was neatly folded in a display box, where it would remain for all eternity, unless he broke the glass to get at it due to some sort of soccer emergency. The nickname "Wingman" was scrawled across the purple velvet backing in bright silver. Cam pretended to like it.

His mom's aunt and her husband arrived next. They were very old and had somehow known him "since before he was born," though Cam wasn't sure how that worked. They talked about other people they knew who were dying from various diseases and touched his face with dry, wrinkly hands like a couple of grim reapers. Cam had grown tired of explaining that he felt fine, for now, and they seemed disappointed that his condition wasn't more painful or interesting, so he began to make up strange sensations. He told them that he sometimes felt like spiders were burrowing through his hair and mentioned with a straight face that he'd had green stool samples lately. He stopped only when his great-aunt told the nurse and she rushed in to see what was wrong with him.

Finally, Mason walked through the door. Mason was his age, but lived in the twenty-four-hour quiet dorms and played Hero-

Quest online instead of soccer. And the odds that Mason would go to the homecoming dance were very low. But Mason had lived three houses down from Cam since elementary school, knocked on the door every Saturday to see if Cam could come out and play, and had been in Boy Scouts with him when they were eleven. Mason had even skipped the end-of-the-year elementary school trip to the water park in fifth grade to play Risk and Stratego with Cam when he'd had his tonsils out. Now that they were in college, they didn't hang out so much, but Mason didn't give Cam grief about his sports friends, and he still knocked on the door once in a while on Saturdays.

"Nice gown," Mason said.

Cam laughed for the first time all day. "You like it? I think they have your size, if you're jealous."

Mason laughed too. He gave Cam a mind reader's salute, holding two fingers to each temple and humming. Then he grew quiet, studying the heart-rate monitor and the chart hanging from the bed. "You get a second opinion?"

"This guy's a specialist. It's all he does."

"So what's your strategy now?"

"What do you mean?" Cam said. "I do treatment, obviously."

"I heard treatment can't save you."

"True. It's very unlikely."

"Hoping for something unlikely isn't necessarily the obvious thing to do."

"Then what do you suggest?"

"Sympathy hookup?"

"Tried it. Didn't work."

"Kristi?"

"Yep."

"Wow. I admire the attempt." Mason tapped his narrow chin. "You know, you've always been a 'doer,' Cam. I remember when we were in high school and you volunteered our crappy little band to play the end-of-the-year party just to scare us into practicing more."

"Yeah. You were so mad."

"It made us good, though," Mason said. "Best thing I was ever forced to do against my will."

Cam watched his friend's face, but there was no sarcasm.

"It seems weird to think of a doer like you lying here in a bed not doing anything," Mason continued.

"Feels weird too."

"So . . . *do* something."

Just then, Dr. Singh walked in. The specialist. The tumor doc.

"I hope you're not giving my favorite patient advice contrary to mine," the grinning doctor said.

Mason gave Cam another salute. "I shall return as soon as I have a plan to vanquish the evil doctor who has condemned you to death." He winked at Dr. Singh, and then exited with a flourish.

Dr. Singh stepped to the edge of the bed. He was Indian. India Indian, not Native American. He hadn't told Cam he was dying at first. In fact, the perpetually chipper doc had come in smiling to talk about the results of the first set of tests. *Smiling!* He had the air of an expert and the credibility of a specialist. He flew in just for Cam's case, knew the disease like the back of his hand, and the local doctors gave him a wide berth.

"You are a remarkable specimen," he'd said in his thick accent. He apparently traveled all over the United States to find cases like Cam's. Confident guy. Friendly too. But "remarkable," in Cam's case, wasn't good, and the smiles didn't keep the traveling doc from eventually delivering the news. Death. A year or less. Ninety-some percent sure, which easily rounded up to one hundred in Cam's mind.

"I'd like to run some more tests," Dr. Singh said. "We're hoping that . . ."

Cam pretended to listen, but he'd already seen the vague image of the killer tumor in his head in the exact spot where the books said a kidney bean–shaped shadow meant you were doomed. It looked more like a pear to Cam, but he was pretty sure any silhouette of a food item in your primary somatic sensory cortex was bad news. The rest of it didn't matter—the name of the disease, how it worked, why it chose his life to mess up. Didn't know. Didn't care. Didn't listen. All he knew was that he sure as heck wasn't going to see the world now.

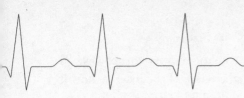

CAM'S PLAYLIST

2. ROADKILL 🔊
   by Suicide Squirrel

3. SOUL ON A STICK
   by Dog Breath

4. WELCOME TO THE ZOO
   by The Way Chunky Monkeys

*"Gotta have fleet feet to
play in the street."*

The sun abandoned Cam, escaping over the western horizon, but he didn't fall asleep. Instead, he wandered through a half-waking dream in which he could feel something coming, but couldn't quite see or stop it. He moved slowly, like he was running through sand, and a strange guy was sitting next to . . .

Cam's eyes popped open. A strange guy dressed in a tan jumpsuit and leather gloves was sitting next to his bed. He was obviously not a doctor or nurse, and visiting hours had ended two playlists ago. He appeared to be around thirty and reasonably fit—neither fat nor skinny. His ears were an irritated red color, and his hair was sticking up. *Like he's been wearing a headset,* Cam thought. The man loomed over Cam's bed, as though inspecting him.

Cam sat up suddenly. "Whoa! Dude! What the hell?"

"How are you feeling, Cam?" the man asked, unfazed.

"Are you a doc?"

"Do I look like a doc?"

"No. So who are you?"

"I'm someone with an opportunity for you."

"Maybe you didn't get the memo," Cam said, settling back into his pillow, "but I'm sorta fresh out of opportunities."

The man grinned. "Oh, but I *did* get the memo. And your medical chart. And your transcripts, your standardized test scores, your application for volunteer service opportunities. I've been a busy guy for the last few days. I even have your soccer stats—no goals last year, but six assists. You're a team player. Your report cards say you also listen carefully and follow directions well."

Cam was fully awake now, all of the cobwebs of sleep suddenly gone. He cocked an eyebrow. "Impressive. So you're a counselor?"

The man nodded. "In a sense, but I'm more than that."

Cam didn't want to be counseled, but he didn't want to be rude either. He let the man keep talking.

"The way I see it, you can spend the last year of your life slowly deteriorating and coming here once a week for uncomfortable, futile treatments until you climb into this comfy adjustable bed one last time like a cat crawling under a porch to die—"

"Wow," Cam interrupted. "Not here to paint a cheery picture, are ya?" He eyed the man, suspicious. "But it sounds like there's an 'or' coming."

"Perceptive." The man grinned. "*Or* you can join our organization and help save your fellow man."

Cam shook his head. "I thought so. Sorry, I'm not interested in joining some religious cult just because I'm dying."

"Ah, but the special young men and women we recruit travel to exotic locations, drive insanely fast cars, and jump out of planes. Does that sound a bit more interesting?"

Cam couldn't help but perk up. "A bit. Yeah."

"What do you want from the last year of your life, Cam?"

"I dunno. Soccer, girls, maybe all that cool stuff you mentioned?"

His visitor chuckled. "Besides all of that."

"What else is there?"

"Anything else. Name it."

"Money, maybe? Or at least the stuff it buys."

"Okay."

"Awesome food? Great workouts?"

"Sure. But those are just *things*. What do you want to do and be?"

"Well, as long as we're dreaming big, I guess I'd like to be a leading man. You know, win the fight and get the girl, cheesy stuff like that."

"You want to be a hero?"

"I guess you could put it that way."

The man nodded. "Ahh. Well, that's the interesting part, because we recruit an elite group of youth. You and nine others just like you. All with glioblastomas. All terminals. All with superior talents. We train you and send you on clandestine operations—secret missions, if you will. It's ferociously dangerous. But then, nothing's more dangerous than what you're facing here, right?" When Cam didn't answer, the man continued. "I'm not promising you your life back, Cam. You'll still die. But we give you the chance to be special, and to live your last year to the fullest."

Cam felt his pulse quicken. He glanced at his heart-rate monitor. Elevated. Over one hundred. Higher even than Kristi Banks had sent it. "What is this?" he said. "The Make-a-Wish Foundation for spy kids?"

"If that simplistic description helps you process what I'm telling you, sure. It's a commitment to do something meaningful with your time here on earth, and the length of that commitment is—"

"Let me guess. One year."

"Right. Or until you die, whichever comes first."

"This sounds crazy." Cam puzzled over the man. He was strangely honest. Blunt even. No sugarcoating. "How do I know you're telling the truth?"

"Your family got a letter yesterday that said if you die they might be eligible to receive two hundred and fifty thousand dollars through a credit card insurance policy you didn't know you had, correct?"

Cam nodded, wondering how the man knew what they received in the mail.

"We sent that. Your credit card company doesn't have such a policy. If you decline to join, the letter becomes junk mail. But if you sign on, the money will arrive within two to three weeks."

Cam's eyebrows rose again. *So much for my poker face.* The money sounded like the sales pitch part, but he had to admit it was a pretty good offer. His parents would be able to retire, or maybe help his evil sister get a house and a real life.

"So you just send my folks a quarter-million-dollar check for my shortened life?"

"We prefer 'condensed' life."

Cam didn't know if he should believe the guy, but the whole thing seemed too outrageous *not* to be true. It was a lot to consider. *I'll need time*, he thought.

The man was nodding, gauging his reaction. "Take some time," he said, as though reading Cam's mind. "Think it over. I'll be back at five in the morning before visiting hours. You'll have one chance to join."

"I have to talk to my friends and family."

The man shook his head. "No, you don't. In fact, if you tell anyone, I won't return."

"But I have questions."

"And *we* are the answer. Good night." With that, he rose and walked out.

Cam struggled to untangle himself from the monitors and bedding. Moments later, he was in cavernous corridor 3C. The nurse was just returning from her break.

"Where'd he go?"

"Where did who go?" she said.

The hallway was empty. The man had disappeared like a whisper.

"Right. . . ." Cam walked back to his room, lay down, and stared at the ceiling. *Time for some thinkin' music*, he decided. He hit PLAY and pushed his earbuds deep into his head.

Cam drifted in and out, glancing at the clock. Soon it was 4:55, and still no visitor. *Dude's not coming back*, he thought. It was all part of a stupid dream, he decided. A figment of his emotional distress. Cam refused to beat himself up for having weird dreams, though. He'd just found out he was dying, and that had to mess with a guy's head. In fact, he figured bad dreams were pretty standard in this wing of the building.

Then he heard the knocking. It came from the window. Not the door, the *window*. It might not have seemed so incredibly odd, except that the window was forty feet in the air.

The clock read 4:59 A.M.

Cam abandoned the comfort of Numo, scrambling onto a chair so he could see outside. There was a face in the glass. Bigger than life. Four floors high. Upside down. It was the man in the jumpsuit. He pointed at his watch. Cam opened the window.

"Decision time," the man said. "Yes or no?"

Cam had been thinking all night, but hadn't decided. His mind was going in too many directions. Now his recruiter was here, dangling four stories up like Spider-Man, which he had to admit was kind of cool. And the organization he represented wanted Cameron Cody. Kristi didn't want him. His soccer team wouldn't be working him into their future plans. No potential employers would invite him to a second interview if he was going to be too dead to work by the time he graduated. In fact, nobody else was going to be picking him for much of anything anymore.

Cam nodded, and the man nodded back. And that was it.

His recruiter rotated right side up, produced a miniature blow-torch from one of the many pockets of his jumpsuit, and went to work removing the safety screen. He chattered as he cut through a rivet, producing an acrid, burning smell.

"You're coming out this way. I'll tie you on. Don't look down if you're queasy."

He slid the screen loose and pulled Cam through. Cam clung to him like a panicked monkey while the man strapped him to his own body with a nylon rope. Then he nonchalantly welded the screen back into place.

"We'll fake your death," he was saying. "You were rushed off in the middle of the night for emergency treatment. Medics heli-ported you across the country. You expired on the way. Quite sad. I saw that your parents signed a form donating your body to sci-ence. Very progressive of them. We'll use that. Your remains will have to be shipped out for preservation and dissection, and no one will try to see them. I'm sorry you won't get to say good-bye. We can arrange for your family to find a note among your belongings, which you wrote to them before you 'died.' What would you like it to say?"

Cam imagined his mother finding his empty bed. She would have wanted to say good-bye. His dad might have understood. It was not the best way to go and not what they deserved, but it was better than the dying-cat-under-the-porch option.

"You were great parents," Cam said at length.

His recruiter nodded. "That's nice, Cam. Best one I've ever heard. Sheesh, I wish I'd told my own mom and dad that. Anything else?"

"No, I guess not."

"Then we're off."

Cam looked down. He was not crazy about heights. "Why go out the window?" he asked, still holding tight despite being roped on.

The recruiter gave him a serious look. "Because it's more fun." Then he laughed. "Besides, we can't drag you through a building full of witnesses and cameras. I already risked being seen last night. Don't want them to record me near you at the time of your departure." He began to ratchet them up the rope using a hand crank.

Moments later, they were running across the helipad on the hospital roof, the tail of Cam's hospital gown fluttering open in the morning breeze, making him glad there were no witnesses.

"Are we getting on that medical helicopter?"

"Yes, but not really. We just painted it that way."

Then they were boarding and strapping in, Cam wedging himself into one of the rear seats and securing the safety belt. The man put on his headset and quickly, but carefully, ran through a checklist. The blades started thumping, accelerating along with Cam's heart. Soon the sound overwhelmed his ears, like a song by the thrash metal band Demonkeeper. It was scary, but exhilarating too. The chopper lurched, Cam felt weightless for a moment, and then they were airborne and all he could think was, *Holy crap, what did I just do?*

As they climbed, his town stretched out below him. First the hospital where he was born, then his neighborhood, his high school, and the sprawling campus of the university. His entire life. For a moment he wondered if he'd already died and if this was his trip to the grand eternity. But he reached up and felt his earbuds still draped around his neck. They were real enough.

His recruiter advised him to get some sleep. It was going to be a long trip. Cam tried to take one last look back, but there was no rear-facing window. He turned his attention ahead. The sun was rising, and he was flying straight into it.

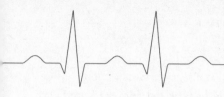

CAM'S PLAYLIST

3. SOUL ON A STICK 🔊
by Dog Breath

---

4. WELCOME TO THE ZOO
by The Way Chunky Monkeys

---

5. SMELLS LIKE MONDAY
by Cheez Whiz

"You all scream like I scream."

Cam was shaken awake, both by his recruiter's hand and the sudden shuddering of the helicopter as it caught a gust of wind. They'd flown straight through the day, stopping occasionally for fuel. He'd awakened during one stop in what looked like a desert village, and then had slept hard again, still exhausted from having tossed and turned the entire previous night.

The chopper bucked again, and Cam leaned to the window to look out. They were flying high over lush trees and thick brush. A jungle. He could see big water ahead, vast and blue. An ocean. Judging from the sun behind them, the waters he was seeing were to the east. There were no jungles in the continental United States, so it was clear that they'd left the country.

"Can I ask you a question?" Cam said to his recruiter.

"Sure, anything."

"Is this South America?"

"Can't tell you that," the man said as the helicopter dipped and jumped in the rising wind. "Ask me anything else."

"Got any Dramamine?"

"I like you, Cam," he said, smiling.

"You got a name?"

"Pilot," the man said. This time he didn't smile. Cam didn't push it. They began slowing down. Cam watched their speed steadily decrease from 120 miles per hour until they were nearly hovering.

"Are we almost there?"

"Yep." Pilot pointed out the window.

Below them, the jungle was a rolling carpet of deep green, but the vast canopy of trees was interrupted by a single, perfectly round blue dot. The dot seemed small from their height, but Cam guessed that it would be more than a hundred feet across at ground level.

"That's your target."

"Target for what?"

Pilot handed Cam a pamphlet. "Memorize this."

"Why?"

"Because your life depends on it."

Cam opened the pamphlet. It said:

How to Deploy Your Parachute

Pull the drogue out of the pouch at the bottom of your pack and let go of it. The pilot chute will catch the air and inflate, pulling out the deployment bag. There will be a popping sound.

The parachute lines are stowed in a zigzag pattern in the deployment bag. As the pilot chute inflates, the lines unfold and stretch out. The wind inflates the main canopy.

You do not want the canopy to open instantly. If it does, you will decelerate from 120 mph to 10 mph instantly. This will injure you and can rip your lines or the canopy.

When the parachute is out and open, look up to make sure nothing is tangled. If there is a problem, pull the reserve chute using the two handles on your shoulders.

Once you begin to glide, grab the two toggles and steer the parachute to the target.

"Wow. That's cool," Cam said. "So that's the training area where I'm going to learn to skydive?"

"You just learned." Pilot handed Cam a heavy pack with sturdy straps. "There's a diagram that shows you how to fasten the buckles and where the handles are."

The diagram was simple. Just the basics. Easy to memorize. His recruiter had done his homework—Cam paid attention and followed directions well. He'd never been a back-of-the-class, spit-wad-shooting, note-passing goof-off.

Cam looked up. He had a sinking feeling, but didn't have to say so. His expression spoke for him.

The recruiter nodded. "Yep. This is the 'jump out of planes' part."

"It's a helicopter."

"Detail-oriented. Good. We like that. Now listen up." Pilot pointed to the chute in Cam's lap. "Buckles across the chest. Primary rip cord on the right, secondary on the shoulders. Count to ten and yank. Pull the left tether to fly left, right to fly right. Head for the center of the big blue circle. When you can make out blades of grass, release the primary chute and drop into the drink without it. You don't want to have the parachute land on you in the water. It can drown you if you get tangled in it. Got all that?"

"You're kidding, right?"

"I'll take that as a yes." Pilot released the latch on Cam's door, and it jerked open. The wind from the vast open sky and the blast of air from the chopper blades whipped Cam's straight blond hair back and forth across his face. A week ago his mom had told him he needed a haircut. *She was right*, he thought.

Cam began to put on the chute, checking each step against the diagram. It went on easily, and too quickly for his liking. They were hovering now, but the helicopter still shucked and jived in the wind.

"Any questions?" Pilot asked.

"About a million."

"About the jump procedures."

Cam took a deep breath. He'd paid attention. He'd followed directions. He was *detail-oriented*. He had no questions about the procedures. He shook his head.

"All right, we're here," Pilot said. "Hop out."

Cam grabbed the doorjamb as though he were confident and ready. All he needed to do was scoot over one foot and he'd be on his way. But he found that it was a long twelve inches between his seat and the yawning door.

Pilot frowned at his hesitation. "This is your stop. I'm going to land somewhere you can't go."

Cam grimaced. "Out? Seriously?"

"Out."

Cam scooted over. Then he was flying.

The helicopter was instantly too far above for him to hear it anymore. The air rushing past filled his ears. He'd told himself he wouldn't scream, but he did, long and loud, like a wailing siren.

Then he realized he was clutching the rip cord and counting to ten. He was already on six. The ground hurried toward him, getting bigger as though he were zooming in on it through a camera lens. It seemed to approach faster as it grew closer. *The blue dot is a lake*, he decided. Perfectly round. *No, wait, it's a sinkhole.* He'd read about sinkholes. Collapsed underground caverns of limestone or quartzite that filled with water.

". . . nine, ten." He pulled.

There was a nasty *pop*. Cam remembered that this was a good thing. The main canopy deployed, his body jerked as the straps bit into it, and the world suddenly slowed down. He was drifting. It was strangely quiet. He could hear the distant thumping of the chopper blades now, but they were fading away. Again came the feeling that he'd crossed over into some strange afterlife. *In a way,* he thought, *I have.*

He looked up. No tangled lines. He groped for the toggles. *Pull left to go left,* he remembered. *Right to go right. Drop into the water when you see the grass.* Simple enough. Falling from a great height had a way of focusing one's thoughts, he decided.

The sinkhole waited below and ahead of him. Apart from a large clearing a few miles to the southwest, it was the only open area in the forest. He was gliding in the right direction, sort of. Steering was more difficult than Pilot had made it sound. Cam yanked too hard left, then overcorrected to the right. *Oh no!* he thought. *I'm going to miss it.* He pulled steadily back to the left, a lucky gust of wind helped, and soon he glided out over the blue pool.

The sides of the sinkhole were sheer solid stone. It looked to Cam like giant aliens had punched a perfect circle in the bedrock with a hundred-foot-wide drill. The water waited, dead calm twenty feet below ground level. There seemed no way to climb the smooth walls. Cam couldn't help imagining himself in a jar where cruel boys killed insects, their legs scrabbling against the slick sides in vain until they gave up. *I can't drop,* Cam thought. *I'll tread water until I drown.* Suddenly, he could see the grass rimming the hole. It occurred to him that perhaps his recruiter had brought him here to die, and he hesitated. Then he saw a dangling rope ladder across the pit. But now it was too late to drop—his momentum would hurl him into the rock wall. *How do I pull up?* he thought madly. *There was nothing in the instructions about that!*

Cam hit the trees that lined the top of the sinkhole at full speed. Branches beat and raked his body as he crashed through them, and leaves obscured his vision so that he couldn't tell if he was going to smash his head open against a trunk. Finally, he was yanked to a jarring stop. Lots of scratches. No trunk. He dangled, swinging back and forth.

"Okay," he mumbled, "that sucked."

He hadn't broken any bones that he could tell, but he'd been well punished for doubting his guide. He'd bruise badly for sure, and he was bleeding in several places. Cam looked up. The chute was fouled among the branches above him.

Cam groaned and pulled himself atop a big limb, where he released the lines with a *click*. One stray cord was still hopelessly tangled around his leg. He pulled himself to a sitting position to get his bearings.

He was high in a massive, gnarled tree, perhaps twenty feet off the ground. He glanced about. The tree had huge seedpods and gray-brown bark on its spindly trunk. *A kapok?* He remembered the strange kapok tree's distinctively large seedpods. He'd read about them in a copy of *Extreme Nature* magazine in his dentist's office. They grew in the Amazon jungle and Africa, and their silky floss was used to wrap poison darts for blowguns. He surely wasn't in Africa. *So this has to be South America,* he decided. *But where in South America? The middle of nowhere,* Cam thought, *that's where.*

The first order of business was to get down. Once on solid ground, he could start by investigating the rope ladder that was obviously intended for people who dropped into the water properly, which he hadn't.

But before he could try to untangle himself there was a rustling in the brush. A man with a machete stepped through the forest understory at the base of the tree.

The man was hard-looking and sun-browned, well equipped with a canteen, a loop of rope, and a bowie knife on his belt. *Militant? Smuggler?* Cam hoped not.

As Cam sat there hoping, the man looked up and frowned, seeming to reconstruct in his mind what must have happened. Then he came up, climbing hand-over-hand with the dexterity of a gymnast. He was strong. His cantaloupe-thick upper arms bulged as though his muscles had muscles. When he reached Cam's branch, he drew the machete again. Cam cringed as it rose, prepared for the worst, then it fell on the line tangled around his leg, cutting his cord.

The man tucked the machete away. "So, did you scream on the way down?"

Cam didn't answer.

"It's okay." The man laughed. "You all do."

"Who are you?" Cam asked.

"Me? I'm your personal trainer. . . ."

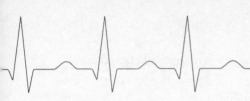

CAM'S PLAYLIST

4. WELCOME TO THE ZOO 🔊

  by The Way Chunky Monkeys

5. SMELLS LIKE MONDAY

  by Cheez Whiz

6. THE OATH

  by Slinky

"You fling poo. That's whatcha do."

"Leave the chute, Cam," his personal trainer said when they reached the bottom of the tree. "It has served its purpose and graduated, and we have to get moving."

Cam nodded, stretching his legs to make sure he hadn't cracked bones or torn muscles. He seemed to be more or less intact.

"So, what did you learn from that, Cam?"

"Follow the directions?"

"Bingo. First lesson. Follow directions."

"Is it all right if I call you something normal, like Bob or Frank, or are you all named after your jobs?"

"Right to business, eh? I'm Ward. But no last name, in case you were about to ask."

Ward faced him, but didn't extend a hand to shake. Instead, he pulled a tube of ointment from one of his many pockets and quickly smeared it on Cam's arms where he'd been slashed by the branches, and on a gash in Cam's face he didn't realize he had. Then Ward strapped bandages across the wounds.

"There. You look better already. Come on."

With that, Ward glided into the jungle understory like a panther. Cam had no choice but to plunge in after him. He struggled to keep up. Pilot had given Cam baggy gray sweatpants, a T-shirt with a picture of a howler monkey that said WHATEVER, and light canvas boots that seemed to be one-size-fits-all.

If I die now, Cam thought, *at least I won't be found in that ridiculous gown. In fact, I probably won't be found at all.*

They circled the rim of the sinkhole, and Cam glanced down into the crystalline stillness of the lake each time they stepped close to the edge. Sunk in the earth and with the cover of trees all around, no wind disturbed it. There were no ripples. The surface could have been a sheet of glass. Cam kicked a rock over the edge. It hit with a violent splash. The water opened up for an instant, then closed over the stone and calmed as though the rock had never existed.

Ward watched him out of the corner of his eye. "Only about half of you hit the water, in case that's what you were thinking about."

"I was thinking that this lake is kinda creepy."

"And kinda beautiful, eh?"

"I suppose. Anyone die in there?"

"Not yet."

They reached the area above the rope ladder and turned into the trees, where the heavy heat of the forest bathed them in a warm layer of instant sweat. Ward seemed to glisten, while Cam simply dripped like a melting candle. When he wiped his face with his shirt, he found the cotton fabric already saturated. Curious yellow flies buzzed around him in a cloud, like insect groupies excited by his arrival. They discovered every exposed patch of skin, and each bite left a pinpoint of blood where they'd worshiped him. They seemed to ignore Ward. Perhaps the familiarity of his flavor bored them, Cam thought. He, on the other hand, was tasty new cuisine.

Cam was pleasantly surprised that Ward spouted information like a happy tour guide as they trudged through the dim understory of the forest. Pilot had told him almost zilch. Ward confirmed Cam's suspicion that he'd landed in a kapok tree, explained why the flies liked him so much—Cam's U.S. diet probably included a lot of sugar and salt, which made his sweat smell especially tasty to them—and he pointed out various flora and fauna as they passed or trod upon it. Cam heard monkeys chattering in the distance, and birds called to each other in full, rich voices unmuted by fear of humans, telling him that he was the stranger here.

"What's the most exotic place you've ever been, Cam?"

"The Tiki Room. Frontierland. Space Mountain. A lot like this place, only with paved paths and hot dog stands."

Ward laughed loudly.

They walked for miles, or at least it felt like miles—the terrain was difficult, and as much time was spent crawling over downed trees and wriggling through thick brush as walking. The beauty of the jungle was wearing off. Cam was hungry, tired, and could feel a blister starting on his left heel.

"When do we get where we're going, anyway?"

"Now," Ward said as he hacked a path through a wall of thorny bushes with his machete.

Beyond the bushes, the world opened up. Light streamed in, and Cam found himself peering out over vast open water. The ocean. They stood atop a high cliff.

"Down there," Ward said, pointing to the beach below.

Cam could see faint dots in the distance spaced at intervals too regular to be natural. Some sort of man-made structures.

"How do we get down?"

"We climb." Ward pulled off his pack and began to unload rope and harnesses. "There's no path to the beach. It's safer that way."

Cam wondered what was safer about climbing down a cliff to get to their destination, and then realized that Ward must mean the destination was safer from *others* trying to get to it.

Ward secured the rope to a sturdy tree, strapped himself in, and motioned for Cam to follow his lead. Cam stepped into the harness, fiddled with its straps and buckles, and then looked up at Ward.

"Is this good?"

"Good enough. Let the rope out gradually as you descend." With that, Ward stepped backward over the edge of the cliff.

Cam was a good athlete, and he could already bench-press fifty pounds more than the year before. But halfway down his teeth were gritted, his fingers were cramping, and his biceps burned. He clung to mouse-sized handholds, not trusting the rope, and the toes of his unsized boots were jammed into cavities in the cliff surface or crowded onto tiny rock protrusions.

"Ward . . . ," he called, groping blindly with his foot. "I'm slipping."

"Don't," came the reply. "I'm not down yet. I haven't got you."

"I am going to fall," Cam said evenly. "And then I am going to die."

"Climb back up to the last good resting point," Ward advised. "Hold out there for one minute until I'm in position. You can do it."

Cam strained upward, his muscles screaming. He was able to reach a better handhold. Then Ward was down.

"Got you!" he called.

"Do I let go?"

"Yep. Trust me."

Cam had no choice. Even with the better hold, his arms were failing. He let go. There was a slight jerk as the slack in the rope tightened, then he hung suspended over the rocks on the beach below, clinging to the rope with his feet braced against the cliff.

"Do you lower me now?"

In answer, the rope began to play out, and Cam rappelled down, his feet hitting the wall every couple of yards. He pushed off and swung out, then swung back, smacking against the rock and flailing to keep his legs in front of him.

"Stop bouncing!" Ward yelled up to him. "Just walk."

Cam settled onto the wall and began to step backward as he descended. Soon he was hiking down at a steady pace. With the proper technique it was surprisingly easy, yet when he hit the beach, he still breathed a sigh of relief.

Quiet waves crept up and swirled around Cam's feet in the sand before slinking back into the ocean.

"There you go," Ward said, "you learned something. Remember to use your feet for support next time. Don't hang by your arms—your legs are a lot stronger. Any questions?"

"Just one. Now that I'm at sea level, I can't fall to my death anymore, right?"

As they walked the beach, Cam marveled at his new surroundings. Behind them, the towering cliffs dove straight into a bed of sand and dozens of scattered boulders shed over the centuries. The blue ocean swept in over the sand and slammed directly into the cliff wall, cutting off any retreat in that direction, which appeared to be south. The waves had carved the rock so that the slope was oversteepened and looked ready to collapse. Ahead of them to the north, the widening tan belt of sand between a high bluff and the sea created a safety zone—a beach that would have looked fabulous on a travel brochure. In this protected flatland Cam saw small thatched-roof buildings on stilts. Five of them.

"Huts?"

"Quaint, eh?" Ward said. "We call them the 'condos.' They stay dry and usually survive the weather. If a storm gets too bad or the moon drags the tide too far up the beach, we move to higher ground. You'll be in the last one there with the empty bed and Ari."

"What's an Ari?"

"Your roommate."

They passed several huts. Cam could see that they were solid one-room structures, not makeshift or rickety. Each was slightly different—all built by hand—but they appeared to be roughly the same size, and about the dimensions of the living room in the house he was supposed to be renting with his friends at the university. Farther up the beach and wedged against the bluff was a large square building built from cinder blocks, with narrow openings instead of windows. It seemed to be the central and primary structure in the compound. Its stark, angular gray walls contrasted with the vibrant and textured green jungle behind it and the churning blue water before it. It reminded Cam of a jail with arrow slits.

Beyond the block building lay a natural lagoon with shallow, calm water protected from the open sea. Cam strode past the drab structure to the lagoon edge, curious. The pool was light blue, like the sky, and so clear that, as they approached, Cam could see flashes of color darting between the rocks that dotted the sand on the bottom.

"Fish!" He stared for a time, fascinated.

Ward chuckled. "Yes, they come with the ocean." He tapped Cam on the shoulder and motioned him back toward the compound. "Let's go. You can come back and visit them during off time or during hunter-gatherer sessions, if you feel like sushi."

Cam followed Ward, wondering what hunter-gatherer sessions were. He didn't ask. There was too much to take in. Past the lagoon, the north end of the beach was hemmed in by more cliffs. Cam noted that these appeared impossible to climb, as they were worn completely smooth, with few visible hand or footholds.

As they walked back toward the main building, a cluster of small, orange monkeys appeared on the roof and began hopping up and down, chattering among themselves and watching them come, like excited fans in bleachers.

"They want food," Ward explained. "The irony is they *are* food. They just don't know it yet."

"Are you saying we eat monkey?"

"If you're hungry."

"I'm not hungry."

"You will be." Ward laughed again.

Cam was disturbed by how often Ward laughed. Not everything he laughed about was funny. If someone told Ward he'd just stepped on a jaguar's tail, he'd laugh about that too, Cam thought. Although, he'd probably also know exactly what to do and wind up with jaguar-skin gloves he crafted himself. Maybe that's why he was laughing—he knew what he was doing. Cam, on the other hand, had no clue.

"When do I meet the others?"

"How about now?"

"Okay." Cam waited, but Ward didn't take him to the big building. "Uh, where are they?"

"All around us."

Cam turned. He saw no one.

"You're fast, right, Cam?"

"Reasonably."

"Do you think you can get back to your condo without getting tagged?"

"Tagged? Like touched?"

"Something like that."

"Last hut on the end?"

"Yep. Ready?"

It was a game. A test. A something. Cam scanned the beach. He still didn't see anyone. "Sure."

"Go!"

Cam began trotting down the beach. He skirted the first of the condos, figuring the others must be hiding inside them. Instead he hugged the bluff on the landward side. He moved quickly, but didn't run at first. He needed to scope things out. With his eyes fixed on the structures, he didn't see the padded pole until it hit him in the head.

The packed sand beach was harder than it looked, and his thoughts were muddled for a moment before he looked up and saw a perfectly camouflaged person separate from the bluff. The figure was male, his age, and taller than him, with a chest and abdomen like a rippled wall. His body was smeared with dirt, and he held a pole with pads on each end. He shook a drooping plant off his head, an ornament that had helped him blend into the hillside.

"Pretty good shot, huh?" camouflage said. "I'm Donnie, and you'll want to remember this. Now stay down and tap out, and I won't have to tag you." He raised the other padded end of the pole. It was red and glistened in the sun.

"Whoa . . . okay," Cam said, stuffing his hands into the sand and trying to rise to one knee.

"You have to tap out," Donnie said impatiently. "Three times on the ground so Ward can see."

"Just a sec. You hit me so hard. I'm loopy. Is this really . . . ?"

Cam threw two fistfuls of sand in Donnie's face and rolled hard to his left. The pole came down with incredible speed and force on the sand where he'd just been, but he was already up and running. There was a short pursuit, but the guy was still rubbing his eyes and stopped at the first hut. He barked a single profanity and gave a loud whistle.

One down, Cam thought, but the whistle sounded an awful lot like a signal. There would be others, perhaps eight of them. He stayed away from the bluff. He had barely started toward the next hut when he felt something was wrong. Nothing was happening. No one emerged to stop him. No one leaped from the bluff. It was a wide open space. Too easy. He glanced left and right. Only the shadow of a bird moved on the beach, drifting toward him. He looked up. A shower of red paint rained down, and he barely had time to duck back under Donnie's hut to avoid being splattered. It hit the beach like a red bomb. Cam guessed that getting painted red ended the game.

The shadow turned away, and Cam peeked out. *Hang glider!* He broke for the bluff as the triangular aircraft maneuvered for another pass. Cam arrived and hugged the wall as the glider dove after him. There was nowhere to go. He'd trapped himself. But the glider couldn't operate near the bluff. Still, it came on. *He's crazy*, Cam thought. He could see the guy now. He was red-haired and grinning maniacally as he flew headlong toward the wall, getting another bucket ready. At the last moment, he swerved, but it was too late. One of the fabric wings clipped the rocks and dirt, and it crumpled, sending its freckled rider to the beach. He tumbled three times and came to rest in the sand, where his second tagging bucket slammed into his back and covered him in red paint.

It was a hard landing, and Cam almost ran to offer help, but he heard the unlucky pilot utter a loud whistle and realized the game was still on.

Cam ran past the second hut. He didn't stop, but instead zipped to the water side of the third structure and kept going. There was movement inside. He twisted sideways, zigzagging into the white fingers of surf groping up onto the beach. A sharp prick in his upper arm told him he'd been right to dodge. He glanced. A dart hung there, its point buried in the flesh of his shoulder.

"Friggin' oww!"

He tried to shake off the dart as he ran, but his arm wouldn't move. A tingle ran through the flesh of his bicep and forearm, but they refused to respond. The entire limb had gone limp and numb, like a cold summer sausage. He grabbed the dart with his other hand and yanked it out, wondering what might have happened if he'd been hit in the neck or face.

His next challenge was sitting on the steps of the fourth hut. Another guy his age, maybe a year younger or older. He stood as Cam approached, rising higher and higher as his long legs stretched out, until he stood at least six and a half feet tall. He was also thick, with heavy apelike arms. Two giant steps later he'd planted himself directly in Cam's path.

With his size, Cam figured he couldn't run. Cam altered his

THE TERMINALS —√— 39

angle and headed toward the bluff again. The giant followed. Speed was Cam's greatest physical asset. He was fast. He had to be to earn the starting right wing spot on a college soccer team. But somehow the big guy kept up. Cam risked a look back. The guy cranked his powerful legs awkwardly, but rapidly, looking almost as though he was unused to his own surprising speed. Cam turned on the afterburners, his feet churning in the sand. Still, he heard heavy breathing close behind. *Impossible*, he thought. *A guy that big running that fast would have to be a pro football prospect, not a dying tumor patient.*

Stopping to grapple the monster was unthinkable, especially with a useless arm. But getting pulled down from behind would be no better, and embarrassing. Cam felt like he was on a breakaway with the soccer ball and being chased. A player was always a step slower when handling the ball. He recalled a move he used sometimes on those occasions. His coach hated it, but it always resulted in a foul by the defender and a direct kick. He slowed just enough to let his mammoth pursuer get within reach of him, and then he stopped suddenly, ducked, and braced himself.

Given his bulk, speed, and inelegant gait, there was no way for his pursuer to stop. He tumbled over Cam and went down in the sand. Still upright, Cam didn't waste a moment. He dashed onward, the seconds he'd gained enough to give him an insurmountable lead.

He passed the fourth condo at a dead sprint, his own now in sight. He glanced waterward and skyward. Nothing between him and the doorway but sand. His numb arm dangled as he ran, flopping against his side. He hoped it wasn't permanent. *I'm right-handed, for god's sake.*

Just then the sand, the only thing in his way, reached out and grabbed his ankle. Cam careened forward. Unable to catch himself with his dead arm, he hit the beach with his face. His mouth filled with grit but he closed his eyes quickly enough that he was not blinded. He flipped over and saw a slim hand wrapped around his leg. Kicking it away, he scrambled to get to his feet. But the sand erupted, and a figure from beneath it rose with him.

She was on her feet before he was. Female. *Obviously* female, given the accoutrements the nineteen-year-old had squeezed into her shorty wetsuit. With the light-colored sand shaken loose, her savagely chopped hair was as dark as her eyes. She was well muscled too. He could see the corded tendons in her legs, and her abs were rippled neoprene. He lost a split second staring at her while she lifted one foot. Then it shot out and struck him square in the chest. Cam flew backward and landed on his butt. She paused to fumble for something dangling from her belt. Cam didn't stay to fight. He was already in bad shape. He didn't need another dart in the arm, pole to the head, or foot in the chest. Wheezing, he pushed himself up with his left hand and staggered onward. He did not look back and didn't hear footsteps behind him. Nor did he risk looking over his shoulder. He was almost up to speed, the condo was a short sprint now, and turning would only slow him down.

As Cam approached, a boy peeked out of his hut. He looked young, had a slight build, and considered Cam through deep-set eyes. He nodded approval and waved Cam on. *Ari*, Cam realized. This was his roommate. Cam also understood that Ari would not be an obstacle. Cam ran the last few yards toward him, until he saw Ari wince.

Cam considered ducking and should have. The cord hit the back of his neck, and the heavy ends of the bolo whipped around his throat so fast that Cam didn't even realize what was happening until the paint-filled balls smacked together beneath his chin, burst open, and painted his chest red.

"Tagged," the female voice behind him said, not without some satisfaction.

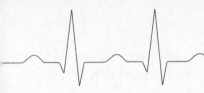

"Dude, it's like ... aww, forget it."

Cam fell to his knees on the beach five yards short of the condo, gasping for air and clawing at his throat. The cord was wrapped ferociously tight, and he couldn't breathe. Nor could he speak to ask for help. As he drifted toward unconsciousness, he was vaguely aware that the girl was standing over him triumphantly. It was Ari who bent to loosen the bolo, although when Cam's flailing hands interfered with Ari's progress, she did help by slapping them away. Finally, a breath rushed into his lungs.

"Here comes Ward," Cam heard Ari say as he blinked and sucked in air. "He'll be asking you what you learned and have a silly catchphrase for it."

"Like 'the hardest part of every journey is the first step,'" Cam wheezed.

Ari laughed. "Bingo. Especially when that step is out the door of a helicopter." He extended a hand in greeting and to help Cam up. "I'm Ari."

Cam couldn't lift his arm. "Sorry, my arm's messed up," he said. "I got stuck with something."

"A dart," Ari said. "If it's just your arm, it wasn't even half a dose. You'll recover."

"You guys poisoned me?"

Ari grabbed Cam's left arm and pulled him to his feet. "Relax. It takes two full doses to kill ya."

Cam wasn't reassured, but he found Ari easy to like, perhaps even trust. The skinny guy was friendly and somehow genuine, not like an instructor with catchphrases. Cam turned to greet his beautiful assailant.

"Hi, I'm Cam," he said stupidly. He added a conciliatory grin.

"You're dead," the woman replied without cracking a smile. "The dead don't talk."

Ari handed her bolos back to her. "Cam, I'd like you to meet your assassin, Zara."

Cam waited for her to extend her hand. She didn't.

Just then, Ward arrived, followed by a small mob of other young adults, all between the ages of eighteen and twenty from the look of them. *My teammates*, Cam thought.

The big fast guy was there. Tough to miss. The red-haired hang glider was limping, but grinning ear to ear. Camouflage Donnie of the padded pole strode up in the back, his narrow eyes assessing Cam. A smaller guy stood at his shoulder like an imp, and Cam decided he must be the dart man. Cam couldn't imagine either of the soft-skinned girls he saw behind Ward sticking him with a needle. One had lips, freckles, and eyebrows so pale they blended with her skin as though someone had smudged them all together with a photo editing program. The other had eyes too big for her nose and a chin too small for her mouth. She looked like a cartoon drawing by a carnival artist who exaggerated his subjects' features so much that they were embarrassed to ever show their friends the picture. Finally, there was a girl with glasses. She didn't look very aggressive either, although her lips were puckered so tight she reminded Cam of his fussy Aunt Eunstice. He recalled that Aunt Eunstice could be a real bitch.

"Zara gets the tag," Ward said. She nodded proudly. "But it wasn't perfect. You had him on his back and mishandled your weapon. Imagine he had a gun. Hesitate and you graduate."

Cam didn't quite understand, but Zara didn't seem too pleased about her potential graduation.

"That was some bullshit he pulled with me," Donnie said.

"Donnie, you also had a chance to take him out immediately," Ward said. "But you chose to hurt him first. Bad choice. Cruelty inspires your opponent, and gloating like a supervillain just gives him a chance to escape. Instead of showing Cam who's boss, he showed you that you're not."

Donnie scowled. "I only clocked him once. I was giving him a chance to tap out, but then . . ."

"But then he threw it in your face?" Ari chuckled.

Donnie shot the smaller boy a menacing look. "No honor, Steiny," Donnie said. "I gave him a break. But it won't happen again."

"There *is* no honor in the individual struggle here," Ward interrupted. "Only in serving the collective good."

"So I failed?" Cam asked, though it seemed obvious.

"Clean up and meet the rest of us up at the bunker. You'll find what you need in your condo." Ward turned and walked off down the beach without answering the question.

The others followed, with the exception of the girl with exaggerated features, who walked to Ari's side.

"Why did that Donnie guy call you Steiny?" Cam asked.

"Because he's stuck in the a-hole stage of grief?"

The girl blushed and giggled. Cam raised an eyebrow. Little Ari had a mouth on him.

"He's a true believer," big eyes added.

"He wants to be a Ward clone. Takes honor, duty, and the mission a little too seriously," Ari said, seeing that Cam needed further explanation. "But you definitely want him on your side in a fight."

"Is your last name Stein then?"

"No. We aren't allowed to tell each other our last names here. 'Steiny' seems to be the numbskullian term for someone who is both Jewish and smart as a physicist."

"Ari has an extremely high IQ," the girl said with a hint of admiration.

"And you have multiple abrasions and contusions, my friend," Ari added, shrugging off the compliment. "C'mon, let's get you some first aid." As he spoke, Ari traced Cam's parachuting injuries with his finger to where the bruising and swelling from the padded pole were already starting. He tilted Cam's head to look at the red welts on his neck. "And some second aid. This is Jules, by the way."

The girl leaped forward and grabbed Cam's arm, shaking it for a moment before realizing it was limp. She awkwardly dropped it. "Sorry!"

"It's okay. Nice to meet you, Jules, assuming you weren't one of the people trying to whack me."

"Oh no," she said quickly. "Calliope and I sat this one out. I did take out Owen once, though. Not really. Tagged him, I mean. It was a melee—all of us in a ring carrying sticks with red paint on the ends. We never did anything like this back in Pine Bluff."

"I thought we weren't supposed to tell each other where we're from."

"Jules, you talk too much," Ari said.

Jules rolled her bulbous eyes. "Like my accent doesn't give it away already." It was true. The twang in her voice obviously had been cultivated in Arkansas or thereabouts, though there would have been no way to guess Pine Bluff.

"Inside, Cam." Ari pulled Cam toward the condo. "You really do look like hell."

The hut was small and amazing. Its furnishings were nautical-sized, designed for tight spaces, but of high quality. Two narrow mattresses on planks were suspended from the ceiling. Ladders of nylon rope and dowels dangled from them for access. A small wooden desk sat beneath each. Atop the desks were pencils and hand-sized notebooks with waterproof plastic covers that would fit in a pocket. No computers, Cam noted. Two footlockers contained clothes—Tec-light water-repellent shirts and a jacket. Expensive. All camouflage or black. Heavy pants and light leggings. Boots and slip-on tennis shoes. No Velcro—it made too much noise if you needed to slide your sneakers off in a stealth situation, Ari explained.

Ari and Jules tended to Cam with a small, portable first-aid kit. They were quick and efficient, obviously trained and drilled. Ari even knew what to look for to determine if Cam had a concussion—he didn't, it turned out. In addition to the cut on his face from his parachuting mishap, his head was swollen from Donnie's pole, his back was sore from the big kid, Tegan, tripping over him, his neck was striped raw from Zara's bolo, his chest bruised from her foot, and his arm was just getting its feeling back. His fingers tingled as warmth leaked back into the muscles.

"Thanks," Cam said.

"Don't mention it," Ari answered. "Standard procedure."

"Guess I totally screwed up my first test."

Jules finished applying a cream to Cam's neck. "Not really," she said.

Ari looked him in the eye. "Dude, you made it farther than anyone else on the entire team, *unenhanced*. That's why Donnie was so pissed. You beat him."

They met an hour later in the bunker, in what appeared to be the main conference room. Inside, first door on the right. They sat in chairs in roughly a V formation. Cam sat at the point of the V, farthest from the board. The new guy. Donnie sat in the front on the left. Zara sat in front on the right.

"She's sure a pretty girl," Cam whispered to Ari.

Ari chuckled. "Pretty girl? She's a goddamned beer commercial, man. James Bond with boobs. But don't bother chasing that tail. If she wants you, she'll come find you."

Just then Ward stepped to the podium. He seemed to occupy the entire room, as much with his confidence as with his wide shoulders. He gave the group a warm smile, and then opened one of the small notebooks and held up a closed fist to arrest their attention. He struck Cam as part counselor, part professor, part drill sergeant, and he had an entire file on Cam's life.

"I hate, h-a-t-e, hate to do things twice," he began. "But Cam is joining us late in the game. We owe him a full-disclosure orientation. And we need his buy-in one hundred percent so we can depend on him. Questions?" He scanned the room quickly. "Seeing none, we're moving on."

He turned to draw a pyramid on the dry-erase board. Cam tentatively raised his hand.

Ari swatted it down and whispered, "You missed questions. Save it."

Ward turned back to the group. "You are all going to die," he said. "It's just a matter of how soon and what you're going to do with the time the doctor left you. In the meantime, I'll try my best to keep you healthy."

Cam had wondered about treatment. The others didn't just look healthy, they looked *extremely* healthy. Zara and Donnie were nearly perfect physical specimens. Tegan was a brute. And though Ari's build was slight, he was spry and full of energy.

Ward began to sketch lines on the board. "As you recruits are diagnosed, you are given a medication called TS-9, which we like to call an 'enhancer.' For the sick, it staves off deterioration and, for you, it will enhance your power, speed, and/or mental acuity. It may affect each of you a bit differently, according to your strengths."

Cam's hand shot up. He couldn't stop it. Ward paused. Annoyance flashed across his face at the interruption, but he quickly pasted a smile over it.

"Hold your questions, Wingman. I'll answer many of them as I go."

Cam put his hand down.

"Wingman?" Ari whispered to Cam.

"I was right wing on my soccer team," Cam grumbled.

"Precious."

"Quiet. This information is for me."

"All right," Ward continued, "as most of us already know, TS-9 is not, I repeat, n-o-t, not a cure."

"It's basically a supersteroid," Ari mumbled.

"Shush," Cam hissed. Ari shrugged an apology and made a zipping motion across his lips, but it was too late.

"Okay, Cam," Ward said. "If you must interrupt, spit out your question."

"Why don't they have this 'miracle medicine' back home?"

"It's not perfected."

"What do you mean, 'not perfected'?"

"The FDA banned research on the TS line before it could be fully developed. There were testing problems—headaches, a few unfortunate deaths. Some doctors went to jail."

"I think I read about that," Cam said uncertainly.

"That was early in the tests, decades ago. But after the bad publicity, it seemed the drug would never see the light of day. Until they created this program."

"We're taking experimental drugs?"

"Not you, at least not until your symptoms get worse. Even then it's voluntary. And any negative effects from enhancers will take almost a year to manifest themselves. That's more time than the doctors say you've got. Any more questions?"

Cam glanced at his teammates. They stared back impatiently. Donnie rolled his eyes. They'd already heard this, Cam realized, and they accepted it. Tegan was already on enhancers, clearly. That was why the big guy was so fast. Probably Zara too, judging from her muscles.

"Nope," Cam said. "I'm good."

"Excellent."

Ward returned to the board and resumed his professorial role.

"We choose candidates for three basic reasons. Additional rule-out factors narrow the field from there. You ten are the result. The first reason is because nineteen years old is the perfect psychological age to accept a new life philosophy. We don't take anyone over twenty-one. Second: only people with nothing to lose would willingly take the incredible risks you're about to take. And, finally, you all care deeply about doing what's right. There are Christian Youth Coalition members, Global Greenways volunteers, and college athletes in this room. Team players. Contributors. Philanthropists without money giving their lives."

Ward's volume and pace picked up as he spoke. Cam was impressed. His soccer coach at Western couldn't have been more inspirational before a big match. And Cam had heard successful politicians with less charisma. *Where did they get this guy?* he wondered.

"Our goal is to do the most good we can in the shortest amount of time. It's that simple." Ward raised his arms like a preacher. "And our first mission has just presented itself. With Cam on board the timing is good. Ladies and gentlemen, innocent human beings are suffering, being exploited, and dying. Our job before we leave this planet is to help as many of them as possible. We're going to save lives, people!"

Cam was surprised when Donnie thumped the desk enthusiastically with his fist. Fussy glasses girl—Gwyneth was her name—sat next to Donnie, nodding like a bobblehead. On the other leg of the V, the red-haired hang glider, Wally, wore a huge cockeyed smile. He looked revved up, and a little crazy. Cam glanced at Zara. She was lightly chewing the eraser on her pencil. *Lucky eraser*, he thought. Her head was nodding too, though not teacher's pet–style like Gwen's. *Buy-in*. The words echoed in Cam's mind. Ward had sold the rest of the team on this stuff long ago. He was merely rallying the troops now. Cam wondered if he was expected to cheer or whistle to prove his loyalty. Probably. He gave Ward a thumbs-up from the back of the room for his performance. His muscular personal trainer acknowledged it with a dip of his square jaw.

Ward moved on, writing in dramatic script on the board. As he did, Cam walked his small notebook between his fingers, a trick he had learned to do with a pen in class to keep his fidgety hands busy—not so different from Zara's pencil chewing. He wondered if he should take notes, but Ward's list was mercifully short. Five rules.

1. Everyone trains.
2. Everyone dies.
3. No one communicates with the outside world.
4. No one reveals the organization.

The final rule was the most important, according to Ward.

5. The good of the many outweighs the good of the few.

Ward also explained that rules three and four were closely and necessarily related. The world, and most definitely their nation of origin, would not understand a system that gave young adults banned experimental medication and sent them off to risk their lives, however short. If the organization came to the attention of certain governments, especially the United States', it would be condemned, dismantled, and unable to do any further good.

After creating the list, Ward wrote the word UNBREAKABLE by each rule, whatever that meant.

"Am I clear?" he asked. Everyone nodded. "This institution is small and tight-knit. Besides me, the only other adult you will have daily contact with is Pilot. If any word gets out, they'll know it was a recruit." Then he softened. "You might feel a bit isolated here at times, but you have the ultimate in loyal friends, I'll take good care of you while you're with me, and you can have whatever you want."

"The food's a bit local for me," Ari whispered to Cam. "But the snorkeling is great, and the tequila is amazing. Twenty varieties."

Cam cocked his head and raised his hand again. "So, no curfew? No drinking age? No chaperones? Stuff like that?"

"This isn't college," Ward said. "You're big boys and girls here. Other than following the rules on this board, the way you live out the rest of your life is up to you. I won't even be here at the compound a lot of the time."

"No supervision?"

"Other than training, no. Just be ready for your missions. Otherwise, you can do whatever you want."

6. THE OATH 🔊
by Slinky

7. HEY, I KNOW THIS SONG
by The Nobodies

8. THE ICE FIREMEN
by Blabbermouth

"Give me your hand, man."

When they were done, Ward announced dinner and they gathered in a dining hall across the corridor. An impressive pantry and walk-in refrigerator were stocked with as much food as Cam thought they'd ever need, much of it prepped and ready to eat. Even better, it was open at all times. On Jules's suggestion, Cam chose a poultry pasta bowl and tossed it in a microwave. Odd-looking greens approximated a salad, so he grabbed those too and smothered them with spicy dressing. The fruit was bizarre, and Jules warned him to stay away from it for the first few days. He was amazed to see several cases of beer and considered taking one—to appear cool and relaxed, if nothing else—but he passed in favor of pasteurized juice. His severely interrupted sleep pattern and the beatings he'd endured didn't make foamy alcohol sound relaxing. The thought of it made him feel queasy, not cool.

He selected a seat, figuring the others would come to meet him when they were ready, and, as he ate, they began to gather at his table. He hadn't expected them to surround him, though. They stood behind him, sat beside him straddling the bench, and Tegan stood across the table, towering over them all. They stared. No jokes. No introductions. Serious expressions all around.

"Whath?" Cam mumbled through a mouthful of salad.

Donnie spoke. "Ward has his rules, but we have our own."

Glasses-girl Gwen hung on one of Donnie's shoulders, and Owen stood at the other.

"You're the last-minute replacement for Pete, our former teammate. We knew Pete. We don't know you."

"Yet," Ari interjected.

"We need you to prove your loyalty."

Cam looked at Ari, who nodded. "Necessary evil, Cam."

"You need to speak the oath," Donnie said.

"The *team* oath," Gwen echoed.

"It's a vow of trust and mutual respect," the freckled girl said. She spoke so softly that he almost couldn't hear her, but her words moved him more than Donnie's. Cam figured that if she and Ari *and* Donnie were all on the same page, it was probably legit.

"We'll be risking our lives together for the cause," Donnie continued.

"Okay, okay," Cam agreed. "I mean I came here, right? So I'm in. What do I say?"

"'Ouch,' probably," red-haired Wally said, and then he cackled with laughter.

"For the good of the many," Donnie said, frowning at Wally.

"Just those six words?"

Gwen harrumphed and adjusted her glasses. "Those six words mean you pledge your life and death to the team and the betterment of the world," she explained officiously.

THE TERMINALS   ⎯⋀⎯ 53

"Okay," Cam said. "A bit grim, but I'll play along. I hereby pledge my life for the good of the many."

But they didn't move or look particularly convinced.

"Seriously," Cam added. "Totally."

Still, they kept him surrounded.

Jules grimaced. "There's a . . . umm, tattoo involved."

Zara pulled a needle-nosed knife from its sheath at her belt. "Where do you want it?"

The bonfire on the beach crackled as the surf licked up into the glowing red embers of the lower level of the wood pyramid Ward had taught them to construct to start fires. Before it collapsed in on itself, it had been taller than Cam, and when it really got going they couldn't approach within five feet of it.

Wally ran and leaped over burning logs, screeching like a wild man until his pant leg caught fire. Then he ran to roll in the incoming waves. Cam was fascinated by his antics, considering he hadn't had anything to drink.

Donnie, on the other hand, had plowed through seven beers in a little over an hour before putting his arm around Cam and declaring Cam's sand-throwing offense during his running of the gauntlet forgiven. Cam thanked him, but didn't know what to make of it. For some guys, drinking together was a bonding experience that lent solemnity to their words. Others simply forgot their promises the next day. He didn't have a good enough read on Donnie to know which type he was.

One thing Cam did know was that Gwen worshiped the guy—she watched Donnie with her lips pursed as though worried he might wander off, and she hurried to retrieve him a fresh can of beer or squeeze herself into the seat next to him when he plopped down on the log they had dragged down from the bluff. She grimaced as she sipped from a sweating silver can of Cerveza Maximo herself, obviously uncomfortable with the taste, but trying hard to fit in.

Tegan watched in silence, his thoughts impossible to read.

Zara, on the other hand, lounged like a great cat, stretching her legs out on the sand and propping herself up on an elbow. She wore a snug T-shirt and confronted the males that snuck glances at it with steady, narrowed eyes until they looked away like losers of a grade-school staring contest. Cam lasted all of five seconds before he withered under her glare.

All in all, it felt like a party in paradise, one meant to welcome Cam to the club, except that they were all going to die, which cast a bit of an unmentioned pall over the celebration.

"What's this organization called anyway?" Cam asked no one in particular.

"Nothing," Jules said.

"I get the distinct impression they don't use an identifiable moniker for security reasons," Gwen explained.

Wally hopped to his feet. "We should name it!"

Ari grinned. "How about Saviors of the Damn Universe?"

"Saviors of the Universe is already a band out of Seattle," Cam said.

"But I added the word 'damn,'" Ari argued good-naturedly.

Gwen's brow furrowed. "I don't think we should . . ."

"Last Gasp?" Owen said.

Jules shook her head. "Depressing. Next."

"Serenity for All," Calliope suggested.

Zara smirked, her upper lip curling like a writhing snake. "That's the worst name for a group of extreme ass-kickers I've ever heard."

"Yeah," Ari agreed, buzzed on the tequila he liked so much. "We should pick a name that kicks ass."

"Like what?" Donnie spat. He seemed ready to challenge anything Ari said.

The Bellingham hospital with its terminal illness ward popped into Cam's head. He'd thought he would quietly expire in dreaded, sterile, empty hallway 3C. He was still housed with other terminals, only now he was at a beach party in another hemisphere, in a tropical jungle alive with color, sounds, and smells, and preparing to go on secret missions. Same concept, different setting.

"Like Deathwing?" Cam said.

Nobody protested or jeered. In fact, nobody said a word. Their silence told him it was right.

After the rest had gone to bed, Cam sat with Ari across from Jules and Calliope, who were roommates. The group would be training early the next morning, and when Donnie had announced his own bedtime, the rest had followed like sheep, leaving the four of them alone.

"My tattoo hurts," Cam said. He raised his unlucky right arm. It had just begun to recover from the numbing poison only to be permanently scarred by a bloodthirsty swimsuit model. The inked pattern was the same for all of them—a series of electrocardiogram heartbeat spikes, followed by a flat line. Cam's ran around his upper arm. Calliope's ran around her ankle, which was smart. A smaller circumference meant less torn flesh. Ari's tat was on his chest. Jules's was in the small of her back—she hadn't wanted to watch. And they said that Wally's lifeline ran straight down his spine until the flat line disappeared into his butt crack, which Cam decided he'd take their word for. The tattooing method was crude—a series of pokes with the fine point of Zara's dagger, which was wrapped with a thin ink-soaked cloth.

"I'm officially no longer turned on by her," he declared.

"I think Zara likes cutting people," Ari said, tossing an empty Maximo can in the dying fire. "She's done all of the tats since I got here. In fact, I think the whole thing was her idea."

"She's so tacky," Jules scoffed. She turned to Calliope. "Don't you think?"

"Well, she's very sexy. And confident."

"Sexy is a spectrum," Jules said. "Friendly, flirty, naughty, dirty, nasty, raunchy, and sleazy. Which do you think she is?"

"Flirty?"

Jules scoffed again.

"*Very* flirty?" Calliope tried again.

"Eh, you're too nice."

"Yeah," Ari said. "Calliope is too polite to bitch about our mission. She joined hoping we'd be saving cute furry animals or the rainforest."

"I want to help people too," she said defensively. "I just thought we'd be building schools or digging wells. Our training seems a bit violent."

"See? All heart, no balls." Ari smiled.

She smiled back, not offended. Cam had a hard time imagining her bitchy or even annoyed. Her demeanor was as soft as her voice, her milk-n-freckles skin, and her wispy strawberry-blond hair, which hung over her face like a veil. Or a shroud.

"Where'd you get the cool name?" Cam asked.

She blushed. "I picked it out."

"Well, it's a great nickname."

"Thanks, but it's not a nickname."

"No?"

"Nope. I was born Alice. It was the trendy name given to me by my dad at the time. I had two other Alices in my preschool, and I was the quietest, so I was 'Alice three.' But when I was six I saw a machine at the circus. It was big, a piano with pipes. Steam came out of it like it was angry, but it turned the steam into music."

"Aha! A calliope organ," Cam said.

"Right. I used all of my tickets making the man play it over and over, and I hummed the tune for months. I wanted one with all my heart, but by then my mom was single. She was a secretary and couldn't afford anything like that. Instead, she bought me a second-hand keyboard and took me down to the courthouse to change my name."

"Cool mom," Jules said.

Ari smirked. "You're just lucky your name's not 'Organ.'"

Cam considered Calliope through the heat of the air over the fire. It distorted her appearance, making her look like a blurred and reddish-haired ghost. Pale. Freckled. The smile on her colorless lips was uncertain. And she was slender. No curves, but she wasn't about that, Cam thought. Not traditionally pretty, yet there was *something* about her.

"You like music?" he asked.

The bunker was open. It was always open. Anything they wanted, anytime they wanted. Calliope led Cam past the conference room and through the dining hall, where they grabbed a tub of chocolate pudding from the walk-in fridge and ate the entire thing with a big wooden mixing spoon.

"It's just ahead," she said, licking chocolate from the corners of her mouth. In the empty hall, even her soft voice was loud.

They passed a small workout room with a heavy punching bag hanging from the ceiling. Helmets hung from hooks, and padded poles leaned against foam walls.

"Defense and attack," Calliope said, anticipating his question. "Kickboxing. Mixed martial arts. That sort of thing. Zara spends hours in here. I don't like that stuff. Ward is teaching me communications method and tech instead."

Cam nodded, wondering what he would be trained to do. Then they stepped into a small room. The only thing in it was an electronic keyboard and a bench.

"Why is there foam on the walls here?" he asked.

"Same reason. In case there's violence," she said. Then she grinned.

"Oh, acoustics," Cam realized. "Duh."

She sat. It was more a slide than a sit, something smooth and natural that she'd done innumerable times either here or back home. Both probably. She leaned to tap the "on" switch as her rump flattened to become a part of the bench, and her slender hands fanned out over the keys like butterfly wings, her fingers alighting on black here and white there.

"Are you going to—" Cam began.

Calliope hit a chord. It boomed, drowning out Cam's voice in the small room. He went silent, and she backed off, transitioning to a light melody. It was her way of telling him to shush, he decided. He complied, and the song built. Her hands danced over the keyboard, starting out playful, but quickly becoming insistent, and then demanding with a hint of desperation. They groped for and pounded the keys. Soon, rather than stroking them, she was punishing them. Her shoulders flexed and tightened. Her breaths came more quickly, her nostrils flaring. She played a series of notes three times through, faster and faster, and then leaped an octave higher. At the crescendo she paused. Cam wondered if she was done, but he didn't dare speak.

She *wasn't* done. She hit a low note—a single note—and held it. Then she sang. Her voice was unexpected. Deep and smoky as she rolled into the lyrics, which were as bitter and ferocious as her hands. As she sang, she hit high notes that proved she was female, but she favored the lower end of the scale, the dark end of her machine. She sang about holding her struggling childhood dog while it was euthanized and wishing for breasts that never arrived—both of which made Cam feel bad for different reasons. There was more, all sad, some angry. At the finish she issued a long, low moan that built to a brief scream that ended abruptly, and when she was done she slumped, spent, as much emotionally as physically. There was a long pause where she simply stared at the keyboard.

"Oh my god," Cam said. "You're . . . good."

She let slip a smile. "You liked it then?"

"Was that song by the band Lisa Ran Away? It sounded like them, but I've never heard it. With the lyrics, it was also sort of like The Dread."

"You know your music," Calliope said. Then she shook her head. "But it's neither of them, although they're both major influences."

Cam cocked his head. "You wrote it," he realized. "You friggin' wrote that!" He smiled at her like an idiot. "And clearly you're a bit disturbed."

She laughed. "We're dying, Cam. Remember? I can't help being a little messed up." The dark admission would have sounded strange in her mouth an hour earlier, but it fit now.

"Yeah," Cam said. "I remember. But for a minute there you made me forget."

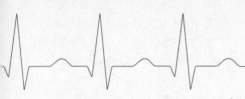

CAM'S PLAYLIST

"Something familiar, but oh so peculiar."

Training came early. They met on the beach. Ward, Zara, Tegan, and Donnie. Four sets of scuba masks and regulators were laid out neatly in the sand just above the high watermark.

"You're athletic, Cam," Ward said. "Let's see if the scuba team suits you for this mission."

After the others had donned and adjusted their gear Cam was still standing there puzzling over hoses and buckles. They helped him while Ward stood with his back to the ocean rattling off steps, rules, and clever sayings.

"SCUBA stands for 'self-contained underwater breathing apparatus'... Don't rise faster than your bubbles unless you want to pop... And do not, I repeat, do n-o-t, not hold your breath...."

The others focused on every word. They were sharp and alert, despite having obviously heard it before. Cam listened hard, knowing from his skydiving experience that his life would likely depend upon it.

"Any questions?" Ward looked straight at Cam.

"No, sir," Cam replied.

"You sure? Tell me now if you're a poor swimmer. There's no shame in acknowledging a weakness."

Cam glanced at his comrades. Zara and Donnie eyed him, evaluating. *Yes, there is*, he thought. "I'm sure," he said.

"Excellent. Donnie, you're team leader. Out to the buoy and back," he said. "Go!"

Donnie, Tegan, and Zara walked straight into the surf, their flippers slapping the sand. Cam followed. The water lapped at his legs at first, and then a swell hit him waist high. Zara was already plunging into the trough of an incoming wave. He bucked the tail end of the wave, then surged forward, inserted his regulator, and dove into the next one.

It was strangely quiet beneath the waves. Cam had to kick farther from shore and dive to get out of the surf, but the tide helped him, the drop-off was steep, and soon he was floating free in the silence of the open ocean. The others were straight ahead, kicking steadily. Donnie looked back, but didn't slow. Cam chased after them. They had to find the buoy without a beacon. "Practice like you play," Ward had said. There would be no beacon on their first mission.

Cam was curious what their mission would be. Saving people was the goal, and a waterborne approach was part of it, apparently. Ari had been sent off with Pilot to drill for his role, whatever that was. When Cam had asked, he'd just laughed and said he had the "cushy job." Calliope was charged with learning the communications equipment. They each knew elements of the plan, but Ward hadn't put it all together for them yet.

Cam had expected to see fish, but the rapidly deepening waters were featureless and dark, very unlike the lagoon, which was shallow, sunny, and teemed with life. The dimness went on as far as he could see, and he couldn't help wondering if this was what death was like. Silent, endless, solitary, eventually a hell of self-awareness without any stimulation. He also realized that he was beginning to get tired and slow down. They hadn't even made the buoy yet. He decided he needed to "focus on the task at hand," as Ward had said several times, and he kicked hard after his team. Perhaps they would surface and rest at the buoy before turning back. But when he looked up, they were gone.

The word "shit" made a lot of bubbles underwater. Cam rotated in place. The dark and distant ocean floor was no longer a good guide for direction. He could surface and find shore, he thought, but the entire point of the exercise was to stay out of sight under-water. He suspected Ward would be watching with the binoculars he'd been wearing around his neck. Drifting with the tide and turning in circles, Cam stupidly and completely eradicated his sense of direction. He chose a heading and kicked for a time, but after several minutes of swimming he still saw nothing.

The surface was toward the light. He knew that much. He cursed himself and kicked upward, careful not to rise faster than his bubbles, and he broke through the waves with a feeling of both failure and relief. The beach was distant, much farther away than he would have guessed. The condos were mere dots on a ribbon of tan below the cliffs. He was also well past the red buoy, which bobbed in the dark blue swells midway between him and the shore. It receded even as he floated in place. *I'm being swept out to sea*, he thought. With the tide against him, the swim back would be harder. He stroked, but made no headway. Kicking with great effort, he found he could make some gains, but if he stopped to rest, he lost all of his progress and more. Soon he was exhausted and farther out than he had been before.

Suddenly, something rose from the water behind him and clamped around his torso. Cam panicked and fought, squirming in its grasp. *Shark!* he thought. He felt a flush of warmth on his upper legs. *I'm bleeding!*

"Calm down! I can't save your worthless ass if you struggle." Donnie's voice was agitated and smug at the same time. He held Cam under the arms in a lifesaving carry and stroked toward shore. "Go limp, and I can drag you."

Cam couldn't decide whether he was relieved or mortified, but he had no options. He had to let the arrogant jerk save him. At least Donnie had no way of knowing that he'd peed himself. Cam relaxed and let Donnie haul him toward shore, trailing behind like a jellyfish. Halfway there, Donnie handed him off to Tegan. And, finally, Zara took him the rest of the way, which was almost as humiliating as having Donnie rescue him in the first place. All three of them still swam strong. Cam was not a bad swimmer, but they were exceptional. *Unnatural.*

"I can take it from here," Cam yelled when they got into the surf. He didn't want to be dragged before Ward like a prisoner. Zara shrugged and dropped him.

But Cam was unprepared and inexperienced in the surf. A wave picked him up like the wind might lift a leaf and bore him to the beach, tumbling him over and over and then depositing him on his head in the packed surf sand, which Cam was rudely reminded was much firmer than the fluffy stuff people kicked up in vacation videos. Rolling over with a groan, he found himself lying at Ward's feet.

"Are you injured?"

"Yeah," Cam said.

"Where?"

"My ego."

Ward nodded, but didn't allow himself to smirk, staying focused on the task at hand.

"So," he said, "not the scuba squad, eh?"

"No!" It was Donnie stomping up the beach, no longer smug.

He was worked up and looked angry. "Total fail! He's not strong enough."

"Failure of one team member is often considered a failure of the team leader," Ward said evenly. "Where were you when Cam started drifting away? You weren't racing ahead to show off, were you?"

Donnie bit his lip. His face looked vaguely purple, and Cam realized he was holding his breath to keep himself from replying. Ward didn't demand an answer. He knew the answer. He turned to Cam.

"In truth, it's not a failure, Cam. It's a life experience, one to be learned from. And I think we've just learned that you are going to be on a different squad."

"Don't sweat it," Ari said, taking a huge bite out of a roasted bird of some sort. "They're juiced. You aren't. It's not an indictment of your manhood."

"I was dragged to shore by the hot gal," Cam mumbled.

"Hot gal on enhancers, pal."

"When do I get some?"

"Some TS-9? Whenever you like, but I recommend you don't start until after your symptoms begin to break you down."

"Is that what Donnie did?"

"I think Donnie was an early adopter. He's aggressive that way."

"What about you?"

"Do I look like I'm on steroids?"

"Yes. I bet you were even skinnier before."

Ari smirked. "You're quick, Cam. And correct. The TS helps with focus too, you know. I've never thought so clearly and quickly."

"It sounds amazing."

"And kills you eventually. Don't forget that part."

"Yeah, but after our natural expiration date."

"I still say hold off until you need it."

"Maybe I need it to keep up."

"Look, I only take it because after they diagnosed me I started to deteriorate. I used to be all natural and organic and stuff, but feeling your body start to decay while you're still alive is pretty goddamned disconcerting. And feeling your brain struggle to call up information you knew by heart just a month earlier is wrong at any age. At nineteen it's a bona fide travesty. The TS fixed that for me. But you're not broken yet, pal."

"What are you, my doctor?"

"Given a few more years I would have been."

Cam considered his roommate. Ari had no reason to lie, unless maybe he was just as competitive about the training as Donnie and Zara and wanted to keep Cam down too. Unlikely. "As soon as I feel even a twinge, I'm having what you're all having."

"And when that day comes I'll buy you the first round. But you can't really go back, so until then just stay gold a bit longer there, Wingman."

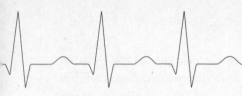

"Melt, melt, melt, like a schoolgirl's dream."

After an hour of rest they tumbled out of their beds and headed for the bunker. The remainder of the crew were already inside, arranged in their V formation in the conference room with Ward at the front. This time Pilot had joined him. He sat in a chair to one side, wearing his jumpsuit as though he might have to scramble the helicopter at any moment. He chewed a toothpick and wore large sunglasses. The chopper wasn't actually at the compound. A beach landing was difficult with the uncertain wind coming over the bluff. Pilot came ashore by boat, a sea kayak he'd paddled from around the southern cliffs.

Zara smirked and Donnie frowned when Cam and Ari walked in. Cam rolled his eyes and headed to his seat in the back. Calliope sat nearby, but she drew cartoons with her pencil and pretended not to notice. Cam wondered if she was embarrassed about having shared so much of herself the night before at the keyboard, or if she too regarded him as a failure. Jules, however, patted his seat enthusiastically and greeted him with a huge smile.

"I'm glad you're not a scoob," she whispered, giving him a smile. "That means you'll be with us."

Ward held up a closed fist, and the room went silent.

"This is the briefing you've been waiting for," he announced. "Today I reveal your first mission. You've all been training for your own specific tasks, except for our newcomer, Cam. And now we put it all together. This is where the whole becomes stronger than its parts."

He pulled a cell phone and aimed it at the whitewashed bricks of the bunker wall. A beam shot out, and a photograph of eight huddled and frightened people appeared on the wall. They were lined up against a brick building—mostly Caucasian, but two Asian women stood hugging each other for comfort, and a tall black woman wore distinctive African clothing. Three looked Scandinavian. The different languages on several T-shirts told Cam they were of multiple nationalities. At least one looked American—a younger man in a Boston Red Sox hat.

Ward's voice filled the room. He sounded like a reporter narrating a news story—yet another impressive skill. "These are doctors from the humanitarian aid collective Worlds Apart, Worlds Together. They were hijacked at sea by pirates. This is the ransom photo WAWT received. Not pictured are the head of the medical team and the captain of their vessel, because they're already dead. The surviving eight are being held not far from our location. You're going to rescue them."

A murmur went through the room.

"Pirates?" Cam whispered to Ari.

"I think I've heard of these assholes," Ari whispered back. "A South American gang just like this was demanding a million dollars from a Korean company to get its ship back not too long ago.

They sent the captain's hand to the company's corporate office. Same ones, you think?"

Cam shrugged.

The other team members were whispering too. Ward had to hold his fist up for quiet again. Then he continued.

"They are being held in a country that is unstable due to its recent political shake-up. Pending new elections, its interim leader controls the military and has declared that any foreign action on its soil will be considered an act of war. No government will touch this." Ward grinned. "But you will."

He tapped a button, and a tactical map appeared on the wall. A group of shapes represented a compound not unlike their own. Waves depicted ocean. The shoreline was a thick solid line. Several simple squares nearby were buildings.

"The infiltration squad will troll the pirate zone by boat with the intent of getting captured. That squad includes Ari, Jules, Calli, Gwen, and now Cam. Owen will fill in as the fourth on scuba."

Owen pumped his fist and patted Donnie on the back enthusiastically. Donnie just shrugged but eventually gave a thumbs-up, seemingly to stop Owen from touching him.

"Scuba will separate from the group at sea prior to contact and follow the vessel in after it has been commandeered. Wally will be airborne."

Ward paused to the let the summary of their mission sink in. There were no more murmurs. Donnie clenched his fists, eager. Jules's brow was wrinkled with concern. Wally had a crooked smile on his face. Cam just stared, bewildered. *Pirates?* He wasn't sure what he'd expected, but certainly not letting a bunch of murderous, gun-toting crazies capture him. The wide-eyed expression on Calliope's face told him that she hadn't expected it either. Gwen seemed less concerned about their mission—instead, she cast anxious glances at Donnie and Zara, clearly unhappy with the groupings.

Ward resumed. "After months of consideration, I've selected the team leader for this operation."

Donnie and Zara eyed each other. Zara grinned. *It's a game to her*, Cam thought. Donnie did not smile. To him this was serious business, a jock's last chance to prove himself a winner. Donnie's expression teetered between supreme confidence and desperation.

"Ari, you're in charge," Ward said simply.

Cam was still considering Donnie, who suddenly looked as though someone had peed in his Pepsi, when Ari nodded as though he'd known it all along. Cam shot him a surprised look.

"Brains over brawn," his roommate whispered with a wink.

"Why not Gwen? She's smart."

"Too rigid. No flexibility."

"Congratulations."

Ari snorted. "Great. Did you notice that these pirates kill the leaders first?"

Calliope frowned and raised her hand tentatively. "Are we gonna have to, like, kill any pirates?"

Ward frowned back. "You're gonna have to, like, try not to kill anyone, pirates or otherwise," he replied. "The rules don't change simply because the danger is heightened or the ethics of the individuals involved are questionable. You only take a life to save more lives. Everyone got that?" He cast a meaningful gaze around the room, meeting each pair of eyes in turn, lingering ever so slightly upon Donnie, Zara, and Wally.

There was more information—two hours' worth. Ward rattled off instructions and logistics, flashing images on the wall. The pirates were a ragtag group, some of them veterans of drug wars, some merely the poor and the desperate—raw recruits. They were armed with a hodgepodge of rifles and pistols. Their modus operandi was to demand ransom and kill a couple of hostages to provide motivation. They were not known to mistreat their captives before they killed them, but Ward advised the females on the infiltration team to wear tampons to help discourage rapes, just in case. Jules and Calliope looked a little green. The team's movements would be coordinated via Calliope's earpiece, but their captors would likely deprive them of any timepieces. "Gwen will keep the time in her head," Ward said confidently, though it seemed an impossible task. Calliope's receivers would look like cheap earrings and her transmitter a tongue stud. They were to acquire the eight remaining doctors and return. Simple goal, yet a murderously difficult task.

The final revelation was that they would all see "the doc" for a checkup before they departed.

A doctor? Cam thought. The presence of a medical professional in the forest hadn't occurred to him before. *But of course they would have a doctor,* he realized. *We all have tumors in our brains busily killing us.*

Ward finished the meeting off with a slogan and admonished them to go have some fun for the remainder of the evening. Cam couldn't imagine how they could think of fun, given the gravity of the mission, but Wally leaped up.

"To the beach!" he shouted.

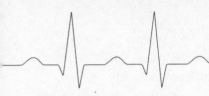

"You sizzle and pop, and you don't stop."

After the meeting they adjourned to the beach, heads swimming and tongues wagging. They chattered as they made their way to the moonlit lagoon, except for Donnie, who marched through the sand in silence with Gwen and Owen buzzing around him. Cam couldn't help beginning to feel excited himself as they arranged themselves on a communal blanket.

The flat surface of the lagoon shone a tranquil silver. Occasional flashes of red and blue winked through it, speaking to the presence of the contented fish. The jungle noises were constant but distant and soothing, like beautiful background music.

"We should get some guns!" Wally said. "*They* have guns."

"Blame her," Zara replied. She nodded at Calliope. "Little Miss Fight Fire with Flowers."

"I don't get it," Cam said. "Why aren't we using guns?"

"I didn't sign up to kill people," Calliope said softly.

"The gun thing was decided before you got here," Ari explained. "We try not to kill people to save people. You can see the philosophical conflict there. And it's hard to incapacitate someone with a bullet in a nonlethal manner. We use darts filled with a local poison distilled from the lovely and hostile native flora and brewed up somewhere off-site. One dose will render you unconscious for hours, but you won't die."

"Yeah," Cam said. "I got a small taste of that lovely stuff in my arm, and it still doesn't feel right."

"Two darts will put a man down for good, though," Zara added.

"Yeah, so the extremists among us can still kill if they really want to," Ari said. "It's a compromise."

"We all want to do good," Jules said.

Dinner came, and they fell to with gusto. Ward delivered pulled pork tacos he'd made from some sort of wild boar he'd killed himself. A "pakira," he called it. They were piled high on a platter amid assorted greens, and the team passed sweet guava juice in a huge wooden pitcher. Cam drank three full glasses, and Wally sprayed a mouthful in the air all over everyone in celebration of the mission. When they'd all eaten their fill and more, they lounged, listening to the waves lap at the sand. After five tacos, Cam felt like he was part of a family of bloated sea lions.

"Now that we've got our first mission, we should go around the circle and all say why we're here," Jules suggested.

Zara smirked. "What's this, some touchy-feely bonding exercise?"

"We all swore the same oath," Owen said. "That pretty much covers it for me."

Cam thought the simple oath probably did cover it for Owen. The round-eyed guy who was already balding at nineteen didn't strike Cam as an independent thinker. He didn't seem to see much past *Donnie strong, Zara hot.*

"No," Jules insisted. "I mean why we're really here. Our personal reasons. It was a big decision for me to join. I'll even go first." She picked up a spiral shell, held it like a microphone, and took a deep breath. "I always wanted to travel. I went to Europe for a year abroad. But when I was diagnosed, my doctor said I had to go home for treatment. No more than a few days away from the hospital until, well, you know. I thought I'd never go anywhere again. But now, here I am."

Yes, Cam thought. He'd feared the same—that he'd never leave his small hometown.

Calliope sat up and took the shell. "I want to help people. Truly help them. Through art or music or education, though. I don't like all this commando stuff."

"We know," Zara mumbled impatiently.

Calliope ignored her. "I talked to Pilot for hours when he came to the clinic. He promised me we would make a bigger difference in a year than most people make in a lifetime. And that I'd have a piano." She passed the shell to Tegan, who sat beside her.

"My dad couldn't afford treatment," Tegan said, holding the shell limply at his waist, and then he fell silent again. That seemed to be the entirety of his explanation.

Gwyneth nudged him, annoyed, and grabbed for the shell. He let her take it, and she rose to address the group, adjusting her glasses. She stood with her back very straight, Cam noticed.

"Upon diagnosis, I was presented with multiple options," she said, her voice sharp and abrupt. "It was a simple matter of choosing the best from among them. One could attempt to prolong treatment in the hope that a cure might be forthcoming, or . . ."

Cam watched Gwen's mouth move, but her words seemed to run together. They were too big and she used too many of them. And her glasses bobbed up and down as she spoke them, which was very distracting. She talked for a long time, it seemed, and she repeatedly touched Donnie's wide shoulder as if to reassure herself that he was still sitting beside her. She was obviously smart as hell.

And if Cam hadn't noticed, he was sure she'd have told him so herself, though without using the word "hell"—she seemed too fussy
for profanity. But when she finally finished, Cam still had no idea
why she'd chosen to join. In fact, out of all of them, only Calliope
seemed a less likely candidate.

Gwen sat and pressed the shell gently into Donnie's palm, making sure to touch his shoulder once again.

Donnie stared at the shell. He hadn't spoken since Ari had been
named team leader. He sat up and looked out past the circle of his
dying comrades and spoke to the night as much as to them.

"I'm here for the mission," he began. "I mean it. I'm all in, and I
don't believe in compromise. That's how you become the best at
something—you commit yourself to it one hundred and ten percent."

"Mathematically impossible," Ari mumbled.

Donnie paused, and Cam noticed he was panting. His face was
red, and a vein in his forehead bulged like a subsurface worm. He
took a big deep breath, bracing himself for his next words. "I accept
that Ari is leader," he declared. "For this mission anyway. You're
smart. I get that. I'll follow you. But ultimately, I serve the mission."

He passed the shell. Cam and Ari glanced at one another. Cam
raised an eyebrow.

"Well, that's reassuring," Ari whispered once Donnie had turned
his attention elsewhere.

Zara held up the shell, then flipped it in the air and caught it
between her fingers.

"Live life to the fullest," she said simply. She looked at Cam and
caressed the shell, then held her finger up in front of Owen with
the shell riding atop it like an elaborate hat.

Owen plucked it carefully from her finger as though nervous
that if he touched her she might practice a judo throw on him.

"I agree with Donnie...," Owen began, and it went downhill
from there, as far as Cam was concerned. Owen next repeated some
things Gwen had said, then a few slogans Ward quoted over and
over. In fact, Cam wasn't sure Owen said anything that was his own.

The shell passed to Ari.

Ari scooped up some sand in the shell, and then tilted it to let the sand drain out slowly. "I think it's a simple matter of what you want to get done while you're on the planet. What's the best use of your time? However much you have. I always wanted to be a doctor and save lives. That or a NASCAR driver. And once I was diagnosed I was pretty sure I could save more people's lives here than I could back home in a hospital. Ironic, eh?"

He tipped the last of the sand from the shell, and then gave it a tap to make sure it was empty before he handed it to Cam.

Cam wasn't sure what to say. It had all been said, and Owen had sounded like a moron repeating it.

"I miss my parents," he said suddenly.

He didn't know why he said it, and he wanted to kick himself as soon as he had barfed it out. *Jeezus*, he thought, *I sound like the scared kid at camp, and I've been here one whole day.* He sounded even stupider than Owen, he decided. But when he looked around the circle he saw the glint of tears in several eyes—Calliope, Jules, and, unexpectedly, Tegan, whose dad couldn't afford treatment. At least he was not alone. He passed the shell without further comment. He didn't want to make it worse.

Ari rescued him. "So Wally, why did you join?" he said, luring both the sympathetic and disapproving eyes away from Cam.

Wally frowned and then grinned. "Why the hell not?" He laughed and leaped up, smashing the shell on a nearby rock. "C'mon, let's go skinny-dipping!"

Wally tore off his shirt and then yanked down his shorts, splashing into the lagoon nude. And alone. Even Zara didn't budge.

Wow, Cam thought, *his tattoo really does run into his butt crack.*

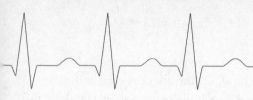

CAM'S PLAYLIST

10. RUSTLE AND WHISPER 🔊
    by Okee Kenochee

*"Your friends are talking 'bout me,
but mine are talking 'bout you too."*

After his disastrous share session at the blanket, Cam snuck off and down the beach back to his condo. As was his habit, he looked for his music as soon as he walked in. He needed a song—something dark that matched his sullen mood, something to help him descend into a full wallow and hit bottom so he could rebound. But his earbuds weren't on the small desk where they should have been.

It was strange. Ari hadn't been to the hut since Cam had left the buds on the desk. And he never misplaced his music. The black buds were like a pair of glasses he rarely took off. The small Clip Chip–brand player that held all of his music had not been separated from them for nearly a year. It fastened easily to his clothing or even to the thick of his sand-colored hair in the hollow of the back of his head, if he was working out shirtless. Everyone had to know they were important to him, even after the first day. He'd worn them all over the compound. Once, Ward had even told him to "pocket the damn things" in front of the entire team. Maybe someone was playing a joke, Cam thought, or sending him a message. He began to hunt, knowing he wouldn't relax until he found them. It was a small hut, and a quadrant-by-quadrant search wouldn't take more than an hour, he calculated. He started with the floor on the south side.

The floor turned out to be a poor place to start. Fifty-four minutes later, Cam found the buds and Clip Chip at the highest point in the condo, on his suspended bunk—the last place he looked. They were tucked neatly beneath his pillow, where, if he hadn't been searching, he would have found them only when he laid his head down at night and thrust his hands underneath. At first he thought Ward might have come to make their beds and stuck them there for safekeeping. The guy seemed to provide every other service. But the covers were still disturbed from the afternoon when Cam had been lounging and chatting with Ari.

He scooped them up and pulled the telescoping wires to length. Out popped a small scrap of paper. It was not folded—the gap in the short wires was too small when they were collapsed. There was writing. A quick scribble. Hurried, it seemed.

"I'm watching you."

What the heck? He flipped the note to see if it was signed. It wasn't. Cam scratched his head. Was it a warning? He read it again, tracing the lines with his finger. Female writing, from the look of it, but he couldn't be sure. Donnie didn't need to leave him a note—he made his challenges out in the open. Frankly, none of the guys seemed the note-writing type. *Calliope?* Cam thought. She'd been distant since they'd bonded in the piano room. She was shy, intriguing. She expressed herself best indirectly. Through song. *Or a note.* Cam's heart fluttered. She was not unattractive. And her voice . . . *wow.* He wondered if a girl could sing while she kissed. Then he wondered if Calliope kissed at all. *Of course she does,* he thought. *We only have a year to live.* He tucked the note away. Even some tuneless kissing would be fabulous. The evening was definitely looking up. Cam selected music that was not sullen in the least and flopped onto his bunk.

Ari wandered in an hour later. "Are you studying the maps?"

"I'll get to it," Cam said. "Hey, did you send me a message?" He didn't mention the note.

"Not lately," Ari said. "Do you want one?"

Cam chuckled. "Sure."

"It's time to start focusing on the task at hand, as Ward always says. *That's* my message for you. He isn't kidding about this being dangerous, you know. And not in the 'you should drive more carefully' way your parents were always saying it."

"My parents didn't always say that."

"Don't tangent on me. This is serious business, bud. These pirates don't mess around. They're not like the Somali idiots you read about on the Internet. These guys are former coca growers who got laid off and had to reinvent themselves. They used to cut off ears, dude—now it's hands and heads. And despite our training, we're not professional commandos. Before you got here Ward said he'd be shocked if he didn't lose half of us on this first mission. And, after reading the background and intel and looking at the maps, I have to agree with him. I'll be up half the night studying."

"Why? Is there a quiz?"

"The ultimate quiz, and I'm the team leader. I'm responsible for all of you poor saps. I don't think any of you wants to check out early, except maybe Wally."

"Yeah, he's crazy."

"You think?" Ari lightened up and laughed.

"Do you believe he's here for the good of mankind, like we all pledged?"

Ari climbed up onto his own bunk and lay looking thoughtfully at the ceiling. "I think he cares, but he certainly doesn't sweat the small stuff, and he doesn't give a rat on a stick about his own well-being. Me, I'm not so eager to die. I think the fact that we have less time on earth makes every moment more precious. Not to be melo-dramatic."

"What about Gwen?"

"Religious zealot."

"Really? The way she paws Donnie?"

"Repressed religious zealot. The worst kind. Won't give up the holy hole, but the word is she'll do anything else for him."

"That's probably more than I needed to know, thanks."

"Incidentally, how are you with g-o-d?"

"He and I had a parting of ways over this whole brain tumor thing."

"I totally understand."

"And what's Zara's deal? She's definitely not repressed."

"Right. I'm guessing she's already had a roll in the sand with just about every—"

"I meant, what do you think is the real reason she's here?"

"Gotcha. She's in it for the extreme experience. If our mission helps others, fine, but she's looking for an adrenaline rush you can't find in a hospital bed."

"Jules?"

"Normal gal. Refreshingly normal. The kind of girl a guy could marry."

Ari glanced away, momentarily self-conscious, and Cam decided to hold his own comment on her appearance—she wasn't pretty, but Ari didn't need to hear that.

"And Calliope?"

Ari grinned. "I thought you'd get around to her."

"Just wondering."

"She's one of my new favorite people," Ari said. "She feels pain deeply and takes things too hard, but has a truly good heart. You like her?"

"I try to like everyone," Cam said.

"Even your scuba friends?"

"As long as they mean well. We're a team, right?"

"Good policy. Wish I could be so accepting. You're all right, Cam." With that, his smallish roommate turned away.

Cam found himself feeling the empty space under his pillow. He hadn't replaced the note for fear Ward would find it. He didn't know why it mattered—Ward and Pilot didn't care if there were romantic shenanigans, so long as everyone trained—but it just seemed best to keep it to himself, so he'd slid it into his toothbrush holder. He was a bit old for secrets and notes, but it was nice to know someone was watching him.

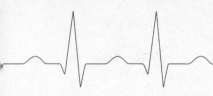

11. LOVE RHYMES WITH SHOVE 🔊
   by Lisa Ran Away

12. BOY FEVER
   by Wind Chimes and Grace

13. SEXT ME
   by Jackie Z

"You love me, shove me, put yourself above me."

The day began with a trail run. Cam had run trails back home in Bellingham, Washington, for soccer conditioning—Chuckanut and Galbraith mountains, five miles up and five back down. But jogging the open paths of the county parks was nothing compared to a jungle run. Half of the time, Cam found himself fighting through underbrush or crawling up muddy hillsides. Ward and Pilot followed them, picking off the slow among them with paintball guns.

Jules was first—shot in the leg. Calliope made the mistake of stopping to see if her friend was okay and was taken next. Three balls of red paint exploded against the side of her ribs so that she looked like a clown wearing a polka dot shirt. The paintballs hurt and left welts, and Cam winced when he saw her jerk sideways. Even as he watched from up the hill, the rest of the team ran on, leaving him in the rear. He turned and scrambled after them.

Gwen twisted an ankle and went down. Cam heard her tell Ward that he didn't need to shoot her, because she was unable to finish anyway. Then she begged. There were two hollow thumps and yelps of pain, and Cam realized Ward had plugged her anyway. Cam wondered where he'd shot her.

Ari shouted for the rest of them to split up into two pairs and a trio. Because he was team leader for the mission, they did as he said without delay or question, as Ward had instructed. Even Donnie bit his lip and complied. He and Owen went south. Ari, Zara, and Cam went north. Tegan and Wally doubled back, attempting to sneak past their pursuers. It was Wally's suggestion, and they dashed off before Ari could object. They were "dead" before they could find hiding places.

With only two groups left, Ward and Pilot could split up and follow them both.

"I'm climbing," Ari said suddenly. He was panting, and he could hardly get the words out. Even on TS-9, he was exhausted.

"You'll be trapped up there."

"I know. But you won't. Zara, leave your pack at the base of the tree. Cam, give me one shoe, then both of you go ten yards and bury yourselves in the brush. No, better make it fifteen. Go!"

They understood and didn't argue. Zara dropped her pack, and Cam handed over his shoe. Then they busted tail through the brush while Ari climbed the tree with the thickest branches and leaves. He went up easily for a skinny guy, hand-over-hand. The two of them found a dense thicket and squirmed into it.

The figure that broke into view was muscular and dexterous, leaping obstacles like a panther. Ward. They were unlucky. Pilot was not as strong and agile or as good a shot. Their personal trainer stopped and surveyed the area, suspicious. He glanced up, spotted Ari, who was easily visible, then circled the tree at ten yards. Ari wedged himself in. Moments later, Cam's shoe tumbled out of the tree and fell right in front of Ward, bouncing on the soft loam of the rainforest floor.

Ward nodded and started up, grabbing the lowest branch. He went up quickly, gun in hand. He was so fast that Cam and Zara hardly had time to break cover and run before he realized he'd been tricked, shot Ari from below, and descended like a monkey. He swung from branch to branch as they tore back toward the compound, putting distance between themselves and their instructor.

"Go, baby!" Ari shouted.

"Shut it," Ward growled as he leaped from the tree. "You're dead."

Cam was fast—college soccer fast—but he was missing a shoe. Zara outpaced him, her muscular legs pumping, carrying her over rocks and roots. She plowed through thick underbrush with such power that she passed Cam and left a trail of snapped branches for him to run through. They made it back to the bluff well ahead of Ward, and Zara went over first, grabbing the rope and shimmying down. Cam paused, overlooking the beach. If he started down the rope, Ward would simply shoot him from above. But hurrying down would be stupid—if he fell he could die for real. Cam grabbed a leaf the size of a garbage can lid from a nearby plant and ripped its stalk free from the stem. Stuffing the stalk down the back of his shirt and hunching over, he took hold of the rope and began to work his way down.

The inch-thick leaf covered his head and shoulders, and it wasn't long before the first paint pellet thumped into it. Red paint splattered from the leaf and fell around him, but didn't mark Cam's flesh or clothing. Even after three more impacts, he reached the bottom unstained. He felt Ward on the rope above, but even their trainer wouldn't be able to hit him while swinging back and forth, Cam thought. He dropped from the rope and ran across the sand, plucking the leaf from his back.

He'd never been so tired in his life, and the anxiety of being a living target drove his heart rate even higher. Cam collapsed facedown on the steps of the bunker next to Zara, gasping for breath. She'd already recovered.

"Good run," she said with a smirk, and gave him a firm swat on the rump.

Ward sauntered up the beach moments later and stood over them, pistol in hand.

"Safe," Cam panted.

"Safe," Ward agreed. "Nice work."

The others filtered out of the jungle over the next few minutes, each with some body part painted bright red. Donnie had been shot in the back. Jules in the torso. Owen had taken one in the neck, which looked like it hurt. Gwen had been shot twice, in the chest and the face, a punishment for trying to quit the game.

When they had all gathered, chattering and telling the stories of their various deaths, Ward addressed them.

"What did we learn today?"

"That we suck?" Wally said, wiping red paint from his orange hair.

"Cam and Zara survived," Ward continued. "How?"

"They're fast," Jules offered.

"So is Donnie, and he's dead." Ward pointed to the red splotch on Donnie's back.

"Sacrifice," Cam said. "Ari gave himself up to help us escape."

"Correct. Ari used his one life to save two others. Simple math. Get it?" Ward surveyed their faces, and then nodded, satisfied that they understood. "Dart practice in thirty minutes."

Cam went to Ari with a high-five extended, but Ari didn't receive it or express any enthusiasm.

"We did it!" Cam said.

"Did what?" Ari said. "I'm dead." He pointed at a red streak of paint on his leg. "That shot would have clipped my femoral artery."

"You were brilliant. We were the only ones who made it."

"Yeah," Ari said, "the only ones. Don't you get it? I was responsible for *every*one. That was a damned cluster! I need to be brilliant *before* eighty percent of my team gets whacked."

———

Dart practice included all of the members of the infiltration team, except Ari, who had disappeared with Pilot. They lined up outside the bunker in front of a human-shaped target. Ward laid out ten darts on a small wooden table. They were odd little things, Cam thought, like tiny syringes with snap-on wings.

"We throw these?" Cam asked

"Two each," Ward said. "Be sure to follow through as if you are throwing it through the target and five feet beyond."

Gwen stepped forward and took her two darts. She flung one at the target. It missed. The second hit the target in the leg. Ward motioned for Jules to go next. She hit once, barely in the foot. Calliope didn't want a turn, but Ward insisted, and she threw her darts halfheartedly, missing twice. For the first time, Ward looked a bit frustrated.

Cam stepped forward and lifted his first dart from the table. It felt natural in his hand—he'd had a dartboard as a kid, a real one his father had brought home from England. The weight of the dart was good—heavy in the forward barrel, light in the shaft. The flights were sturdier than they looked, and the point was needle sharp.

"These are disguised as syringes," Ward said. "One of you will carry them on your person. They'll be labeled 'medication' in English and Spanish. It's our hope they won't confiscate them. If you are interrogated, these are injections for serious allergies."

Epi weapons, Cam thought. *Clever.* He cocked it to his ear and hurled it into the chest of the target. Sweeping up the second, he delivered it to the target's head in one smooth motion.

Jules whistled, and Ward scribbled something in his small notebook.

With an athlete's ego, Cam looked to see if Calliope had noticed his proficiency. It was a mistake. Hitting another human in the head and heart with a sharp object from a distance did not impress her.

It did impress Jules, however. "Wow, Cam, you're good!"

"At stabbing people," Calliope muttered.

"Just lucky," he said, trying to play it down. "I was on a baseball team in elementary school before I had to commit to soccer." But it was too late. He'd made his reputation as a pigsticker in two throws.

They threw more rounds, with Ward donning padded gear and running at them or leaping out as they walked the halls of the bunker. Cam found his mark every time. The rest were inconsistent, and Calliope never hit him at all. Cam couldn't tell whether it was on purpose and in protest or simply because she was a miserable athlete. Perhaps some of both, he thought.

When they broke for lunch, Ward went to work with the scuba team and Wally. And Ari returned from his outing.

"*They* get air-powered dart guns," Ari complained. "Nobody's going to search them when they sneak into camp and start poking pirates."

The mealtime mood was somber. The mission was coming, and everyone felt it. They didn't gather at one table. Ari and Jules sat together. Gwen sat nearby but buried herself in salad and soup, undoubtedly fretting that Donnie was getting an eyeful of Zara. Cam found a seat next to Calliope, who sat noticeably apart from the rest.

"Can I join you?"

She shrugged. Cam sat and began chewing his sandwich. Calliope didn't look at him.

"You seem apprehensive."

She didn't look up. "I am. I won't lie. This is *not* my kind of mission."

"We're going to save doctors, and they're going to save others. We're saving lives exponentially."

"I always get killed first in training. Dying second today was a huge improvement. I know I'm going to die this year. I accept that. But I'm not ready to go this week. I haven't accomplished anything yet."

"That's why we're here. We're accomplishing something."

"I mean my music. No offense, but I didn't want you to be my only audience. Music was something I could leave behind, a way to live on, a sort of immortality. But now nobody will ever hear me."

She still hadn't looked at him. Cam could understand her anxiety. They were only days away. His instincts told him to drop it for now and talk to her another time, but the fact that there might not be another time was impossible to ignore.

"Did you leave me a note?" he asked.

"A note?"

"A secret note."

"You mean like a high school girl with a crush?" She snickered. She didn't mean to be cruel, but it stung a little. "No. But if it said 'meet me out back for a good time,' it's probably Zara."

"It didn't say 'meet me out back,'" Cam said defensively.

"Then what did it say?"

"Something mature and intelligent," he lied.

"That sounds like Gwen," she said.

"I doubt it. Never mind. And please don't tell anyone."

"Don't worry," Calliope said. "I'm a vault. I keep it all in." She glanced up at him for the first time since he'd sat down and gave him a sad smile.

"Hey, you two," Ari called from across the room. "The scuba crew and Wally are back."

Across the room, Gwen leaped up so fast to run out and meet Donnie that she whacked her knee on the table. She limped through the door. Calliope rose and took her tray to the sink, seemingly grateful for an excuse to leave their conversation. Soon everyone was out in front of the bunker.

The scuba team and Wally sauntered up, toting small plastic pistols that looked like toys. Wally spun his gun around his finger, then gripped it and aimed above Cam's head, his brow furrowed and extended arm still as a metal pole for a split second.

Thwip-thwip! Two darts sprang from the barrel. Cam winced as they flew over his head.

"Watch it, dipwad," Ari snapped.

Just as Cam began to relax, an orange monkey dropped beside him, and he jumped again.

Wally shrieked with laughter. "Bull's-eye! Monkey's-eyes!"

One dart had indeed pierced each of the monkey's eyes. *Incredible*, Cam thought. Wally's unnatural focus and steady hand had delivered the needle-tipped ordnance with absurd accuracy, and the two doses killed the monkey almost instantly. *Maybe even just one, for a small animal.* It seized and spasmed and then stiffened, its little lips curling back in a toothy grimace.

"You jerk," Calliope said.

"That was a needless death," Ward agreed. "We only kill one if it saves others. This is a waste. Inefficient and cruel."

"Not if we eat it," Wally said.

"Yeah, if you're fond of paralysis, genius," Ari said. "Eat that, and you ingest what you injected."

"Give me your weapon, Wally," Donnie said. "You're a loose cannon."

"Piss off," Wally said. "You don't own me."

"I'm scuba leader," Donnie said.

"I'm not scuba," Wally pointed out. "I'm aerial. I'm on my own."

Ward watched the exchange, but didn't intervene.

Ari put his hands up in a "calm down" gesture. "Wally, I'm just gonna ask you to please not randomly kill any more cute or cuddly wildlife. Okay?"

The entire group fell silent. Ari was team leader, and the sudden quiet moment between him and Wally was a test of their system, Cam thought, an example of authority problems that could arise during the real action. If there was to be order, Wally would have to relent. Otherwise, the chain of command would be weakened before the mission even began.

Wally frowned and then handed Ari his pistol. "Okay," he said. Then he grinned. "What else we got for lunch besides monkey?"

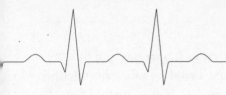

"You make me feel hot, weak,
and a bit like throwing up,
in a good way, in a good way, in a good way.
Yup!"

Three more days of heavy training followed, each more specific than the last. Ward and Pilot became constant dart targets, and the team's jungle survival runs improved steadily. In the final run, six of them survived, with Donnie selflessly lying in wait to tackle Pilot and take his paintball gun. He was then quickly killed by Ward, but the delay allowed the rest of the party to escape. More briefings were held with satellite views of the pirate compound and careful analyses of the likely interior layout of the buildings. The final day was a day of relative rest entirely devoted to live scenarios with no runs or swimming. Instead, they were bound, blindfolded, and dragged from place to place in the bunker and condos, while the scuba team moved in to free them.

"The one constant is variability," Ward quipped at them.

Zara pierced Calliope's tongue with a hot nail to help fit it with a tongue stud transmitter, through which she could report her position and give directions to the team. Cam was amazed that she could talk with her mouth closed and that Wally and the entire scuba team could understand her.

Cam fell into a supporting role, but due to his proficiency throwing darts he was selected to have extra needles and flights sewn into his clothing. He was also given a beaten strap-on water bottle full of poison in the hope they wouldn't think it important enough to take from him.

"Don't accidentally drink it," Ward warned him quite seriously. An athlete's habit of sucking on water bottles almost without thinking would be deadly for the next forty-eight hours.

And, suddenly, the training was done.

The doctor visit was off-campus. Pilot flew them to the facility blindfolded, where they crunched down a gravel path. Once inside, they were unmasked and waited together in a windowless room with Ping-Pong and pool tables and all the soda they could drink. Ari called it "the gli club," named after the malignant glioblastomas they all carried in their heads.

Cam was good at both table games. He'd had a pool table with a removable Ping-Pong top in his house growing up, and Western Washington University supplied several of each in its dormitory common area. In fact, he'd been dorm champ sophomore year. Yet he struggled to keep up with Zara and Owen in Ping-Pong. They returned his slams with razor-sharp reflexes. And Donnie beat him outright. Ari then schooled him in pool, playing the angles with concentration and precision the likes of which Cam had never seen.

A doctor met with them individually in a room full of equipment. Shelves with bottles and beakers lined the walls. It looked less like a doctor's office than a laboratory. Cam's doc was older, maybe fifty, and wore khakis with boots. Her hair was pulled back so tight it stretched her face into a taut mask. She and a male doc had come into the game room and pointed at them one by one, not using their names. Tegan first. Each took over an hour. Cam and Jules were last.

When it was his turn, she marched him down a short hallway into another room. Before Cam could even say hello, she shoved a pencil and some forms at him. The forms didn't have his name at the top. Instead, there was a number and letter—9K. *Anonymity*, Cam thought.

He spent the first ten minutes filling out a survey while the doc took his heart rate, checked his blood pressure, and drew blood into a tube. The survey began with questions about symptoms not associated with his disease. Were there aches in his head? Was there blood in his stool? The questions segued into performance inquiries. Did he feel stronger, faster, more agile? "None of the above" was his answer du jour. He wasn't taking enhancers and, now that he thought about it, his cancer symptoms were not acting up at all. He felt pretty much the same as when he'd arrived, only now he had a better tan. One of the most curious questions asked him whether he felt more "compliant" or more "rebellious." He puzzled over it for a moment and then finally wrote "both" in the margin and moved on. The whole thing seemed like a waste of ten minutes of his short life.

The doctor sat watching him fill out the form, studying him so that he felt like he was taking a proctored college entrance exam. He supposed it was her job. He handed her the finished papers.

"All right. Turn around and drop your trousers."

"For what?"

"There are a dozen diseases in this geographic region that you don't want to catch," she said completely without humor, hoisting the biggest syringe Cam had ever seen. "Now drop them."

"So when would you advise me to start taking TS-9, doc?" he said while he stuck his bare butt in the air. He copped a smile and tried to sound conversational.

"All questions should be directed to your personal trainer," she said. Then the injection came.

"Holy . . . !" Cam couldn't help wincing. It was the most pain he'd experienced by way of his butt since he'd pulled a glute freshman year. It wasn't the "quick pinch" his doctor at home used to tell him was coming when he was a boy getting flu shots. She worked it back and forth for what seemed an eternity before sliding it out and slapping a patch over the hole.

She ran her eyes down his survey answers while he pulled his pants up. "You may go."

Cam stood, confused. "But you didn't examine me."

"You responded here that there was no change in your condition." She pointed at the survey.

"Yeah, but I'm dying of a brain tumor."

"That's not a change, is it?"

He looked around. Among the medical equipment was a treadmill, a weight bench, a tube thing with a mouthpiece to blow into. She'd not had him use any of them. "Everyone else took over an hour."

"You may go," she repeated.

Cam exited and closed the door behind him. *This checkup wasn't for me*, he thought. Suddenly, he was angry. He didn't know where it came from, but he felt it boiling up and decided not to stop it. *I'm dying! And they don't bother to examine me? And they won't even offer me the wonder drug they're handing out to everyone else like candy?* He started down the hall toward the game room, and then stopped. He realized he had wanted some answers, and they hadn't even let him ask questions. He turned and walked back down the hall to the examination room. He reached for the handle, but paused. Beyond the examination room was another door. *Screw it*, Cam thought. He walked past the exam room and shoved the next door open.

Three startled men whirled and stared at him. They were dressed in lab coats. Before them on the table were nine vials of red fluid. *My teammates' blood*, Cam thought. Behind them was a gurney. One of the men quickly pulled a sheet over it.

"Oops," Cam said cheerfully. "Wrong room."

The men glanced at each other.

"Down the hall," one of them finally said through gritted teeth. "The other way."

The second man nudged the first, and he hurried across the room to escort Cam out.

"Sorry," Cam said. "The doors look the same."

"No problem," the man said thinly, turning Cam around and walking him toward the game room. "Right down here."

"Got it," Cam said, and he smiled at the man. "Thanks."

The last beach fire before the mission was quiet and short. No booze. Cam pulled Ari aside and asked him about the exam. He was surprised when his roommate grew testy.

"It's impolite to ask for people's private medical information, Cam," Ari said.

Cam rolled his eyes and went to ask Jules, who blabbed every detail. As he suspected, the doc had done a number of physical tests on her that she hadn't bothered to administer to Cam. Jules said their prior exams had taken several hours each, and they'd poked and prodded them much more extensively. Cam didn't tell her about the other room. He wasn't sure what he'd seen, and she didn't seem the right person in whom to confide.

Cam hit his bunk exhausted and sore from the week. His feet ached from running over the uneven ground and debris in the forest. His legs were as tired as they had been for the first week of fall soccer practice after every summer. He had bruises where Zara had worked him over with the padded poles during a melee workout, and the tattoo she'd inflicted on him hurt and itched. His teammates were sore too. Even Donnie had complained a little, though only under his breath when he thought no one could hear. But Ward assured them all they'd be well rested after their day of light work and a good night's sleep, and they all went to sleep early. Cam wondered if he'd dream of pirates.

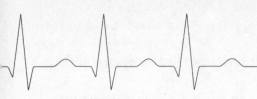

"The image of me in your head,
or that snap of me on my bed.
Which one do you fantasize to?"

Pilot woke them at dawn. "The boat leaves in fifteen minutes. Grab a shower, brush your teeth, and meet on the beach with your gear. You'll eat breakfast at sea."

When Cam tumbled out of bed he found that Ari was already up and gone. He brushed his teeth quickly, then pulled on the swim trunks he wore daily and headed for the outdoor shower. He had to wait for Gwen. Watching her shower in her swimsuit was surprisingly uninteresting. She was frowny, all business, and had a routine—first her feet, then legs, torso, and hair last. Systematic. No surprises. Nothing missed, and nothing lingered upon.

"I have finished," she announced curtly. She stepped out, groping for her glasses almost before the water stopped flowing. She straightened them carefully, content only after they were perched on her nose just so, providing her with two little windows on the world. *Or windshields*, Cam thought.

The team gathered at the shoreline. No Ward. No Pilot. Ari was nowhere to be seen either.

"What the hell?" Donnie complained.

"Still two minutes," Gwen said, tapping her cell phone. They'd all been given cheap phones just for show. They'd almost certainly be taken immediately and weren't meant for use, but the simple gadgets told time and had an overhead map of the pirate compound that could be accessed only with the code word—DEATHWING.

"Look," Owen said. He pointed out to sea.

A rigid inflatable boat approached, its outboard motor humming. Donnie said he could see Ari's black hair from a distance before Cam could even make out the shape of a person.

They murmured among themselves, speculating, but Cam knew that Ari would fill them in as soon as he arrived, so he didn't bother to take up any brain space wondering. The ten-person craft surfed an incoming wave, and Ari tilted the engine out of the water at the last minute so that it glided entirely up onto the beach and lurched to a stop right at their feet with him perched on the bow like a ship's figurehead. The little guy certainly liked to make an entrance, Cam thought.

"All aboard!" he shouted happily over the surf.

"We're all going to cram into a rubber kiddie raft?" Gwen said, frowning.

"This is a Zodiac," Ari said, indignant. "Top of the line."

Gwen climbed in, unimpressed. Minutes later, they were all bouncing out past the surf. Ari drove like a kid with a new toy, his smile broad and genuine. Cam stood beside him while the others sat.

"Johnson outboard," Ari explained. "American made. This craft is the consumer version of what the military uses."

"How do you know that?"

"You know that kid who had every toy car, boat, and plane? The dorky one who built models and had a bunch of remote control crap?"

"Yeah."

"Well, I was that kid. Only now I'm old enough to drive the real thing." Ari tilted his head back and whooped into the spray as they hit a wave. "Woo-hoo!"

Ari steered toward the southern cliffs, and the boat climbed over the rolling water. Cam put his headphones on and punched up a song, taking note of the landscape south of the compound. It was treacherous, steep and heavily forested. Trying to get to the condos and bunker wasn't only difficult because of the cliffs, it was almost impossible because of the terrain that preceded it. Cam noted that it was probably also impossible to go the other direction.

They came around a point, and Ari looped into a protected cove. To Cam's surprise, a sizable white yacht floated at anchor ahead of them. It was a sixty- or seventy-footer—one or two million dollars' worth of vessel, Cam estimated.

"Ward says we should avoid contact with civilians," Donnie advised as they motored into the cove. He pointed at the yacht.

"It looks empty to me," Ari said. He winked at Cam and steered directly toward it. When Donnie began to protest again, Ari raised a hand to silence him. "Trust me, Donnie."

They pulled up to the stern of the yacht, and Ari shimmied up the ladder hanging down the back.

"Anyone there?" Cam called up.

"No one but us," Ari said.

They all glanced at each other.

"You're kidding, right?" Cam replied.

Ari held up a set of keys.

"Yes!" Wally yelled, and he flew up the ladder.

The others stampeded past Cam, who stood in the Zodiac, stunned.

"Cam, throw me the line and let's haul that dinghy up here," Ari called down. "We are going pirate hunting in style!"

The yacht was spacious for ten young adults. The main deck had a kitchen and common area. The lower three cabins held two bunks and two large beds. Ari stood at the controls on the upper deck and took her out.

"You know how to operate this thing?" Cam asked.

"This 'thing' is a Ferretti 630, I'll have you know—a million five worth of boating goodness. And what do you think I've been doing all week while you chumps were playing darts and going for swims? *This* was my training."

The cruising time was nearly ten hours, according to Ari, and so they had eight hours free before they needed to start their prep.

The refrigerator was fully stocked. Ari and Pilot had made some inroads on the food supply during the week to make the boat look lived in, but there was still plenty.

Jules decided to prepare a meal for everyone, explaining that she cooked for her family back home and missed it. "It's hard to believe I've only been gone a couple of months," she said, her eyes tearing up. Then she excused herself to the kitchen to get started.

The others scattered about the large deck. Cam stood out over the ship's prow with his arms spread and fists thrust forward, listening to "Ace in the Hole" at near maximum volume. It was an anthem of sorts, but a touch discordant and not for everybody. He found he preferred bands' less famous songs and wondered what that said about him.

Donnie, Gwen, and Owen sat around a deck-side table in the stern, continuing to review strategies and scenarios. It wasn't required, Ari said, but it wouldn't hurt them any either. Tegan had found a deck of cards and played solitaire, although he seemed to spend most of his time chasing stray cards that the light ocean breeze slid askew. Wally had gone with Pilot in the helicopter. He would be launched miles away with a radio receiver and hang glide into the action if necessary.

"Relaxing is a good idea too," Ari said to Cam when he came into the cabin.

"You going to drive all ten hours?"

"If I can." Ari still had the big smile on his face.

Cam decided to visit the girls. Calliope was helping Jules create a sort of chicken Parmesan out of frozen breasts and a hard cheese they'd found in the crisper. Music from a satellite channel blared from portable speakers. They made small talk as they worked, avoiding the topic of the mission. But the kitchen was not big enough for the three of them. Cam lingered a bit, but found he was mostly in the way.

Everyone seemed able to occupy themselves except him. But he didn't believe anyone was honestly relaxing in the face of the impending raid. Even those who were no longer prepping couldn't ignore that it was coming.

The ship's cabins were downstairs in a short hall. An escape of sorts. Cam trotted down to check them out. There were three doors. One of them stood slightly ajar, just a crack, and light leaked out. Cam frowned and walked over to investigate. He pushed it wide and stepped into the room. A bedroom. But something was wrong. The door swung closed behind him suddenly, and he was thrown forward onto the bed. The person on top of him pinned one arm. He flailed with his other, until his fingers were forcibly bent backward.

"Oww! I give!"

"You gonna be that easy for the pirates?" Zara said. She straddled his legs, held his arm behind his back, and shoved his head down.

"I think the idea is to *let* them capture us," he mumbled into the pillow.

"Well, now I've captured you. The question is: what shall I do with you?"

"Let go of my fingers?"

Zara chuckled and gave them one last painful yank for good measure. Then she slid her hand from his arm to his shoulder and flipped him over so that she was sitting on his stomach. Sweat trickled down her arms and dripped from the tip of her nose onto Cam's chest.

He squirmed beneath her. "Someone's going to come investigate."

"The music is too loud and the door is locked," she said, and she wiggled her eyebrows.

Cam felt his heartbeat quicken. Zara panted on top of him as she held him down. He could feel her heat rolling off her. It was suffocating.

"I'm not sure this is the right time or place," he heard himself say.

"Are you kidding? We're on a million-dollar yacht in an exotic country, we're young and hot, we have no girlfriends or boyfriends to be faithful to, and we're all going to die within a year. Maybe even today. This is *exactly* the right time and place."

She has a point, Cam thought. There was no reason to hold back. And she was right about herself being hot—it didn't even sound like bragging coming from her. Still . . .

"How many of the guys on the team have you done this with?" he asked. "The romance, I mean, not the assault."

Zara just laughed. "It's not romance."

"So I'm not the first."

She just smirked. Her nonanswer told him what he needed to know. Donnie for sure. Probably others, though they were hard to imagine. Tegan or Owen. Calliope maybe? Certainly not Ari. Or Wally—Cam shuddered.

"I hate to ask if you've tried this on Ward."

She hesitated, and Cam could see that she was way ahead of him.

"Ward is a Boy Scout," she complained. "You're not a Boy Scout, are you, Cam?"

"I was."

"Oh my god! This doesn't need to be complicated. You're like a lady."

"And you're not."

Cam wanted to take it back even as it came out of his mouth. There was hurt in her eyes for a moment. But as quickly as it appeared, the look vanished. She scowled and climbed off him, her lips drawing a delicate line between defiance and uncertainty.

"Have the decency not to tell anyone about this, okay?"

"Okay," Cam said. Being decent wasn't a problem for him. Then again, he thought, it was exactly his problem sometimes.

Zara stepped to the door and grabbed the handle. She paused, and Cam marveled at how the back of a woman's head could look sad. She spoke without turning around. "Don't you think I'm pretty?"

"Yes," Cam answered. "Very."

It seemed to be enough. She nodded and slipped out.

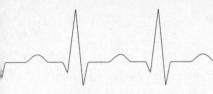

"Don't come at me cocked and locked unless you're ready to rock."

Two hours out Ari revealed a hidden trapdoor in the floor of the boat.

"This used to be a smuggler's vessel," he explained, and he instructed the scuba team to tuck their gear away. They'd soon be ducking into the hold also. There was a watertight exterior hatch through which they would exit when the time came.

Very nice, Cam thought, impressed, and he suddenly wondered where the organization got their funding. He'd ask Ward later, he decided. Some things weren't talked about, but Ward was always open to questions and, when he answered them, he was brutally honest.

The yacht cruised into darker waters. It was hoped they would be taken in the evening so that they would spend as little time in the hands of the pirates as possible before their nighttime assault. Ward had warned them that despite their preparation, there would be "variables." Pirate recruits came and went. Leaders changed. Their methods evolved or deteriorated. Some of them were on drugs and erratic. Some were erratic without drugs. There was no way to predict exactly where they would be ambushed or what the pirates would do with them. The hope was simple—they'd be walked through camp without blindfolds and housed with the doctors. They could direct the scuba strike team, which would then know the defenses, would find them easily, and bring them all out together. Unfortunately, Ward also said, things usually weren't simple.

A skiff with POLICÍA stenciled on the side in drippy paint approached near dusk, sending the scuba team scrambling for the secret hold. Gwen and Jules snapped the faux-wood floor back into place over them and then stapled a carpet over the top of it.

Ari stepped to the rail to meet their guests, who pulled up alongside and flashed badges as though they were law enforcement officers. It was a ruse, and they all knew it, but Ari pretended to believe. To Cam's surprise, he spoke Spanish to them as they demanded to come aboard toting different types of guns. Cam frowned—they didn't even look like cops. At least one appeared to understand Ari's Spanish, though they spoke to each other in a language Cam didn't recognize.

"I'm scared," Calliope whispered.

"Me too," Cam said. "But you've been training for a month. You're ready. Just focus on the task at hand."

Calliope's task was communications. She nodded, appearing reassured, and moved near Ari, keeping her ears and earrings open. Cam saw her mouth moving subtly, communicating the events to the scuba team below, and Wally, if he was in range.

Ari's task as team leader was to determine their opponent's leader and negotiate for any advantage he could gain. He was already asking questions, feeling them out to see which of the bearded men was in charge of the skiff. There was likely a different man on shore who was in charge of the entire compound.

Cam's job was to count weapons, decide which men seemed aggressive or unstable, and keep track of the locations of the gun toters as best he could. He turned his attention to his own chore, which turned out to be easy. They all had guns, and they all looked unstable. There were three pistols in the boat and two rifles. The lead man—the talker—appeared confident and held a rifle casually at his side. Cam and his friends looked like stupid rich kids, after all. Two other men sat with their hands under their shirts, clearly gripping pistols, eyes darting about, hardly more than boys. They were scared, Cam thought, but no less dangerous. In fact, they were skittish, like nervous dogs, and potentially trigger-happy. He made a note of it. The last man was running his eyes over their vessel. He recognized its value, it seemed, or at least could see that it was extremely valuable, possibly worth more than a ransom. He wore a floppy hat and carried a nicer rifle. He was the real skiff leader, Cam concluded. He glanced at Ari, who met his gaze with an eyebrow twitch—Cam's roommate already knew. Floppy hat man hung back, letting the talker take the risk of being identified as leader and shot first if there was a confrontation.

Ari managed to surrender the boat without any pointing of guns. He even got their captors to agree to let him steer it into their ramshackle dock. It was better than being taken by force, for both sides. By pretending to believe they were a police outpost, Ari was even allowed to continue speaking with his own team.

"They will take us to wait with other 'trespassers' while they contact our authorities to determine why we've 'violated their waters.' I told him we were sorry we strayed into their jurisdiction, and by morning we could gather money to pay any 'fine' they deem reasonable."

Bingo! Cam thought. The other trespassers would surely be the doctors.

As they were escorted ashore, Cam continued counting pirates.

Multiple men stood about the compound eyeing them as they were marched in. Ari's tact also meant no blindfolds. Another advantage. Two men on the roof, Cam counted, and one at the gate. All armed, but they appeared bored and inattentive. That made seven so far. *Ten of us versus seven of them*, he thought. Reasonable odds, assuming they were not tied up—Ward had thought they would not be. More probably they'd be trusted to a locked room. Gwen's job was to count and memorize the layout of the place as they were led through. She was good with maps. Cam could see her studying the walls and counting her paces. The team was on task. Whether it was their enhancement, the training, or the sheer terror of the situation that focused them he couldn't tell, but all were certainly doing their best to execute the jobs they had been assigned, which was good, he thought, because their condensed lives surely depended on it now.

There was a courtyard. Brick walls. Cam spotted a faded chalk outline on the bricks beside the door they were headed toward. The chalk formed a rectangle of familiar size—approximately eight feet high and, he guessed, twenty-four feet wide. A soccer goal. Their escorts hustled them through the door into a large room with chairs, a fan, and a primitive-looking toilet.

"Wait in here," the talker said to Ari in Spanish. Floppy hat nodded behind him, and the door swung closed. An ominous click signaled a deadbolt being thrown on the outside.

"Gwen," Ari said immediately, "do you have the layout?"

"Of course," she replied, and she dropped to her knees to quickly draw in the dirt floor with a pencil she produced from her shoe. "It's nearly a square around the courtyard. The exterior and interior walls are ten feet apart on three sides, meaning those three sides are only one room deep with no hallways. I saw two doors on each wall and one beside the entrance. So six rooms. Judging from the cheap construction, they probably mirror each other. Two other doors were propped open. We're in one. That leaves four others the doctors could be in. My money is on the one to the right of us as we exit, because it has a deadbolt like ours."

Cam was impressed. He thought he'd done well just counting the guards. *She's hyperfocused*, he thought. *Better than me.* He'd been admiring a stupid soccer goal while Gwen had been vacuuming up critical information with hawklike eyes.

"Good work," Ari said. "They're probably discussing what to do with us now that they've got us tucked away. They said we'd wait with others, but they could change their minds."

Jules looked around the room, concerned.

"What are you thinking, Jules?" Ari asked.

"I'm *not* pooping in front of you guys," she said.

"I think that's the least of our worries," Gwen snorted.

"For you, maybe. But if we die, I want my dignity intact."

"We shouldn't be here that long," Ari assured her. "A couple hours, tops. Donnie will be here with his team as soon as possible. They released from our vessel just before we docked. Keep your eyes and ears open. Gather all the info you can so we can relay it to them. Any detail could be the difference between success and failure."

Cam watched Calliope repeat everything they were saying inside her own mouth almost without moving her lips, like a ventriloquist without a doll. She waited for a moment and then nodded. The tongue transmitter had sent, and she'd received confirmation back through her earrings.

"The scuba team is holding just offshore," she said quietly. "The pirates are sweeping the vessel, and there are too many lights on the dock to come ashore near it. They're going to drift down the shoreline and look for a more secluded angle of approach."

Just then the bolt clacked open. They quieted as the door jerked wide, revealing one of the nervous boys from the dinghy. He stepped inside and sat heavily in a chair beside the door, where he fumbled out a fake tin badge. Ari acknowledged his phony authority with a polite nod. It was weakly returned. The boy didn't want to be there. Upon closer inspection, he appeared even younger than Cam had first thought. His faint mustache struggled for a foothold on his upper lip, and adolescent acne dotted his forehead. *No more than sixteen.* He reminded Cam vaguely of a nervous boy named Simon at his high school who the other kids picked on.

They sat for half an hour, until their teen guard grew bored and slumped in his chair, staring at the floor. The boy's superiors were undoubtedly discussing what to do with the rich Americans they'd captured, and this little pirate wasn't important enough to be included. Instead he'd drawn babysitting detail. Gwen kept track of time by tapping her foot methodically, her concentration almost total. Calliope carefully listened to her earrings, but rarely talked for fear of being caught with the microphone. None of them carried their cell phones. They'd been taken anyway, as expected, after each of them had been quickly frisked. The younger pirates had immediately begun snatching small electronic devices from them and the boat. More evidence that they were cheap hirelings in the endeavor and not partners who shared the real money. The syringes had been left alone. The pirates didn't want an ill captive, it seemed. Ward had been exactly right. After the search, Cam had quickly assembled two darts and passed one to Ari, who tucked it in his shirtsleeve. Now two of them had weapons.

There had been no move to put them with the doctors, however. And the scuba team was still circling, not yet approaching the compound, according to Calliope's covert reports, which she gave in hand signals Ward had taught them in the briefing room. They were allowed to talk, but they were unsure how much their guard understood, and so they said nothing of their mission. Instead, they spoke fictitiously about how worried their families would be that they were missing and whose fault it was they'd strayed off course. Then Calliope gave a hand sign that meant she needed to tell them details she couldn't signal.

Ari glanced at their guard. "Do you need to use the toilet yet, Jules?" he asked.

She shot him an annoyed look. "None of your business."

"I just wondered if you needed some *privacy*," he clarified.

"Oh! Yes. Yes, I do." She stood suddenly and crossed her legs like an elementary school child in need of a hall pass for the restroom.

"Bathroom," Ari said to the guard in Spanish, and he pointed at Jules. He motioned toward the door and indicated that he, Cam, and the guard should step outside.

The boy stood and thought for a moment, his brow furrowed. It was clear he had no authority to deviate from his instructions, and the privacy of their new female guests hadn't been discussed. Jules grimaced and gave him a pleading look. Reluctantly, he moved to the door and turned a simple key in the lock. The deadbolt slid aside, and he let the boys out, motioning for them to stand against the exterior wall. Then he closed the door behind him.

Ari whispered to Cam, "I need a moment to hear what Calliope has to say. And I need it pronto."

Cam thought hard. He ran his hand along the chalk line of the goal on the bricks. "Football?" he said to the boy finally.

The boy turned to him, curious.

Cam pointed toward the chalk. "Goal?"

The boy answered with halting Spanish.

"What'd he say?" he asked Ari.

"He says they play here in the courtyard. Penalty kicks mostly, but there's another goal on the opposite wall for scrimmages."

"Ask him if he wants to play with me," Cam said. "Tell him I'm very skilled."

Ari rattled off a sentence in Spanish. The boy shot back an answer, and Ari translated. "He says he is the best in the compound, even at his age."

"Tell him, 'maybe not anymore.'"

Ari translated, and Cam smiled good-naturedly so the boy could see that he meant it as a friendly challenge. Their guard brightened. After a stretch of nerves and boredom, the simple gesture seemed a welcome relief, and he couldn't hold back a childish grin. He motioned for them to stay and jogged across the courtyard. Moments later, he returned with a tattered ball.

Ari knocked on the door and asked loudly if Jules was done, and then opened it and went inside, quickly closing the door behind him. Cam hopped in front of the goal chalked on the wall and gestured for the boy to kick the ball before he could stop Cam's roommate.

The boy glanced toward the door, torn between following Ari and having some sport with Cam.

Cam pointed to his own chest. "Steve," he lied.

"Ranuel," the boy said.

Cam crouched in front of the goal. "Shoot, Ranuel." The irony of his request was not lost on Cam, but he didn't smirk. He was working. Calliope would be reporting Donnie's position to Ari right now. Dart guns were being loaded outside the wall. Poison was waiting in needles.

The ball came low and left, just as Cam had expected, though a little harder than he'd have guessed for a skinny kid like Ranuel. Cam wasn't a goalie, but he'd shagged enough balls in goal to dive and punch it wide of the chalk. He rose, spitting dust and smiling, and then touched the ball back out to Ranuel with a flick of his toe. "Again," he said. He didn't know how much time Ari would need, but the more the better.

Ranuel juggled the ball, showing off, then trapped it and fired it high and right. Cam gauged that he could reach it, but he let it slip past his fingertips. It thumped against the wall just inside of the chalk line.

Cam shook his head. "Whew! Nice shot."

Ranuel nodded, smiling. Cam retrieved the ball and dribbled it out to where Ranuel stood, but when Ranuel started toward the wall, Cam continued across the yard toward the other goal. Ranuel hesitated, and then followed. Cam glanced up at the guards on the walls. There were two. No guns visible, but they were undoubtedly within reach. The man to the east sat looking outward and never turned. The other stood on the west wall and frowned down at him and Ranuel disapprovingly, but didn't interfere. *Another minion*, Cam thought. Soccer with the prisoners was not part of the compound protocol, clearly, but the wall man apparently had no authority to correct their teen guard, and management was still in a meeting somewhere.

Cam found the penalty kick spot, a worn area in the dirt. It gave him a thought, and he glanced about, examining the doorways while trying not to look like he was examining them. The dirt was worn into a smooth trench in front of one door. That would be the one with the most foot traffic, he thought. Ergo, that would be the meeting room. It was time to get back to Ari and the others.

He lined up for a penalty kick and waited until Ranuel stepped into the goal. His first shot smacked the wall in the lower right corner almost before the teen could move. Ranuel stumbled sideways only after the ball had already bounced back out toward where Cam stood. Cam quickly lined the ball up again. He eyed the lower left corner, and then sent the ball there just fast enough that Ranuel had to dive after it. Ranuel flattened out and reached, getting a hand on it and knocking it wide. He came up smiling. When Ranuel rose, the pistol was visible in his waistband.

Cam noted the weapon's location and extended a hand to shake. *"Gracias!"* he said. He'd shown Ranuel his skill and then let the boy feel like he'd risen to the occasion. A tie meant they were peers, not opponents, and a handshake would cement the relationship.

Ranuel adjusted the pistol, and then took Cam's hand and shook it vigorously, babbling excitedly in Spanish.

You don't get out much, do you? Cam thought.

Cam took the ball and dribbled it back toward the waiting room. When he reached the door, he knocked and announced himself.

"It's Cam. And our new friend, Ranuel, is right behind me."

He entered and found his teammates standing in a semicircle around the door. Ranuel stepped in after him. Ari's dart hit the unsuspecting teen in the left breast. Ranuel reached for his pistol instinctively, but Cam knew he wore it on his right hip and secured his right arm. The teen grabbed the door with his left arm to steady himself as his legs began to buckle, and he stared at Cam with sad eyes, betrayed. Cam almost felt badly, but the boy was an outlaw, and the bullets in his gun were meant for them. Cam kicked the door closed, and Ranuel dropped to the floor.

"I take it Donnie's team is here?" Cam said.

"Four minutes and thirty seconds," Ari replied. "Things are about to get interesting."

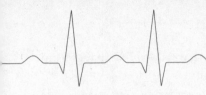

CAM'S PLAYLIST

"Chaos. Total loss. Run! Hide! It's chaos!"

"Is he dead?" Jules gently turned Ranuel over.

"Of course not," Gwen snapped. "One dart. He's just out." Gwen resumed counting. "Four minutes left."

"What about his gun?"

"Disable it. Flush the bullets," Ari instructed.

"I know where the pirate brain trust is gathered," Cam said. "The door to the right of the gate."

"How certain?"

Cam hadn't evaluated his degree of certainty. "It's the most likely door," he tried.

"'Most likely'? That's it?" Gwen complained, her eyes bugging out behind her glasses.

"I need a percentage." Ari's brow was wrinkled like that of a kid concentrating in a chess match.

Cam could almost see his roommate's mind ticking off the odds and possibilities. "I dunno. Eighty."

"It's enough."

"Two up on top," Cam added. "One over the gate and one on the west wall." He began to assemble and hand out darts. He was quick. One hundred repetitions of inserting needles and attaching flights during training made it second nature.

"Calliope, tell Donnie."

"Already doing it," she said. She relayed the information and awaited a reply. "They see the sentries and think they can dart them both."

"Okay, last mystery. Where the hell are the docs?"

"There's the one other door with a deadbolt," Cam suggested.

"That's obviously it," Gwen interjected without losing count.

"What about the gathering room?" Ari asked. "They all have guns. If scuba storms it, there are likely to be casualties."

"The doors open outward," Cam said.

Ari thought for a moment, and then nodded. "Yes. I see what you're saying. But we need to move before scuba raises a ruckus. Calli, tell scuba to give us two minutes after they dart the walls."

"We'll need something heavy," Cam said.

He and Ari tried shaking the toilet to see if they could pry it loose.

"Wall sentries are down," Calliope reported moments later.

"We have two minutes, starting now." Gwen began her count at zero again.

Cam went to the door. He almost threw it wide, but some instinct told him to peek out first instead. A large man was walking toward him, already halfway across the yard, his rifle on his hip. He glanced up, looking for the sentries, frowning.

"Someone's coming," Cam hissed, and he slid the door shut again.

"Shit!" Ari said, and they all reached for darts at once.

"He's got a rifle. Finger on the trigger. If he opens that door and sees Ranuel lying here someone's gonna get shot."

Jules breathed a desperate prayer, and Calliope shrank behind her.

"This is what we signed up for," Gwen said, gritting her teeth and gripping her dart white-knuckled. "This is the mission."

"We'll need a moment," Ari said. "Just a moment."

"The toilet!" Cam said. "Help me get Ranuel up!" When Jules hesitated, he grabbed her by the shirt and yanked her down to the teen pirate's body. "Quickly!"

Together they hauled their limp guard up onto the seat. Cam propped Ranuel's elbows on his knees and let his head drop into his chest. Finally, he yanked down the teen's worn trousers.

The man opened the door to find them all standing along the wall, politely looking away from Ranuel, who sat on the toilet with his pants around his ankles and his head down. By all appearances, Cam thought, the teen pirate was taking an especially difficult dump. The man spoke, and, when Ranuel didn't answer, he stepped across the room, turning his back to Gwen. She leaped on him from behind and buried a dart in his neck with such force that a thin stream of his blood spurted across the wall. The poison acted quicker than it did with Ranuel, and the man collapsed before he had time to raise his rifle. Cam almost stuck him with his own dart too, but held off at the last possible second. He was glad he did. It would have killed the man. Instead, the pirate merely joined his mate in unconsciousness.

Calliope was already relaying the events into her tongue ring.

"There you go," Ari said to Cam. "Something heavy."

"One minute to scuba," Gwen said.

Ari pointed to the door. "Go!"

Cam and Gwen grabbed the heavy man, while Ari and Jules hauled Ranuel off the toilet half-naked. They didn't even pause to pull up his pants.

The moments during which they dragged the bodies across the yard were the scariest. If the door on the far wall opened, the pirates would step out to find them hauling their slumped companions along the ground. They would likely be summarily executed, Cam thought. The door was out of dart range, their hands were full, and scuba was still forty seconds away.

The big man was heavy, and Cam was surprised that Gwen was pulling her side more easily, *much* more easily. She glared at him, almost running with the large body while he struggled to haul it along.

"I thought you were an athlete," she hissed.

She's juiced, Cam reminded himself. He strained, willing himself to keep up, sweat springing out on his forehead, his calves and biceps aching. It felt strange running toward danger, and his instincts complained almost as loudly as his muscles. Then they were at the door. They slowed and quietly eased both bodies against its base. Cam estimated the limp weight of Ranuel and the big man at nearly four hundred pounds. It wasn't a permanent fix, but it would keep anyone from bursting out suddenly.

When Cam turned, Donnie and Owen had appeared in the yard like ghosts. They made no sound, proceeding with hand signals only. They'd drilled with signals for months before Cam had arrived in camp, and they were proficient, while Cam had trouble deciphering their rapid arm movements. They flashed a signal to Ari. He answered, flashing three and five fingers back, which meant "three to five enemies behind the blocked door." Donnie waved, and Owen took up a sentinel position beside the door.

Across the yard, Zara was already trying another door, looking for the docs. Tegan covered her, his dart rifle on his shoulder.

The pirates' upper hierarchy still hadn't tried to exit. *Dinnertime*, Cam realized. *They're eating.* He glanced at Ranuel. The boy didn't get dinner. Instead, he was twisted beneath a fat man with his arm bent behind him in an unnatural position, his privates hanging out, and his face shoved in the dirt, lips pulled back to reveal surprisingly straight and white teeth. He looked, Cam thought, like a whinnying horse trying to cry out in alarm.

"We had a guard," Cam said to Calliope suddenly. "So will the docs!" He had no idea how to signal the information to the others across the yard without yelling. Calliope looked at him, puzzled, and then realized what he was saying. Gwen was at the door across the yard with the deadbolt. Cam whistled for her attention, and she turned to look at him just as she swung it open. It was a mistake. A large, hairy hand reached out and grabbed her by the back of the neck.

The team drifted toward her and her captor, except for Cam, who ran. He didn't realize he was sprinting until he skidded to a stop only five paces away.

The pirate walked her out into the courtyard, his big hand gripping her neck. He wore cutoff jean shorts and a dirty T-shirt. He was older, maybe forty. His facial hair was long, thin, and scraggly, and he was nearly bald. It looked as though the hair that was supposed to cover his head had slid down the sides of his face, like he was melting. His eyebrows rose as he looked around and saw the scuba team with their strange-looking dart rifles, and he shoved the barrel of a pistol into Gwen's back so hard that Cam could hear her grunt. She flinched, but didn't pull away. She didn't dare—the muzzle was snuggled up against her.

The man called out in Spanish for his comrades, glancing up at the walls where the sentries should have been.

"Shut him up!" Zara hissed, breaking their sign system.

She was looking directly at Cam, and he realized she didn't have a good shot with Gwen in her line of fire. Nor was the sliding-hair man focused on him—he was staring at the scuba team's weapons. Cam was also closest. He already had a dart in hand. "*Hesitation kills,*" Ward had taught him. "*If you're going to be wrong, be wrong decisively and promptly.*" Cam whipped the dart to his ear and hurled it at the pirate.

The needle sunk into the pirate's bald head with a light thunk. Cam smiled. It was a good throw. Then the gun roared.

Cam staggered, his ears ringing. When he looked down, he found himself covered with blood. *I'm shot!* he thought. But there was no pain. The pirate lay in a heap in the dirt, Cam's dart still jutting from his head like a large, persistent mosquito. Beneath him lay Gwen.

Cam stood shell-shocked, and Zara reached her first, yanking the man off and flinging him aside with one hand. At first Cam didn't understand what he saw. It looked like Gwen, but a motionless version that only looked straight ahead, the way a mannequin stared out a store window.

"She's done," Zara said simply, and she hopped back up to cover the open door with her dart rifle.

The blood on me is hers, Cam realized. He felt suddenly and intensely selfish for worrying that he'd been shot himself. *I killed her.*

The gunshot had echoed through the compound. Shouts and foreign profanities rose from behind the blocked door, and there was furious thumping on the other side. It nudged open an inch. Owen stepped out and neatly pumped a dart through the gap. Donnie stayed with him, the butt of his own gun against his shoulder, the muzzle trained on the door.

"Some of the doctors are in here," Zara announced. Her voice shook Cam from his stupor, and he edged past Gwen's still form to look inside.

Flies buzzed. The collection of three severed heads was strangely tidy. They were arranged in a row—a generically Caucasian man, a Scandinavian, and the young man in the worn Red Sox cap. The hat was still on his head, a bizarre mockery of his U.S. heritage. The heads sat upright on the dirt floor, open-eyed and staring ahead. Except for their grimacing expressions, they might have been beachgoers whose kids had playfully buried them in the sand.

"Only three," Zara said. "Where are the other seven?" She ticked off the inventory of missing physicians, while Cam fought the urge to retch. "Check that cabinet," she said, unfazed by the aura of death in the room. Then she ducked out to tell the others to keep searching.

Cam stepped gingerly past the line of heads. He felt like he was violating an invisible barrier, and he tried not to look at them as he opened the top drawer of the cabinet. Nothing inside. He fumbled with the second drawer, eager to be gone. The events were so bizarre and happening so fast that he would be paralyzed by fear if he stopped to think about them. There was nothing of interest in the second drawer—a stapler and some documents. The third drawer, however, held a bulging backpack. Cam reached in and unzipped it, hoping it didn't contain another head.

It wasn't a head. It was money. Tidy stacks of bills bound by rubber bands. U.S. currency. All hundreds, from the look of them. More cash than Cam had ever seen in his life. He pulled the pack out of the drawer and looked around nervously, like a shoplifter, but the watchful heads on the ground did not complain or shout in alarm.

Cam emerged from the room with the pack on his back, still shaky, and he jumped when Calliope put a hand on his shoulder. Ari was there too.

"Wally says there are lights coming our way from the south," Calliope reported to them in a quavering voice.

"Dammit!" Ari muttered. "They must have called the nearby camp."

Cam had forgotten about Wally, who was hovering overhead somewhere in the darkness. *Crazy redhead*, he thought.

Across the yard there was a loud boom, and a fist-sized hole appeared in the blocked wooden door. Given the size of the hole, it occurred to Cam that someone had a shotgun inside the room. Donnie, who stood beside the door, leaned out and stuck his dart rifle in the ragged void. He pumped two more quick shots into the room and then leaped back. A second shotgun blast created two holes, one in the door and one in Ranuel's torso. The body of the young pirate who'd only wanted to show Cam how good he was at soccer shuddered beneath the heavy man atop it.

I've killed him too, Cam thought.

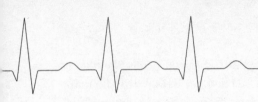

CAM'S PLAYLIST

16. BACKPACK FULL OF SOUL 🔊
   by C. Aspen B.

17. DRIFT
   by Slurpy

18. CAN'T BEAT ME
   by Two-One-Two Zone

"Puts me in a sad mood.
But I can't cry 'cuz I'm a dude."

Tegan found them—seven docs, alive and well. Truthfully, they looked incredibly screweddyi up. Their dazed expressions reflected how Cam himself felt. He watched them stumble across the yard toward the gate like zombies. Tegan hustled them along, flashing a signal to the group without slowing a step.

"Departure!" Ari snapped.

Cam started to run.

"Wait," Ari said. "Help me grab Gwen."

"Grab her?"

"Recover all fallen teammates. Ward was very clear about it."

"Ari, we are *leaving*!" Donnie shouted from across the yard. Another shotgun blast ripped through the blocked door.

Cam bent over Gwen's body. Her glasses lay on the ground beside her, surprisingly intact except for a single perfect bubble of blood on one lens that looked like a cranberry. He reached out and plucked them from the dirt, sliding them into a pocket before helping lift her. He took one leg and an arm, while Ari grabbed the others.

Cam couldn't help feeling that being ordered to carry Gwen was a punishment for having killed her. Once they got moving, he had to run to keep up. Her head lolled and she bled on his feet. Ari had said she was extremely intelligent, but she'd had that idiotic crush on Donnie, who was little more than an adult manifestation of some popular football player she could never date in high school. *No need to reconcile her brains with her poor preference in men now,* Cam thought.

He made it halfway to the boat before stumbling and dropping her. Cam lay sprawled beside her until Donnie shoved him aside with his foot.

"Useless!" Donnie growled, kneeling and keeping his dart gun trained on the compound entrance. "Just get to the boat. Owen, help here!"

When they made it to the yacht, they quickly stowed Gwen's limp body in the Zodiac and stretched its cover over her. The rest of the team had already swarmed aboard, sweeping the decks with dart guns at the ready. They found only one pirate on the craft. He was sleeping in a cabin and smelled strongly of alcohol. They pulled his gun, then Tegan hauled him from the room like a rag doll and flung him over the side. Scuba had already disabled the pirate boats, and Ari had them launched and out to sea minutes later, just in time for Wally to ditch his hang glider in the water nearby. They scooped him up, and Ari lavished praise upon him for dropping flares in the trees to distract the pirates who'd been coming from another camp.

Wally laughed. "I had those idiots wandering around trying to find phantoms in the forest like Scooby-Doo!"

No one else laughed. They were too shaken up, and Wally wasn't particularly funny.

Jules was still shaking. "Oh-my-gawd, oh-my-gawd, oh-my-gawd!" she kept saying.

When they finally calmed her down, she asked about the doctors they'd saved. "How are they doing? They must be terrified." Zara had taken them below and admitted them to one of the larger bedrooms with no more explanation than that they were being rescued.

"Their debriefing is not part of our mission," Donnie reminded her.

"And why did the pirates kill the other three?" Jules persisted. "Maybe these survivors know."

"We don't talk to them," Donnie said more firmly. "Those are the orders."

"That's true," Ari said reluctantly. "We're all probably curious, but we're just supposed to free them, not interrogate them."

"They thanked me," Jules said, her voice still quavering.

"They should thank Gwen," Calliope said quietly.

The words stabbed at Cam's conscience like a dart. "I'm sorry," he said suddenly.

They all turned and looked at him. There was silence for a moment.

"For what?" Zara said finally.

Cam looked from face to face for accusation or blame. He saw none, but that didn't mean it wasn't there. "For Gwen," he said.

"We're all sorry," Ari replied, his tone strangely matter-of-fact.

"But I'm especially sorry."

"Why?" Donnie said. "Were you looking to hook up with her?"

Owen giggled, and Jules shot Donnie an angry look.

"No," Cam said, incredulous. "I got her killed."

Ari didn't even look up from the wheel. "No, you didn't. You kept that dude from killing *all* of us."

"It was a good throw," Zara added.

Cam glanced at Calliope, looking for a softer opinion, but she afforded him none. Her face was blank, her eyes empty—the emotion of her musical soul was buried somewhere behind them. Only Jules seemed outwardly distressed, but she didn't blame him either.

"It's what she wanted, Cam," Ari assured him. "It's why she signed up."

"A quick, easy death," Donnie snapped. "That's the deal here, or didn't you get the memo?"

"Yeah, I got it," Cam said, growing testy.

Ari intervened again. "She went out a hero."

"With a bang," Donnie said.

"And she sure doesn't have to worry about that tumor anymore," Owen added, looking to Donnie for support. Donnie rewarded him with a smirk.

"Jerks," Jules mumbled.

They're punchy, Cam thought. *Jacked up. One more bad joke and they'll descend into a giggle fit.* It was tough to condemn them—anyone might be half crazed from the insanity and adrenaline rush they'd just lived through. He didn't feel so good himself, although he thought he was more likely to puke than laugh.

It suddenly felt crowded and hot in the pilothouse, and Cam's head began to swim. He excused himself and slid out onto the deck for some air.

Feeling his way along the rail in the moonless night, he wondered if he might fall overboard and drown. *A quick, easy death*, he thought. No such luck—he found himself on the bow again. The sea and the sky were black together, and the yacht bore him blindly through both with a steady hum and a rhythmic rise and fall. It made him think of the metal band Necromoor and their song "The Endless Nothing." It was not so different from falling out of the helicopter, a weightless headlong rush into the unknown.

Even after Cam returned to the pilothouse, they cruised for another half an hour with no lights, trusting a fluorescent compass Ari kept below the dash. When Ari finally switched the interior overheads back on, there was a collective sigh of relief. The team found seats, and each sat quietly with his or her thoughts, or they mumbled about what was left to do on the mission checklist. Jules and Calliope had gone to the stern to busy themselves cooking food that had not been taken by the pirates. They were all waiting for Ward to check in, and they no longer spoke of the loss of Gwen.

Their guests were quiet and confined to the big bedroom where Zara had tackled Cam. Their spokesperson had banged on the door and demanded to speak with whoever was in charge. But Donnie had gone down and made it clear that there would be no speaking except among themselves, apparently while brandishing his dart gun. *Nice*, Cam thought. After the terror of the pirate camp, the last thing they needed was someone with a gun locking them up without any explanation. The survivors were all women, a fact Cam hadn't realized until he'd had a chance to calm himself. The Scandinavian man, the young doc in the Red Sox hat, and the boat captain had all been reduced to heads in the dirt. Perhaps some bizarre notion of chivalry among pirates had saved the women, he thought. The image of the surprised face of the young man in the Sox cap leaped into his head. Just out of med school, from the look of him. Like a future version of Ari. And, like Ari, his life had been condensed before he could reap the benefits of his intelligence and hard work in school.

"We're out of pirate waters," Ari announced. "Ward should be checking in any moment now."

Moments later, the yacht's phone rang. Ari turned and wiggled his eyebrows.

"Good call, boss," Zara said, reaching over to flip on the speakerphone.

"Ari? You there, kid?" Ward's voice was easily recognizable, even with the poor connection.

"Right here."

"So you're alive. Great. And the outcome?"

"They killed another doc. We rescued seven."

"Understood. How many team casualties?"

"Gwen."

The room went silent while they waited for Ward to comment, and Cam realized that they had no idea whether the mission had been a success or disaster.

"That's it?" Ward said finally.

"And one pirate," Cam added, thinking of Ranuel and the yawning red shotgun hole in his torso.

"That dirtbag doesn't count," Donnie growled.

"Yes, he does," Ward said. "Cam is correct. All people count. But is two truly the sum total of the collateral damage?"

"Yes."

"Wow!" Ward exclaimed, sounding genuinely impressed. "Excellent job, everyone. Top notch. I'll look forward to receiving you upon your return. In the meantime, quarantine the doctors, and there's champagne for all of you hidden behind a false panel in the cupboard to Ari's right. Raise one glass for Gwen's graduation and stow her in ice for burial here. This is the only time we'll use the yacht, so enjoy the cruise back. See you at home."

Home? Cam thought. A compound on a remote beach with nine—*no, eight*—other college kids whose last names he didn't know sounded cool, but it didn't sound like home.

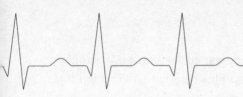

CAM'S PLAYLIST

17. DRIFT 🔊
by Slurpy

18. CAN'T BEAT ME
by Two-One-Two Zone

19. BROKED APART HEART
by The Shitkickers

*"If you look to the sea, you'll find me
drifting, drifting, drifting."*

Gwen's ceremony was brief. Celebrating felt wrong, so they didn't open the champagne for it. Ari said a few words, ending his eulogy with their spoken oath, "My life for the good of the many." Cam recovered his Clip Chip player from its hiding place and played "Cool Cruel Sunset" by Shocking Pinkies over its tiny speakers. Then they covered her with ice to keep her corpse from rotting, as Ward had suggested.

Ari said it had been a quick, painless way to go. Cam thought it terrifying, horrible, and violent, but didn't say so. He kept her glasses. He wasn't sure why. Perhaps because of the anonymity of her death. Without a token of her, it might feel as though she had never existed at all.

Four hours later, they unloaded the docs to a waiting skiff oper-

ated by Pilot. Afterward, celebrating seemed more appropriate. They
found plastic cups and passed the champagne. Donnie shrugged off
a small cup and took pulls straight from a full bottle. Wally opted
out, but chattered incessantly despite being sober. There was even
some laughter. It was then that Cam chose to summon everyone to
the large quarters.

"I found something at the pirate camp," he said once they'd all
gathered, and he hoisted the backpack onto the same bed where
he'd denied himself access to Zara's incredible body.

"I was going to ask you about that," Ari said.

Cam didn't explain, but simply upended the pack and dumped
its contents onto the bedspread. The bundles of hundreds tumbled
out like green bricks, spilling over the bed and onto the floor. They
kept coming, and Cam had to shake the pack to dislodge them all.
The team stood and stared. Wally giggled. Jules reached out as
though wanting to touch it, but her hand just hovered over the pile.

"How much?" Zara asked.

Ari scanned the pile. "Figuring one hundred hundreds per
bundle, and given that this is one hell of a big stack of bundles, I'm
gonna guess a million." He looked up. "Remember the Korean ship
I read about, Cam?"

Zara whistled.

Cam glanced up to find Donnie's face turning purple. "Dude,
your face is turning purple," Cam said.

"Why didn't you tell us about this, Cam?!" Donnie exploded, as
though Cam's words had popped him like a balloon.

"I'm telling you now." Cam's hand slid instinctively to the front
pocket of his shorts. At the bottom of the pocket was a velvet
pouch. His teammates had no way to know he'd removed it from
the backpack, but having all of their eyes on him made him nervous. There were diamonds in the pouch. Big diamonds. And he
didn't know why he'd taken them anymore than he knew why he'd
taken Gwen's glasses.

Donnie remained ignorant, still fuming about the cash. He

picked up a bundle of bills. "This money is part of the mission. You should have given it to Pilot!"

"And we will," Ari assured him. "Cam is simply conferring with us, his teammates, before taking that action, right, Cam?"

"Listen, little professor," Donnie growled, "you don't tell me—"

A bundle of hundreds hit Donnie in the head. It bounced off and landed at his feet. He turned slowly, steaming.

"Money fight!" Wally yelled. He tore open a second bundle and showered Cam with the bills.

Cam didn't react as the bills silently drifted down around him. Nobody else joined in either, but Ari saw his chance to duck out.

"I'd better get up to the helm," he said. "Pack this stuff back up."

Cam had killed the celebratory mood. Or Donnie had. It wasn't clear who was at fault. Cam picked up the backpack and began to gather the cash. Jules helped. Donnie couldn't bring himself to either help or leave the room, and so he stayed to observe, perhaps thinking someone might pocket a portion of the loot. Cam couldn't fault the guy's instincts. He was dead right—Cam already *had* taken a cut.

The hours of tension were followed by a mellow ride back to their own stretch of coastline, where they piled into the Zodiac to go ashore.

"I'm gonna miss her," Ari muttered as he ushered the others in.

"Yeah," Cam said.

Then Ari patted the rail, and Cam realized he was talking about the yacht.

"Ward says we won't use her again," Ari said. "Her name was *Harsh Mistress.*"

"Still is. Says so right there on the back."

"The stern."

"Whatever. Say good-bye, pal."

"Good-bye, pal," Ari said to the yacht, and he stepped into the Zodiac.

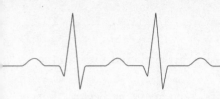

CAM'S PLAYLIST

"I've got a pass to kick your ass!"

Cam awoke in the afternoon to Ari's humming. His roommate's song was an imitation of the tropical birds in the distance, and it was a pretty darn good rendition.

"Dude, you are entirely too chipper," Cam groaned.

"Lunch in ten minutes. Briefing afterward. You don't want to miss that."

"I'm coming. I'm coming."

"And shower up. You still have blood on you."

Cam had the outdoor shower to himself. It felt odd. He'd showered with Gwen just the day before. Today he washed off her blood.

Lunch was breakfast food—omelets and mango juice with a slab of peccary on the side. Ari drank coffee, which he proclaimed "excellent." Cam passed—he'd always thought coffee tasted like warmed-over liquid dirt. Afterward, Ward gathered them in the classroom to debrief.

"I'll be meeting with each of you separately," he began. "But first I'd like to tell you a few things about your mission that you might not know. In their careers, these seven doctors you rescued have already saved more than one hundred lives between them. Now they will live on to save at least that many more. You lost one dying teammate and possibly one pirate. Ergo, you are dozens of lives in the plus column. Congratulations."

He began to clap, slowly and then more insistent. Donnie joined first. Owen followed. Then Zara and Tegan started in. Soon they were all clapping—even Cam, though mostly because he didn't want to be the odd man out.

Ward continued. He was enthusiastic, like a happy coach after a win. He reviewed their success. By all appearances, a bunch of rich college kids had been captured by outlaws and simply busted out, taking the other hostages with them. They'd left no evidence, save a couple of odd syringes, which could be accounted for by the presence of the doctors. There was no way to trace the team's identities. And because it seemed an escape and not an apparent political incursion, there would be no repercussions from the volatile, newly formed government against the United States.

As Ward's recap wound down, Donnie turned and pointed at Cam. The backpack sat at Cam's feet. Donnie had threatened to tell Ward about it himself if Cam didn't bring it to the debriefing. Cam reached down and hauled it up into his lap.

"Ward, we brought you something," Cam announced.

Ward nodded. "I see. What is it?"

"A backpack."

Wally laughed. Cam walked the pack to the front of the room and sat it before Ward like an offering.

"It was in a cabinet behind three severed heads."

Ward lifted the heavy pack. "Those are usually meant to ward off intruders."

"Yeah, well, I would have been warded," Cam said, "but Zara made me go in."

Ward zipped open the backpack and looked inside. His face was a mask, except for one eyebrow, which shot up. "How much?" he asked after a moment.

"One million even," Ari said.

Cam walked back to his seat, relinquishing any claim to the fortune. The fact that it was an even amount of cash ensured that Ward wouldn't think he'd taken any. *Why would I?* Cam wondered. They had everything they could desire in their beachside paradise. Besides, where would they spend it? There was no reason to want money. But he *had* taken the diamonds, and he'd told no one, not even Ari. He'd even hidden them in the sand under his condo. An animal had burrowed a small space beneath the rear wall, and he'd wriggled underneath to bury them there.

He wondered if Ward could somehow sense that he'd lifted them. The guy had instincts like a panther. If he did, he didn't say anything. He simply slung the pack full of bills over his shoulder and dismissed them.

"All right then. I'll donate this to the cause. Good work, Cam. In the meantime, we are off the clock. I'll take Ari first for individual debriefing. The rest of you go relax. You've earned it."

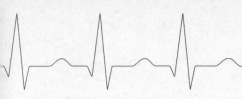

CAM'S PLAYLIST

19. BROKED APART HEART
      by The Shitkickers

___

20. DOWN TIME
      by Robo Dork

___

21. PERFORMANCE ANXIETY
      by Crush

"I love your face, your place,
your body in lace . . . just not you."

They filed out of the bunker, and Jules caught Cam on the way to the condos.

"I talked to them," she said in a conspiratorial whisper.

"Who?"

"The doctors."

"They thanked you, right?"

"No. I mean, yes, but I talked to one of them some more. On the yacht."

"That's against the rules."

"Not the 'unbreakable' ones."

"Yes it is, actually—contact with the outside world."

Jules rolled her eyes. "They're people. Scared people. One of them told me her headless husband was getting out."

"Out of what?"

"I dunno. The people she works for, I guess."

"Worlds Apart, Worlds Together?"

"That's not who she said they worked for."

"So who did she say she worked for?" It was Zara. She'd snuck up on them so quietly—*unnaturally quietly*—that she was part of their conversation before they realized she was there.

Cam shot Jules a look—*time to shut up*. But she didn't catch it.

"We didn't talk long enough to get that far," she said.

"What else did you talk about?"

"Nothing."

"Nothing?" Zara used her stare-down technique, meeting Jules's eyes. Cam watched Jules wither.

"Not much. Just that they're in drug research. That's all. Nothing much."

"That's not nothing," Zara said.

"Really, that's all. The woman was just a bit freaked. She blabbed some stuff out. I told her everything was going to be okay, and she didn't need to explain."

"I'm sure you did." Zara's eyes were narrow. She was thinking. Cam didn't like it. Finally, she shrugged and walked off.

"That was stupid!" Cam snapped at Jules once Zara was gone.

"What?"

"You need to watch your mouth. And keep me out of your rule violations. We weren't supposed to talk to them."

"I didn't 'reveal the organization.'" Jules made little finger quotes in the air. "Or tell her what we do. I just comforted her. So I listened to someone upset—what's the big deal?"

"I don't know. Nothing, maybe. It's just that everything has suddenly gotten so serious. People are dying."

"Duh! *We're* dying. That's why we're here." Jules spotted Ari coming out of the bunker as Wally was summoned inside. She turned and left Cam in favor of his roommate, but not without taking a parting shot. "Not to get yelled at."

Cam found himself walking up the beach alone. The door to Zara's condo was open. It would have been polite *not* to glance inside, in case she was changing, but he did. She sensed him, whirled, and met his eyes. Caught, he was forced to say something.

"Can I come in?" he asked. It was lame, but it was better than *Sorry, I was trying to get a look at you in your underwear since I missed my chance on the boat.*

"Free country," she said. "At least, I think it is."

He stepped inside. One bunk was made, its sheets tucked so square and tight that the mattress looked like an uncomfortable white box. *Gwen's work.* The other bunk was mussed, its sheets crumpled and bunched at one end, like an angrily discarded Dear John letter. *Zara's.* Cam had to wonder what sort of wild midnight thrashing could so thoroughly ravage them. The rest of the place was immaculate. Zara had not had the opportunity to disorganize it yet, it seemed.

"So . . . I haven't been in your condo before," Cam said. "It's nice."

"Why are you here, Wingman? Don't trust me? Worried I'm going to rat out your ugly girlfriend?"

"I know you won't," he said, hoping she wouldn't. He watched for a hint of her intention, but there was nothing except an uncomfortable silence. He glanced at the empty bunk. "Gwen was your roommate. I just wanted to say . . ."

"No need. We weren't exactly close."

"And I'm sorry about what happened on the boat," he blurted out. "Between you and me, I mean. I do think you're a very pretty woman."

Zara cocked her head. "No, you think I'm a tramp. Well FYI, sport: I'm not the person I was before I came here. None of us are."

"I know."

"You *don't* know. You don't know a thing about me."

She was almost shouting. It annoyed him.

"Okay," he snapped back, "what don't I know? That you never got the chance to climb Mount Everest? Or that you were going to try out for the Olympic kickboxing team? Congratulations, you're extreme, harsh, and intimidating."

"You don't know that I loved a boy once."

The word "love" sounded so strange on her full, salacious lips that Cam fell silent. He sat down. It was a simple gesture, but it was enough to let her know it was okay to continue.

She spoke without looking at Cam. "He was my best friend. He and Kate. We were a trio, really. Grew up on the same street in the same small town. We did everything together. I started to like him in high school, and by college I was full-on into him. But we never hooked up—I thought that might ruin it. He was one of those nice-guy types, and I imagined us married someday, buying dishes and decorating a house and crap. Cheesy, huh?

"Then one day Kate comes to me. She tells me he's in love with me. For a moment I was in heaven. Then she got this incredibly sad look on her face. She said I was prettier than her, that I was more exciting, that I would have my choice of college boys. I didn't know where she was going with it until she suddenly asked me if I would walk away from him. He was her soul mate, she said. She would never meet another guy, and he would never be with her if I was available. She cried and declared me her best friend forever. Cheesy again, eh? But I felt bad for her. Sympathetic. Even flattered. In the end, I did it. I told him I didn't see him as a boyfriend, just as a friend—you know the drill."

"Yeah . . . I get that."

"To seal the deal I said, 'and I'm doing an older guy.' I actually said that."

"Oh no . . . you didn't. That kills love-struck teenage boys, you know?"

"I know. And I wasn't even actually doing anyone. I deliberately caused him pain. I crushed him. I crushed myself." She looked away.

"But you're beautiful. I'm sure you met lots of boys in college, like this Kate girl said."

"Yep. Lots of jerks. Had my choice of them." She coughed up a laugh, but there was pain there—a bad experience. Maybe several.

Cam tried to move her past the memory. "What happened to Kate and, uh, the guy?"

"They're engaged. Ridiculously happy. She preferred that I didn't hang out with him anymore, since they were together. So I didn't see her much either after that. Now she's with him studying abroad in Italy. And I'm here with a fatal tumor and an ex–soccer player who thinks I'm a loveless slut."

"I'm sorry." Cam didn't know what else to say, but he said something else anyway. "I won't tell anyone."

"If you do, I'll beat your ass." Zara's words were firm, but she said them with damp eyes.

Cam reached out to her, offering a hug, but she pushed him away.

"No. You had your chance."

Wally sat in the lagoon up to his chest watching the blue and red streaks in the clear water. He stared, focused, and didn't look up, even when Cam arrived at the pool's edge.

"You're always so overstimulated," Cam said. "It's strange to see you relaxing."

Wally smirked. His hand shot into the water like lightning and came up dripping with a small wriggling fish clenched in it. Wally popped the fish into his mouth and gulped it down.

Cam shook his head. "Like I said, *strange*. What did Ward ask you in there?"

"Nothin'. He just wanted to know if I had any questions."

"He didn't quiz you?"

"Not really."

"Did he say *anything*?"

"Said I saved all your tails with my flare drops." Wally tapped the surface of the water above the gathering school of fish with his hand, sending silver, green, and yellow flashes in all directions.

"Then he said how proud he was of me. Haven't heard that in a while."

"So what did you ask him?"

"Nothin'."

"Don't you wonder about some of this stuff?"

"Why mess with a good thing?"

Cam didn't push it. He left Wally sitting in the calm pool and headed for the bunker. It was his turn to debrief with Ward. A lot had happened in the past twenty-four hours, and he fully intended to ask some questions.

Ward was seated in the lounge, an artificially comfortable alternative to the briefing room. Two hammocks hung in the corners, and padded chairs were scattered about, intentionally askew. Ward held no gear or manuals. The backpack of money was gone, already spirited away.

"Hey, Cam," he said in greeting. "Come on in. How are you holding up?"

Cam decided that somebody who preceded him must have gotten upset. Probably Jules. "I'm fine," Cam said. "Rested. What's the purpose of this meeting?"

"I just wanted to provide you with a sounding board in case you want to talk about anything. Maybe things you don't want to discuss with your teammates. Or if you want to ask any questions. By all reports you had quite an extreme experience."

"No kidding."

"Anything bothering you?"

"No. Why? Should there be?" Cam spoke evenly, but he could feel his temper rising. He didn't know exactly why, and he couldn't stop it.

"Okay, I'm sensing some tension now."

"People died, man! You sense that?"

"Every day. All over the world."

"You still say this is all for good?"

"The reason you're here is bad. But what you're doing is good," he said decisively and promptly. "You're a hero, Cam. Very few people get to live a life where, at its end, they know they've made the world a better place. It's supposed to feel positive. Let it."

"At our medical exam they didn't review my condition at all."

"You've already accepted that you're dying. It's a basic tenet of our philosophy."

"I'm not showing any symptoms. What if I'm recovering?"

"Cam, if they chose you, you're not going to recover."

Cam sighed. Ward had a pithy answer for everything. He was like the bastard offspring of a therapist and a public relations official.

"Were those doctors working with you?" Cam said suddenly.

Ward's eyebrow twitched, and Cam could see his trainer thinking. *No clever saying for that, eh?*

"Of course the organization has doctors working for it, Cam," Ward said at length. "That's how they evaluated you, helped you disappear, and continue to care for you. What's your concern?"

"We weren't told."

"You're not told a lot of things. That doesn't change your purpose here."

"To save this organization's own employees." It was a statement, not a question.

"In this case, yes."

"Who were pretending to work for a global charity."

"We *are* a global charity. Cam, you know this has to be a clandestine operation. We have secrets."

"But you're assuring me it's all for the good of mankind, right? Scout's honor?"

"How can saving the lives of many at the cost of a few be anything but good?"

Cam thought, but he couldn't come up with a rebuttal. He wondered if Ari could have.

Ward laid a hand on his shoulder. "Scout's honor."

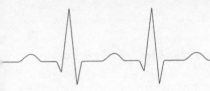

"Refresh, rehash, restock my stash."

Cam climbed the ladder and flopped onto his bunk. He'd been explicitly ordered to relax, feel good, and enjoy paradise for the time being. The breeze that blew through the condo felt good on his hot skin, which was still flush from his exchange with Ward, and the thin sheets were cool to the touch. He shoved his hands under his pillow to get it right for his head. Something crinkled at his touch. Paper. The note had not been hidden in the earbuds this time. Bolder by an increment.

Cam sat up and looked for Ari. His roommate was at the desk below and couldn't see up into the bunk. Cam slid the note out and cupped it against the pillow to examine it in secret. The message was longer this time.

*Glad you're still alive. I'm looking for someone I can trust. Is it you?
PS: Don't drink the Kool-Aid.*

Cam went through the girls in his head again. Jules, Zara, Calli.
It wasn't Gwen—of that he could be certain. There were reasons
why it could be any of the rest of them and reasons it shouldn't be
any of them. *A mystery,* Cam thought. He tucked the note away. It
didn't suggest a way to answer. Perhaps he needed to stuff his answer back under the pillow. But the note was annoyingly vague.
"Trust" me for what?

Cam leaned over the side of the bunk. "Hey, Ari, what does
'don't drink the Kool-Aid' mean?"

Ari pushed back from the desk and looked up at him. "Jim Jones."

"Jim Jones?"

"Cult leader from the seventies. He got a thousand of his follow-
ers to commit mass suicide by drinking cyanide-laced Kool-Aid."

"Holy crap."

"Yeah. Even the children. Most awful thing ever. Why do you
ask?"

"Just heard it somewhere."

"That's interesting, because it happened right here in South
America."

Cam stuffed the note back under the pillow. The Kool-Aid
was clearly the TS-9. It had to be. *But who doesn't want me to drink it
and why?* The thought occurred to him that the note writer could
be a male.

"Who was around our condo while I was talking to Ward?"

"I dunno," Ari said. "I was in the kitchen. Jules was making a
chocolate cake." He uttered a low hum to indicate the cake's tasti-
ness. "You know, I kinda like that she has a traditional side. Zara's
hot, but she wouldn't be caught dead in the domestic fairy tale."

She might have, Cam thought. *Once upon a time.* But she'd dared to
dream of a husband and a house, and she'd broken her own heart.

Then she got sad, screwed, and sick, and the white picket fence fantasy went *poof!*

"She might be more normal than we think," Cam disagreed. "Maybe we just need to get to know her a little better."

"Good luck with that. Sounds like an excuse to try to get to know her butt a little better. You're better off chasing Calliope, though you don't know what you're going to get with her from one day to the next."

"I'm not chasing anyone."

"Too bad. You're a good-looking young man." Ari chuckled. "And fast."

"You're all nearly as fast as me. And stronger."

"Is that what you want? Artificial strength?"

"I just want to keep up."

"You're fast enough." Ari jotted some notes on a road map he was studying.

Cam glanced over his shoulder from atop the bunk. "I can't believe I gave away a million dollars this morning."

Ari shrugged. "Monopoly money to us. Means nothing."

"I guess you're right."

"Changes your priorities when you realize your term here on earth is finite, eh?"

"Ward said he was going to keep the money for the program. If we're so righteous and good, why didn't he send it back to the Koreans it was stolen from?"

"It would probably go to some insurance company, and that isn't going to make the world a better place."

"That simple?"

"For me, yes. I'm quite fond of simple. I haven't got time for complicated. And we only have a day to kick back."

"Before what?"

"Mission number two. We leave tomorrow." Ari held up the road map. "And I was promised a fast car."

─────────

When tomorrow came, Pilot flew them several hours away and deposited them in an open field. Cam was surprised to find that they'd left the forest. A dirt road led out of the field, and trees had been cleared all around. A bus awaited them nearby. It was painted green and had a banner plastered across the side with words in what looked like Spanish to Cam.

"What does that say?" Cam asked.

Ari interpreted. "'Friends of the Rainforest.' We're ecotourists."

"Lovely," Zara grumbled.

"I kind of like it," Calliope said.

Ari found the door open and ushered them aboard. "If any of you spoke Portuguese we wouldn't have to be tourists."

Cam climbed in as Ari took the driver's seat and located a hidden key. Cam whispered to his roommate on his way past, "Not exactly the insanely fast car we were promised, eh?"

"Hey, it's a nice bus." Ari grabbed the intercom mic. "All passengers, take your seats, please," he announced. "My name is Ari. I'll be your tour guide today, and this excursion is under way!"

The doors closed with a *whoosh*, and the bus lurched onto the dirt road. Rutty, packed dirt became gravel, and a right turn took them onto a paved surface.

"We're in civilization!" Jules exclaimed, clapping her hands together.

Donnie cleared his throat to get their attention. "No contact with the outside world, except for what's necessary for the mission."

Jules looked at Cam and rolled her eyes.

"What is our mission?" Cam asked loudly. He addressed everyone, but directed it mostly to Ari.

"Our mission is to attend a soccer match," Ari said. He grinned and offered no further explanation. Demands from the team for further details and even mild threats from Zara couldn't wrest any more info from him. "Hey, that's most of what I know," he claimed.

After another half an hour, more cars began to appear on the road. The team chattered and pointed out the windows at passing sights. Fruit stands, vendors, and even small stores began to dot the road. Ari narrated, telling fictitious stories about the increasingly urban features whizzing by.

"Coming up on our right is the fabled Sausage Man of East wherever we are. He cooks his famous *chouriço* right there in that rusty half barrel. And, on the left, you'll see a fine example of the exotic local wildlife, a feral *bos taurus*, if I'm not mistaken."

"A what?" Jules asked.

"A loose cow," Cam said.

Jules was up on her knees in her seat like a third grader on a school bus, her head snapping back and forth. The others had their faces pressed to the glass too, drinking in roadside art and advertisements alike, eager for both the greater and lesser offerings of humanity after months of isolation in the forest.

"I'm going to get me one of those sausages," Donnie said.

"Me too," Owen echoed.

Even Cam felt a twinge of excitement. It felt like coming back to the real world from their surreal beachfront heaven. Soon they turned onto a road that was legitimately busy, and Ari quieted, concentrating on his driving. He'd obviously not trained behind the wheel of a ponderous bus, Cam decided, and the local drivers didn't seem to pay much attention to lanes of travel.

"Maybe this is a reward for the good job we did," Jules said.

Cam nodded. "Maybe." But Ari had said it was their second mission. He looked to Calliope, who just shrugged.

They were driving into the center of a city of some sort. Not a huge city, but not a mere village or town either.

"That sign said 'Amazon' something," Jules pointed out. "Are we in the Amazon?"

"It doesn't matter where we are," Donnie said. "We're not supposed to know."

"We're going to know as soon as we step off the bus, genius,"

Zara said. "Maybe before." She pointed to a huge billboard that featured a soccer team.

"That must be the region's football club," Ari said. "That's who we're going to see."

"Mystery solved, everyone!" Wally shouted from the back as another road sign appeared in the distance beyond Cam's sight. "Macapá, Brazil, one hundred kilometers."

Ari unfolded a sheet of paper containing handwritten directions, which led them into the city. Once among the packed buildings, they wove south through surface streets in a light rain that hung in the air as though it never left. The team was looky-looing in all directions, including down on the small cars of the locals— *every bit the tourists we're playing*, Cam thought. Then Jules gasped.

"Oh my gosh!" she exclaimed. "Look-look! The river! Is that . . . ?"

The Amazon, Cam realized. *The biggest river in the world.* It could be nothing else. The vast expanse of water was not the ocean, for he could see a distant shore. Nor was it a lake—two children in a canoe drifted at surprising speed on its powerful current. They slid past in water the color of heavily creamed coffee, reminding Cam of children who paddled a boat through molten chocolate in a book he'd read in grade school.

The street leading to the stadium was named Avenida Equatorial, and Ari informed them over the intercom that the Amazon River lay almost exactly on the equator. His commentary was interrupted a few blocks before they arrived at the stadium when he received a call. Ari quickly donned a headset and pulled to the side of the road. He listened and then summoned Cam.

"Come help me with something."

They left the bus and walked to the rainforest banner decal. Ari picked at one corner, and it began to peel off.

"Grab the other corner."

Cam helped him peel the entire banner, and then Ari told him to flip it over. The rest of the crew watched from the windows above.

The reverse side read CALLI! in huge pink letters. Cam cocked his head.

"Stick the decal back on, but with this side showing," Ari instructed.

Cam did as he was told, smoothing it as he went. He didn't ask what it meant. He knew better. Ari disclosed information when he was good and ready, never before.

"Great," Ari said. "Let's do the other side."

"That's my name out there," Calliope said when they returned.

"Sort of," Zara pointed out.

"Look," Ari said, "I honestly don't know any more than you do at this point. Pilot just called and told me to turn the decals over."

"No other instructions yet?" Donnie asked, suspicious.

"He did say to enjoy ourselves."

"I'm not a big soccer fan," Donnie grumbled. "But maybe they sell sausages at the game."

They were an hour early when Ari pulled into the section of the lot reserved for large vehicles. A dark, well-dressed Brazilian woman met the bus and waited politely for someone to step outside. Ari shrugged and exited to chat with her. Moments later, he climbed back into the bus and asked for everyone's attention.

"What's going on?" Donnie demanded.

"Apparently, we're special guests."

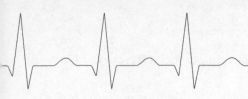

21. PERFORMANCE ANXIETY 🔊
   by Crush

22. HAMSTER WHEEL
   by The Fluffy Bunnies

23. REVELATION
   by Breathe

"Give me a moment!"

The seats were good, down low in Zerão Stadium's bleachers. When the game started Cam felt like he was practically on the field with the teams. He couldn't help feeling spirited. He'd root for the local team, he decided—the black-and-white-striped Amapá Clube. The raven-haired woman who'd escorted them in had led them past the food vendors, souvenir booths, and a more modern Internet kiosk to their section. She spoke English and explained that the midfield line was exactly on the equator so that each team defended one hemisphere. The stands were full, and the crowd behind Cam was raucous—an important match, it seemed, or at least a hated rival. Cam wondered if the organization had planned the outing especially for him. He was the soccer player of the group. Mere weeks earlier he wouldn't have imagined himself at a Brazilian regional match on the Amazon River. He laughed privately—he might not have gotten his fast car, but this was certainly an adequate substitute. He wondered if they sold zebra-striped replica jerseys.

Jules sat next to him, clapping along with the crowd at times, though Cam didn't think she knew much about soccer. She spent the other half of her time wandering around seeing the sights or visiting the restroom. Donnie sat one row back, polishing off his second sausage and tipping back a beer. They didn't sell sausages at the stadium, but the woman made a call, and a nearby street vendor hurried over with nine of them, which they paid for with money Pilot had given each of them. Calliope had passed, willing hers to Donnie before she disappeared with the woman, taking Ari with her to translate.

The first goal came in the twenty-third minute on a corner kick to the head of an Amapá midfielder, who drove it into the back of the net, and the crowd went crazy. Cam was pleased to see the others enjoy the moment too. Even Donnie cheered. Zara rocked back and forth to a song the crowd had taken up. And Wally was folding paper flyers into airplanes and trying to drift them out onto the field of play. Fortunately, they banked left or right and flew in slow circles instead until their short flights ended and they were trampled underfoot.

Then it was halftime.

The teams retired to the sidelines for the break, and several stadium employees hauled a platform onto the field. Next came sound equipment, quickly hooked up by scrambling young men in collared shirts with a logo on the breast. Finally, three big men wheeled a piano out onto the platform.

Donnie rose. "I'm going to go find the bathroom."

"I gotta go too," Owen said.

"Wait." It was Zara. "I think you might find the halftime entertainment interesting." She pointed down to the platform, where a woman in a long red dress was approaching the piano. She strode to the bench and slid her hips onto it in a practiced manner Cam recognized immediately.

Jules jumped out of her seat. "It's Calliope!"

Two young girls unfurled a CALLI banner, and then Calliope began to play. It was not the song she'd performed for Cam. Not so dark. A catchier rhythm. More accessible. Still, it was unmistakably a piece she'd written. After the upbeat piano intro, she slowed it down and began to sing. Quiet at first. The audience strained to hear, affording her the courtesy of a minute's chance to win them over and intrigued by what they couldn't quite make out yet. She pulled them in, and then, just when a murmur might have begun or the restless might have started shifting in their seats, she blasted them. Her voice rang clear—a scream drowning any conversations about finding the bathroom or stepping out for sausage. They were stunned.

After the initial shock, her voice fell back in with the steady beat of the song, and the crowd embraced the reprieve with eager relief. She gave them a clear refrain and then began another build, an implicit threat to scream again. But when she reached the song's moment of greatest tension, she didn't. She spared them, and for that they were grateful. They clapped along as she led them through a verse and back toward the refrain, and then delighted them by signing it in Portuguese. *She had to have practiced this*, Cam realized.

The song rose and fell, and rose again higher, and when she had built it to its limit and it strained for release, she pointed out at the waiting fans, and they screamed for her. She played three final, emphatic notes, and then she was done. There was a moment of silence as they made sure that she was finished, or perhaps they were simply marveling over what they'd just heard, and then the stands erupted. They didn't stop cheering until Calliope had waved two good-byes and disappeared beneath the stands. Cam looked around. The crowd nodded and smiled, still clapping. The entire Deathwing team stood, stunned.

Their phones all rang at once.

Cam hurried his headset to his ear while the others did the same. It was Pilot. He spoke to them all via conference call.

"Time to go to work," he said. "And you need to move fast. Take the stairs to the VIP area. There is a dressing room. Calliope will be receiving a man there. He has guards with him. They are to be incapacitated when Calliope calls for you. We prefer they are not killed."

"Prefer"? Cam thought.

"Who is he?" Jules asked.

"There's little time. Are you moving?"

"Yes," Donnie reported, pushing the others toward the stairs.

"Good. He is an owner of bauxite mines. An aspiring politician. Very powerful in his own country, but vulnerable here. He has a weakness for soccer and female singers. Good luck."

Pilot hung up as they descended to the lower level. A long hallway was lined with doors. Their well-dressed hostess stood at the first door. She smiled as they passed, and she pointed halfway down the hall to where Ari was waiting. A large man stood beyond him at the far end.

"One way in, one way out," Zara observed. "Not great."

Ari met them midway between the woman and the man, out of earshot of both. "Four more bodyguards inside the lounge," he said quietly. "No guns—they don't carry them in this country."

"What are we doing?" Cam asked.

"Getting ready. Our little performer will call when she needs us. In the meantime, just look like Calli's roadies, because that seems to be what we are. She's the lead on this one, my friends."

"She didn't say a word about any of this," Jules complained.

Cam nodded, understanding what Jules did not. "She's a vault," he said.

Jules's phone rang. She tapped it. "Yes?"

Cam watched her shake her head, and then her eyes filled with tears.

"I know," Jules said. "We love you." She turned. "Cam, she wants to talk to you."

Cam took the headset. "What's happening in there?" he asked suddenly and loudly. Ari had to shush him.

Her voice was strangely calm. "Relax, Cam. I want to thank you."

"For what?"

"For being a nice guy. For making me feel special." She paused. "And I'm sorry I didn't leave you that note. Whoever did is making a wise choice."

"Thanks, but this is an odd time. Everyone is standing here listening to me."

"I don't care. I have to go. And you have to come. Now. Goodbye, Cam."

"Calliope . . . ?" He didn't understand. He wanted to talk some more. There *had* been a connection. He hadn't imagined it. Cam looked up to find the team staring at him and realized that he had no idea how long he'd been standing there holding the dead phone.

"Well, what did she say?" Donnie demanded.

"She said come now."

They started for the door. In the other direction their hostess's phone rang. She answered, and her face paled. She rushed from the hallway, tapping the screen on her phone furiously.

"Go time!" Donnie said, and he strode toward the man at the end of the hall, fists balled in anticipation.

The team followed. The man watched Calli's friends come, unconcerned.

"Calli called us," Ari announced as they approached.

The man admitted them to the waiting room just as a feminine cry of alarm rose from behind the dressing room door on the far side of the room.

"Something's wrong!" Ari shouted, and he started toward the door.

The four guards were lounging on couches. They leaped to

their feet, one going to the door, another moving to stop Ari. But Donnie and Tegan were already among them like wolves, moving even faster than Cam remembered from training. Donnie wrapped himself around a guard's arm and yanked upward with a popping sound. The man went down immediately, his elbow bent backward, forearm flopping loose. Tegan grappled another and flipped him over a couch. They moved so fast that they disposed of their initial opponents before the others had time to turn on them.

The man from the hall stepped into the room to enter the fray, but Zara whirled and planted her heel square in his jaw with a sickening crunch. His head snapped back and rebounded from the doorframe. Cam winced. He'd felt the impact of her foot himself—it had practically caved in his chest, and she hadn't been trying to injure him.

All of it happened before Cam had a chance to move. Two men remained. One faced Donnie, who still had his foot on the guard with the broken arm. Cam shoved the man from behind. He went down, but came right back up, flicking out a telescoping rod. He swung it at Cam's head.

"Club!" Wally shouted. He grabbed a pillow to catch the blow. The silver rod flashed like a darting fish, striking foam as Cam fell backward on the couch. The pillow saved Cam, but the cudgel was deflected into Wally's own face. It smacked flesh and bone. Wally howled, but fought through the blow to grab the man's hand. He pulled it down and smashed it against the coffee table once, then again, and again. Bone splintered against wood, the rod long gone. The man lay writhing on the ground as Wally straddled his arm and began to hammer his unrecognizable hand into the table like a small red sledge, until Jules and Owen pulled him off.

The violence ended suddenly. The guards were all incapacitated. None were dead. Wally bled profusely from his nose, which sat askew on his face, obviously broken. Ari hurried to stanch the bleeding with the pillow, while Jules calmed him down. He'd taken a glancing blow that might have broken Cam's skull.

There was another shout of alarm behind the dressing room door, male this time.

"Calliope!" Cam gasped, and he leaped to the far door.

It was locked, but cheap and flimsy. Tegan's size-thirteen shoe made short work of it. It burst open, and Cam shoved his way inside.

The man kneeling on the floor had to be the bauxite politician. He was at least fifty and wore a suit. He yelled for his guards, but Cam shook his head, making it clear they wouldn't be coming.

Calliope was sprawled on the floor before him like a sacrificial offering. Cam's heart sank. The woman who'd given such life to a crowd of thousands lay still now, her eyes open but empty, the knife that ended her song nearby on the floor. Her crimson dress was puddled in the corner, and a pool of equally red blood widened slowly on the floor beneath her nude body, so pale by contrast that she might have been carved from a single piece of alabaster.

"You killed her!" Donnie barked.

The man was panicked. "No!" he said. "She asked to see my knife. She stabbed herself!"

Donnie and Cam started for the man at the same time. But there was a commotion in the hall behind them. Their hostess had returned with stadium security.

Ari grabbed them both by the shoulder. "No! It's over," he said, casting a sorrowful glance at the unreal scene. "Pilot says to go."

"What's happening?" Jules wailed in the doorway.

"Time to go!" Ari insisted.

And then they were pushing past stadium security hurrying in the opposite direction.

"In there!" Ari shouted to the bewildered officers on his way out. "He stabbed her!"

Jules was sobbing. Zara kept looking back over her shoulder, as though she burned to go back and wipe the floor with the bauxite man. But it was too late. They'd been too slow.

And it's my fault, Cam thought. Calliope had said "now," and he'd hesitated. He had stood debating her affection like a needy pubescent boy instead of saving her life like a man. Not focused. Not strong enough. Not fast enough. A failed knight cringing behind a foam shield wielded by a lunatic who was a more worthy male protector than he.

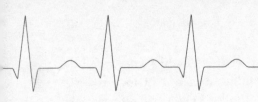

CAM'S PLAYLIST

22. HAMSTER WHEEL 🔊
   by The Fluffy Bunnies

---

23. REVELATION
   by Breathe

---

24. GROWTH SPURT
   by The Lucky Ones

"I try to reach the top, but it just won't stop."

They were in the parking lot, the commotion of the match and the sinister events beneath the stadium behind them. The team was focusing on the task at hand—exiting, escaping. Purpose kept the insanity at bay. Ari trotted to a stop at the large empty parking stall.

"What the hell?" he barked.

The bus was gone.

Their phones rang. Pilot spoke. "Vehicle change. Three cars. Keys under the visors. Directions on the GPS. Get out of there. The police are coming."

They found the cars quickly, two BMW sedans and a black Dodge Charger. But Pilot was wrong. The police weren't coming—they were already there. Two patrol cars burst into the parking lot, sirens blaring. One proceeded to the stadium. The other slowed and turned their way.

Ari ducked. "Shit! Don't show them which cars you're taking. I'll draw them off." With that, he threw himself in the driver's seat of the Charger. Jules followed, and though he waved her off, she got in anyway. The rest of them waited to climb into the BMWs as Ari tore out of the lot past the oncoming patrol car.

The police car accelerated after him. Moments later, Cam was in a BMW with Wally and Zara. Wally climbed into the driver's seat.

"You're *not* driving," Cam said, horrified at the prospect of riding in a car with Wally at the wheel. When Wally started to protest, Cam pointed at his ruined nose. "You're injured."

Zara pushed Wally aside and secured the keys. "I got this," she said.

"The GPS should take us on the same route as Ari," Cam pointed out. "No need to catch up. Just keep it calm, inconspicuous."

He didn't feel calm or inconspicuous, but it seemed like the right thing to say. They drove through town unnoticed, following the speed limit and the GPS on the dashboard. Zara drove efficiently and with razor-sharp reflexes, snapping in and out of her lane to avoid the less-than-careful local drivers.

At the edge of town they went north, followed the highway for a time, and then turned onto a secondary road. It was only a mile before they came upon the police car. It was parked on the side of the road just beyond two horrendous potholes, its lights still flashing. The other BMW was tucked in behind it. Owen waved them down, and they pulled over and hopped out. The officer sat in the back of his own car behind the safety cage with a deep frown. Owen quickly explained that Tegan had stuffed him inside after they'd confronted and overpowered him.

"Where's Ari?"

Owen took a deep breath. He pointed off the road at a reddish dirt field. "Over there."

Cam gasped and started into the field.

"Wait!" Owen called after him. But Cam saw the problem, and he didn't wait.

The Charger lay on its side. It looked unremarkable, entirely unlike car wrecks from the movies. No smoke. No ominously spinning tire. It was as though a giant child had simply left his toy car on its side when he'd been called to dinner. Donnie and Tegan stood atop the Charger, wrenching on the bent passenger door. Metal squealed, and then gave, and the door came loose. The two of them hauled it open. They leaned in and dragged Jules out. She was in hysterics, babbling about Ari.

"Shut up!" Donnie barked as he and Tegan lowered her to the ground. "She can walk. Get her out of here."

"No! I'm staying. Ari!"

Owen stood by the police car, casting anxious glances at the officer in the backseat. "Hurry up!" he yelled into the field. "He's sure to have called for backup or an ambulance."

Zara and Wally arrived at the Charger to help. They took charge of Jules and led her back to the BMW. Cam stayed, trying to see Ari through the cracked windshield.

"He's tangled," Donnie said. "Let's just turn this thing over."

Donnie hopped down, and, with Tegan, began pushing on the car to turn it upright. *Two guys shouldn't be able to flip a car,* Cam thought. But when they set their feet in the dirt and shoved together, the Charger immediately tilted, and then went over with the tortured squealing sound as the ruined passenger door swung on its broken hinges, and a heavy thump as the tires hit the ground.

"Hurry. Get him out!"

Donnie was inside. "Come on, teammate," he was saying. "Hang in there."

In spite of Donnie's encouragement, Ari died. It was clear to Cam as soon as they brought him out. Too wilted. Too broken. He'd seen death several times now, and he found that he recognized it immediately. It was not so much the injuries as an absence of energy. The Ari he'd known radiated life. The body they held was a shell. Empty. Inert. Cam didn't need to be told. They laid it at his feet, and the head lolled to one side. Donnie listened at his chest, and then felt for a pulse. Finally, he looked up at Cam.

"Hey man," he said, "I'm sorry. I know you liked him."

That was all. Tegan threw Ari's body unceremoniously over his shoulder and ran for the cars.

Pilot had them back at the beach in under four hours. Jules was still dazed, either from the horrific events or the sedative Pilot had given her. Cam tried to walk her to her condo, but she shooed him away.

"I need to think," she mumbled.

Ward warned her that thinking too much after a mission wasn't a good idea. "Just relax for now. Wind down. We'll debrief in forty minutes," he said.

Cam was left to trudge down to his own condo alone. He'd made peace with their losses during the four-hour trip, but the small place still felt empty without Ari. His roommate's dirty clothes were still piled in the basket beside his footlocker. His notebook still sat on the desk. Cam turned it over, and then picked it up. There would be notes in it, he thought. *Smart-guy notes. Strategy and survival notes.* Maybe he could learn something that would keep him alive for a few more missions. Cam eased it open. There was indeed writing, and lots of it, the sort that poured out when the hand couldn't keep up with the brain. Cam flipped through. Months' worth of hurried-looking script filled page after page. It was a narrative, not just notes. A *diary*, Cam realized. He flipped through it until he reached a page where Jules's name caught his eye, and then he read too much before he could stop himself.

They'd done it. Sex. In the condo before Cam had arrived. Cam wondered what it must be like on TS-9. Three lines later, Ari answered him with a single word. "Unbelievable." Jules was passionate and emotional, the diary said. Cam believed it. He could immediately picture her demonstrative face showcasing each emotion as it came and went—her big smile so open and welcoming, her oversized eyes so wide with delight, her gasping breaths so deep and abrupt that her eyelids would suddenly mash together tight. She was a bundle of exaggerated feelings. *Enhanced feelings.* Ari's physical description of her was also complimentary, almost poetic, like a mortal worshipping a goddess.

Cam closed the notebook. He suddenly felt guilty peeking in on Jules's heart and body without her permission. *Although she might give me permission now.* She and Cam had both lost their roommates. They were both available. It could work. She was sensitive—she'd need companionship, and not the cold sort Zara offered. With Ari gone, Cam was the obvious choice for her anyway, and though she was a little odd looking, she was by no means ugly. Besides, she was the only person who could have left him the suggestive notes.

He suddenly hated himself for what he was thinking. His best friend was dead, his body only a few hours cold, and Cam was already raiding his memories. Worse, he was using them to make plans to scoop up his girl.

"You are such an ass," he swore at himself.

Then he heard a sound. A sigh or a scrape—he couldn't tell—but it was definitely under the condo. *The burrowing animal,* Cam thought. He tossed the notebook on his bunk and hurried outside.

He stopped short of the hole to study the ground. He had to cock his head and squint to make it out, but when he did, he saw that there was definitely a disturbance in the sand along the beach, a subtle but regular pattern leading from the cliffs to his hut, or vice versa. Some sort of vague tracks, Cam thought.

He bent to peer under the condo. It was dark, and he had to drop to his hands and knees. He heard a shuffling sound. Something moved deeper into the hole away from him. Something large. He glanced back at the tracks. The sand was swept back and forth. A boa constrictor, maybe. He shuddered and scooted away another foot. He didn't want whatever it was to come barreling out at him. His eyes were beginning to adjust. He could make out a dark lump in the far end of the hole—not a snake. There was a low growl.

"Easy there," Cam cooed. "Don't want to have to get a dart gun."

The thing shuffled its feet, adjusting itself, perhaps for a charge. *A large monkey? A boar? Do they have jaguars in the Amazon or leopards? And what's the difference?* Ari would have known, Cam thought. The thing was crouched. Too big for a monkey. It was a jaguar, he decided. Nothing else he knew growled.

Cam's heart began to beat faster. He backed away slowly, speaking in a soothing voice, "Okay, Mr. Jaguar, stay cool. I'm going to go get some help."

"No!" cried the jaguar.

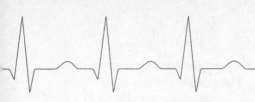

"You were something I didn't expect . . ."

"Who are you?" Cam asked.

The girl was halfway out and squirming through the sand. "Don't tell! Please. Don't call for them."

"Who the hell are you?" Cam repeated.

"My name wouldn't mean anything to you if I told you," she said, spitting dirt and climbing to her feet.

She was Caucasian and spoke English. Her physique was slender, with wiry muscles, and she crouched as though ready to bolt or spring. She glanced around the corner of the condo toward the bunker.

Cam took a step back, wary. "Well, *what* are you then?"

"Can I trust you, Cam?"

"How do you know my name?"

"I heard it from under there."

"You've been spying on me!"

"Spying." The word lingered on her tongue, and she looked like she wanted to chuckle, but couldn't. "Isn't that what we're all here for?"

She was dirty, Cam saw. Her fingernails were black, and her ratty brown-red hair hung over her face like limp yarn. Her worn clothes were ripped in places.

"You're the one who left me the notes," he realized.

"I left the notes," she confirmed. "I won't lie. I need help. Your help. But I'm trying to help you too."

She gave him a piteous look. She wasn't just slender, Cam realized. She was downright skinny. *Malnourished.*

"Did you growl at me?" he asked. "Because that was weird."

"I was scared."

"Me too. I thought you were a jaguar. What did the notes mean? And what do you want? And where the heck did you come from?"

"So many questions."

"Well, maybe you should start answering some of them."

"You should be asking questions about your trainers, not me."

"We have asked questions. Lots of them."

"Not the right ones."

Cam heard a whistle and turned. They were gathering. It was time to debrief with Ward.

"I have to go," she said, her eyes darting past him, watching for the others. "I'll contact you again soon. I have to trust you. Don't tell them about me." She was pleading.

"I trust my teammates more than I trust some stranger who appears from nowhere and sneaks into my hut."

"I understand, really I do." She started up the beach toward thick foliage at the base of the cliffs, wiping her tracks away as best she could considering the hurry she was in. "Because this used to be *my* hut."

Then she was gone. Cam stood for a moment, puzzling over her last words. Then he began to get a sinking feeling. He leaned under the condo, reached in, and felt around. His fingers sifted through sand, but found nothing. *Dammit!* he thought. *She took the diamonds. . . .*

Cam was late, and the room was in an uproar when he walked in. Jules and her powerful emotions and goddess body were up front. She stood, facing Ward, tears pouring down her face. The sedative had obviously worn off.

"Take me home! I wanna go home! I'm done with this! All of it!"

Ward was in damage control mode, his arms open in a comforting gesture.

"Everything is fine."

Jules wouldn't let him near her. She waved her own arms for space, trying to control her breathing. "It's not fine! It isn't! My best friend was murdered. My boyfriend was killed in a car wreck."

"I can field all of your questions," he said calmly. "Please sit."

"I don't have questions! I understand 'dead'!"

"I have questions," Cam said.

Everyone turned at the sound of his voice. They hadn't seen him enter. Jules stopped sobbing.

"And I have answers," Ward said. "Can you help your teammate, Cam?"

Cam went to her, and she seemed to calm, but when he tried to help her into a chair, she shoved him away and stormed out. Ward let her go.

"We're moving on," he said. "Take your seat, Cam."

"I'd rather stand," Cam said. He didn't really want to stand, but he didn't want to take orders just then either.

"As you wish. Please stand there." Ward pointed to a space against the wall. "So that everyone can see."

It was a compromise. Cam accepted it and moved to the wall.

"I'd like to start by congratulating you," Ward said.

"But the mission was a massive failure," Cam said.

"We don't even know what the mission was," Wally mumbled.

"That's why you're going to calm down and listen up," Ward said patiently. "Look, I know this process is hard. You are losing teammates. But stay strong."

Donnie glared around the room. "Yeah, shut it and listen to Ward."

"The mission," Ward continued, "was a complete success."

They did listen this time. And the statement was so contrary to the experience that Cam wasn't sure how to argue.

"We sent you to end the political ambitions of a man secretly backed by militant rebels who would have ousted all foreign businesses from his country and driven his people into poverty. His election is in two weeks. Thanks to you, he was found by local police in a room in a foreign country with a naked young girl. He had her blood on his hands. His knife killed her. And this team right here kept his guards from doctoring the scene until the police arrived."

Ward paused to let it all sink in.

"He was probably traveling anonymously, which will look suspicious. But he won't be anonymous after the Brazilian police take him into custody. There will be full news coverage. It doesn't matter whether they find him guilty. The scandal will be enough. His career in politics is over."

"How did Calliope get him to stab her?" Owen asked.

"She stabbed herself," Ward said, eliciting stunned silence. "Don't worry, she coated the knife with poison from the dart she was carrying. She will have felt almost nothing."

Cam put a hand against the wall to steady himself. "Why didn't you tell us?"

"Would you have let her do it?" Ward let the question sink in. "You're a bunch of heroes. You would have tried to stop her, to 'save' her. But this is what she wanted. This was the time she chose. I wasn't there, but I understand she received a standing ovation."

Zara was fascinated. "She died a rock star."

"But what about her body?" Donnie asked. "We didn't recover it."

"When we set up the gig, we gave them a phone number. They'll call it to tell us what happened. The autopsy will be quick—fairly obvious cause of death. We'll give them instructions to deliver her body."

"And Ari? What about him?" Cam asked. Calliope was being efficiently explained away, but he still felt empty, and he wanted something to remain angry about.

"He drives too fast," Ward said simply.

"Drove," Donnie whispered to Owen. "Past tense."

"Killed by a pothole," Owen snickered back.

Cam shot them a dirty look.

Ward held up his fist for attention. "He made a mistake, but he died helping the world and doing something he loved, Cam. His actions were philosophically consistent with our purpose here, and he was precisely on task. He kept the police from detaining all of you at the stadium. Correct?"

Cam nodded. He had to. Ward was right.

"Do you see what we're doing here?" They all nodded, except for Cam. "Do you get it?" They nodded again, satisfied.

It still felt wrong to Cam, but he couldn't figure out why.

Ward saw that he'd won the others over. He looked directly at Cam. "Are we missing something, Cam?"

Diamonds, Cam thought. *He's missing some diamonds and a note-writing girl from the jungle.* Cam wondered if Ward knew he was keeping secrets. As far as he could tell, he wasn't breaking any of the "unbreakable" rules. But the man sure could stare. Like Zara. Everyone was staring. He felt the collective weight of their gaze. *I'm the odd man out, here.* Perhaps it was time to 'fess up, he thought. Time to get with the program.

"Can I talk with you privately?" Cam asked Ward.

"Of course. We'll debrief individually. We can talk then."

They moved on, and Ward filled in the details of their mission.

It all made sense. And except for crappy Brazilian roads, it would have gone exactly as planned. A "variable," Ward called it. "Unfortunate."

When the meeting ended, Ward told them the order of their individual debriefings. Cam was second to last, which meant he had some time, so he went to see Jules. When his turn came, he'd tell Ward about the diamonds and the girl under his condo, he decided. He didn't want the group hearing about it. Donnie would fault him for not coming clean, for not being a team player, and he sure as heck didn't need that.

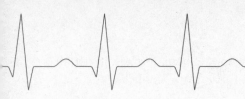

24. GROWTH SPURT 🔊
   by The Lucky Ones

25. MY HEART OR YOURS
   by Love-n-Stuff

26. DICE
   by One Shoe Magoo

"Gotta grow into these wings."

Jules looked up. She sat in a pile of fern fronds she'd arranged into a sort of soft chair. Behind her, shells were arranged decoratively on a shelf. Her eyes were red from crying, but tears were no longer flowing. It appeared as though she'd cried so much that she'd cried herself out.

"I can't do it anymore, Cam," she sniffed. "I can't."

Cam moved to comfort her. He joined her on the pile of fronds and held her, trying not to think of Ari's glowing description of her goddess body as she pressed it against him, which was not easy.

"Can't do what?"

"I can't stay. I have to go home."

"We can't go home. We're dead, remember? This is our home." It sounded as wrong when he said it as when he'd heard it, and he hated himself for lying to her, but there was no choice. If they didn't pretend this was a home, they had no home.

"They'll let me go," Jules insisted. "I'll tell them I sent a message. Then they'll have to."

"A message?"

"To my sister. At the Internet kiosk at the stadium."

"No! You didn't."

"Cam, I had to. I just had to."

"What did you say?"

"Just that I'm okay."

Unbreakable, Cam thought.

Jules frowned at him, reading his concerned expression. "I didn't tell her about Deathwing, if that's what you're worried about. Like that even matters anymore."

"It matters to the organization. You shouldn't even tell them you contacted her."

"It's the only way they'll send me home. Now if they keep me here it'll be kidnapping."

"You're going to blackmail them?"

"No." She harrumphed. "I'm just going to tell them I have to go. This is a special situation."

Cam sensed something. He turned and jumped, startled. A figure stood in the doorway. Zara.

"Dammit, woman. Don't do that." He wondered how long she'd been standing there.

"Jules, it's your turn to debrief," she said.

Cam met Jules's eyes. He shook his head—one last warning. She shrugged—one last defiance. Then she stood, turned her divine body away from him, and went to meet with their personal trainer.

Cam's turn inevitably came. The last debriefing had been easy. Just an opportunity for him to ask questions. They hadn't grilled him about diamonds or secret notes. So when he was called this time, he felt reasonably calm.

"I hope you don't mind if Pilot sits in," Ward began.

"I don't mind," Cam said. *This is different*, he thought. Ward talked a lot, but Pilot *listened*. He wore sunglasses and held his head at an angle like a bird of prey. It was unnerving.

"I want to ask you about your teammates," Ward said. "How are they doing? Anyone seem troubled?"

He obviously meant Jules. "I think Jules is upset. She really liked Ari and Calliope."

"So did you, Cam. Are you upset?"

"No. I mean, yes, of course. But I'm not . . ."

"Not what?"

Ward was probing. They wanted to know what Jules was doing. Or maybe they already did know and wanted to test Cam to see if he'd lie about it. "I'm not crying like a baby about it. It's all part of the philosophy, right?"

Pilot nodded.

"Right," Ward agreed. "Did Jules say anything to you? We're concerned about her."

"No. Did she say anything to you?"

"She was upset, like you say."

"Anything else?" Cam went on the offensive, asking the questions.

Ward and Pilot glanced at one another. "Details about the mission," Ward said quickly. "It's nice to get it fleshed out. It sounds like you did well."

"Thanks," Cam said. It was bullshit. He'd frozen during Calliope's phone call, costing them precious seconds—they might have saved Calliope's life in spite of her intention. He'd also been ineffective in the room. Wally had to save his sorry butt. Cam hadn't even driven the car. Zara had. He was dead weight. "I think it's time to get me some TS-9, though."

"Are you having symptoms?"

"Yeah. I'm experiencing some muscular weakness when compared to my teammates, and a relative slowness in my movement. And my mind isn't as sharp as it could be."

Ward scowled at the sarcasm. "You want to be enhanced. Is that it?"

"I want to be an asset to the team."

Ward's expression lightened. "That's our Wingman," he said to Pilot, and Cam felt relieved to be moving the conversation away from Jules. "We'll let the doc know. She'll consult with you next visit."

They had more questions. Ward asked for details of the trip to Macapá—who went where and when. How the confrontation with the bodyguards progressed, blow by blow. Who was quick or strong. Cam was honest, hoping to match his story to what Donnie and Zara and the rest had likely told them. It was best to be as accurate as possible, in case they asked about Jules again—if he was honest enough for most of it, he might earn enough credibility to pull off one lie. And, finally, Ward asked the question Cam had sensed was coming.

"Did Jules ever say anything about an Internet kiosk?"

Cam pretended to think. "There was one at the stadium," he said vaguely. "We didn't stop at it. We got sausages. Donnie had two. He's a pig, you know."

Ward chuckled.

Pilot nodded and spoke. "Be that as it may, we just want to make sure everything is all right with the team. If a member isn't on board, we'd like to know. You're still with us, aren't you, Cam?"

Cam forced a laugh and hoped it didn't sound too forced. "Where else would I go?"

"Home?" Ward suggested.

Cam sat back in his chair. "Naw. I'm dead. This is home now."

Cam went straight to Jules's condo, where he found her gathering her things. She looked up. Her smile was as big as he'd imagined it while reading Ari's journal. It finally matched the size of her eyes nicely.

"What's going on?" Cam asked, stepping inside.

Jules peeked out the door behind him, and then ducked her head back inside and whispered. "They told me not to tell anyone. But I'll tell you. They're sending me home!"

"What?"

"I asked, and they said no. Then I demanded that they at least let me go to Scotland where I did a semester overseas. I'm sure the local family I stayed with will take me. And they said yes!"

Cam was stunned. "I can't believe it."

"I told you, silly."

"How will that even work? What are you going to tell people?"

"They're making up a story for me. I obviously can't tell about this place, but don't worry, I can totally keep a secret."

Just then, Pilot called for her to come to the Zodiac.

"I have to go before they change their mind. They don't want me shaking up the team—the whole 'stay focused' thing, you know." She suddenly leaped at him and gave him a huge hug. "I'm glad I knew you, Cam."

Jules exited, and Cam stepped out of the condo to watch her skip down the beach to the waiting boat. Pilot glanced up and saw Cam in the doorway. He frowned until Jules arrived at the boat, and then smiled and helped her in. Pilot waded into the surf to push off, hopped in after her, and they headed to sea. Then she was gone.

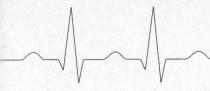

CAM'S PLAYLIST

25. MY HEART OR YOURS 🔊
    by Love-n-Stuff

26. DICE
    by One Shoe Magoo

27. OH YEAH, MAKE ME
    by So It Begins

"My heart, your heart, torn apart, fresh start. Oh-oh-oh!"

"Where are they going?" It was Tegan. He sat nearby, far enough away that Cam was sure he hadn't heard the conversation, but close enough to see Jules depart.

"I don't know," Cam said. It was partially true and partially a lie. "I'm sure they'll tell us at our next meeting."

"Yeah," Tegan agreed. "They'll tell us what they tell us."

"What do you mean?" Cam said.

"You're a snotty college boy. You figure it out."

"College boy?"

"Aren't you?"

"Yes, but . . ."

"You all are. Not all boys, but all rich school kids."

"We're all on the same team."

"Kind of. But it's no different here than anywhere else. The brainy kid, the athlete, and the good-looking girl argue over who they think is running the show, but they don't realize it's the people with the real money who pull the strings. They tell us what's what and where to go and what to do. We fight their battles. We die for them. They don't teach you that in college, do they?"

"Is there someone you'd rather be dying for?"

"Naw. One boss is as good as another. Mill operator. Mine owner. Army sergeant. Prison supervisor. Personal trainer. Makes no difference. We work for them, and then we die. It's just quicker for us here."

"Coming here was our choice."

"We didn't have much choice. You wouldn't have come if they hadn't told you that you were dying."

Cam cocked his head. He hadn't heard more than a sentence from Tegan the entire time he'd been here. But it was the same amount that he'd heard anyone say *to* Tegan, he realized. Cam sat down in the sand to join him.

"What's your story, man?" he asked.

"We ain't got stories, do we? We checked those at the door. Just first names here. Not supposed to talk about where we're from or what we did before. I thought it might be a kind of fresh start. But I was wrong. People are still who they are."

Cam nodded. "How is it rooming with Wally?"

"He's crazy."

Cam laughed.

"Not a bad guy," Tegan added. "But pretty much a mental case."

"Maybe it's his way of dealing with all this."

"Maybe."

"Sorry I haven't been friendly," Cam offered.

"It's okay. You've been taking sides and chasing skirt. I'm just doing my time."

"Your time?"

"I'm the farthest along."

Tegan set his jaw, and his eyes narrowed. It was tough for him to say. He meant the disease. His diagnosis was worse than the rest. He had less time to live.

"I'm sorry," Cam said.

"Not your fault. I blame the docs." Tegan grinned. It was the first time Cam had seen him smile.

"I'm thinking I'm ready for the TS-9 myself," Cam said suddenly.

Tegan thought for a moment. "Naw. I get these headaches. They suck. You don't want them."

"But you're strong and fast."

"Yeah, that part's fun. But it's unnatural. It's not me. I feel wrong, and when my head starts thumping like it's gonna burst out of my skull, I feel *really* wrong. I think when the end comes you'd rather be you than TS-Cam."

Cam nodded and rose. "Thanks for the chat, man. I'll try to be less snotty from now on."

Tegan smirked, and Cam saw that, if he hadn't completely won over the big guy, he'd at least made a sort of peace with him.

Cam carried the split half of a roast fowl to the rear of his condo. The plastic wrap stretched over its surface kept the sand off as he slid it underneath. Then he headed inside.

Owen showed up ten minutes later. "Hey," the Donnie imitator said in greeting. He stood in the doorway carrying a large canvas bag.

"What's that?"

"They're rearranging the roommate situation."

"And . . . ?"

"And I'm here now." Owen didn't look confident. He lingered at the entrance, not bold enough to step inside yet.

"They've assigned you to me?"

"To this condo, yeah."

"I thought I'd get it to myself after . . ."

"I guess not."

Cam puzzled over it. "There are five condos and six of us left. Who's Donnie bunking with?"

"I think he's alone now."

"Wally?"

"Alone."

"Zara's alone, obviously. Tegan?"

"Alone."

"So we're the only roommates."

"I guess so."

Cam frowned. It made no sense, unless . . . *They're watching me*, he thought. Owen had been sent to spy on him. He remembered what the skinny girl from the jungle had said. *That's what we're all here for.*

Cam forced his frown into a smile. "Throw your stuff over there. Welcome to château Cameron."

Owen looked relieved. He ambled in and began to set up shop. Cam began to climb up to his bunk. Then he saw Owen reach for Ari's diary.

"Dude!" Cam barked.

"What?"

"Toss me my notebook, would ya?"

Owen picked up the diary. He turned it over in his hands, and Cam was certain he'd open it. "Sure," Owen said finally, and he threw it up to Cam, who shoved it into his pocket.

Cam laid back and let himself slide into sleep. Owen couldn't find out anything about him if he didn't do anything. Besides, the diamonds were gone. If Owen went poking around, all he'd find was half a cooked bird.

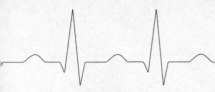

CAM'S PLAYLIST

26. DICE 🔊
by One Shoe Magoo

27. OH YEAH, MAKE ME
by So It Begins

28. THE ENDLESS NOTHING
by Necromoor

"Roll 'em, roll 'em, roll 'em again."

Cam awoke to a narrow, grease-stained face. Female. *The girl from the jungle.* He sat up quickly. She stood on his rope ladder, leaning over him the way Pilot had those long weeks ago in the hospital.

"Fank-roo," she mumbled through a mouth full of dark meat.

"You're welcome," Cam said. "What are you doing in here? I thought you didn't want people to find you."

"It's dark out, and your new buddy is off at a beach fire." She tore another hunk from the bird leg.

"He's not my buddy."

"No?"

"No. I don't trust him."

"Why not?"

"Because you've made me paranoid. By the way, you took some-thing from me."

"You don't need it. Or do you?" She cocked an eyebrow. "What's your plan?"

"Plan? I don't have a plan."

"Well, you should."

"I want some answers. And I don't want you to get me into trouble."

"Why are you so worried about getting into trouble? This is all for good and justice and blah-blah-blah, right?" She paused to eat again. "Well, I'll tell you why. Because you sense it. I know you do. You can feel that something's wrong."

"I don't know," Cam said defensively. "People are dying. Some of it is hard to take. It makes a guy think. But it's an intense pro-gram. That doesn't mean something's wrong."

"You didn't tell them about me. I would know if you did."

"No. I didn't."

"Can I trust you?"

"I gave you a chicken, or whatever that bird was."

"*They* give you food. Do you trust them?"

"I have so far."

"So did I."

"You're one of us, then?"

"I was. Last year's batch. TS-8."

Prior teams? Cam thought. *Why not?* Ward had never said there weren't—he just never talked about them.

"Why are you hiding?" Cam asked.

"I'm not with the program anymore, and they didn't exactly provide me with transportation out of here."

"You went AWOL. Wow. But what does this have to do with me? I can't help you go anywhere. I'm here until I die."

"Until you die, huh? God, you are dumb. You don't get it, do you? And I thought you were smart. A year and a half ago they di-

agnosed me with the same life-sucking, brain-eating thing they say
you have. But look at me. What do you notice?"

"You're skinny and dirty?"

"I'm not dead."

Her name was Siena Black. She was from Eugene, Oregon, the only
child of an architect and a teacher. She was about to declare her
major in environmental studies at the University of Oregon when
she was diagnosed with malignant glioblastoma out of the blue.
She'd been on a team just like Cam—ten college-age kids. But she'd
bailed and fled into the jungle. Siena talked machine-gun fast,
spilling more personal info in a few minutes than his teammates
had in weeks. But she didn't linger. It was a trust offering, and she
was eager to get to business.

"So that's a bit about me," she said. "Now I need your help getting out of here."

"You're telling me you're not sick?"

"I'm not a doctor. I'm just saying I haven't died, and they said I
would."

"From the tumor or the TS?"

"They said both would kill me. But a tumor hasn't killed me, obviously. And I stopped taking the TS-8. I couldn't get it after I went
AWOL. That was hell, by the way. I went through withdrawals. Lots
of barf. Not pretty. That's part of why I look like an anorexic runway
model. My body's so screwed up I don't know if I'm sick or recovering or going to die in five minutes. But I'm still kicking. I know that."

"Proves nothing."

"I didn't say it proved anything. Just said I need to get out of
here. They aren't very understanding about the desertion thing."

"They let a friend of mine go home."

"Did they?" She looked genuinely surprised, and there was a
hint of hope in her expression, but mostly doubt.

"That's what she said. She begged and they agreed. She was a mess. Maybe you should have just cried a lot if you didn't want to be part of the team anymore."

"Right. The almighty 'team.'"

"They're my friends. You're a stranger. No offense."

"Your friends aren't that great. You don't even trust your room-mate."

"That's because he's a tool."

"The rest aren't much better."

"How do you know? Eavesdropping? Sneaking under huts?"

"I just know."

"Yeah. How?"

"Because they hunted me."

"What?"

"There were two of us. We were the leftovers. I started the TS last, and he wasn't on it at all. They didn't have any more missions for us. They were bringing in new kids, but keeping us isolated from them. Pilot told me I was going to be going away for some 'individual training.' He said to meet him at the boat the next morning, but I started getting a bad feeling about it. We agreed to run. Ward, Pilot, and some of your friendly teammates came after us."

"Then where's the guy?"

"I don't know. I haven't seen him since we separated to split up our pursuers."

"Maybe he's lost in the jungle?"

"Maybe."

"You say 'hunted,' but what if they were just trying to find you?"

"The athletic guy threw a dart at me while I was in a tree. A fall from that height would have been fatal."

"Donnie? He's an ass."

"His minion and the big guy were after me too."

"Tegan and Owen? Why would those guys hunt someone who hadn't done anything wrong?"

"Because Pilot told them to? And Ward could make up anything in a team briefing. How do you know *your* targets were bad guys?"

"Oh, please," Cam sniffed. "Our first mission was to rescue doctors from pirates. Pirates have been bad since time immemorial. Three severed heads pretty much confirmed it."

Siena went to the doorway to make sure no one was coming. "Look, idiot, *I* was your team's first mission. You weren't there because you were the last-minute replacement for the poor sap that fell over the cliff chasing me. And I know damn good and well that I'm not a bad guy."

Cam fumed. It was interesting information, he had to admit, but was it true? And he didn't like losing the logic fight. "Are you going to give me my diamonds back?"

"No. I'll need them when I get to civilization. If you're staying here, you won't."

"Fine. You're right."

"You're right, I'm right."

"I mean about the diamonds. About the rest, I'm not sure."

"Who do you think is funding all of this? They're still testing TS. On us."

"Not on me."

"You ever heard of a control group? You're the athletic, smart, normal human guinea pig they compare your enhanced teammates to. They're not going to give it to you. Ever."

"Ward told us that the TS was experimental right up front. We knew that when we signed up."

"Then you know that the organization has to be a fucking pharmaceutical company, right, Cam?"

For a moment Cam couldn't speak. The idea was so overwhelming that it bounced around in his head and he had trouble getting hold of it.

"Just because there's money behind all this doesn't mean it's evil," he said.

"Unless we were never dying to begin with."

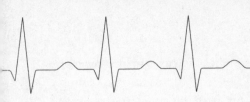

27. OH YEAH, MAKE ME 🔊
by So It Begins

"I wouldn't wish me on your worst enemy."

Cam groaned and rolled over. Owen was up and annoying him already.

"So what's on the agenda today? Got plans? I'm just hanging out. What are you doing?" Owen had black hair, Cam noticed, the blackest he'd ever seen, so dark that, from behind, his head looked like a hole in reality perched on his sunburned neck.

"I was thinking I might explore the jungle a bit," Cam said. "Maybe find some coconuts."

Owen looked confused. "Okay. Cool."

It wasn't cool. It was stupid and a lie. Cam dressed and headed off toward one of the climbing ropes strung up on the bluff. There were three, including the southern one on the cliffs he'd come down initially with Ward. It was the highest. The others were plenty tall as well, but not so harrowing. They were the two used for practice runs in the jungle. Cam walked toward the one in the middle. Owen watched him go, and Cam watched Owen watch him go out of the corner of his eye. When his roommate ducked inside the hut again, Cam hurried back and slid underneath into Siena's hollow space.

Owen was already in Cam's footlocker. Cam could hear his dark-haired roommate emptying it and then stacking everything back inside. The floor was thin, and though he couldn't see through it, he heard every step. Owen went to the desk next. He was looking for the notebook, Cam realized. Cam had Ari's diary in his pocket, but he'd left his own, which said almost nothing. He'd been tempted to write "Screw you, Owen!" on the last page, but decided it was better not to let his roommate know he was onto him. He might be able to learn something. Thirty minutes later, after Owen had made a thorough search of the condo and Cam was getting cramps in his legs, he slid out from underneath and backtracked to the bluff.

"Hey Owen!" he called, approaching the condo. "I'm back!"

When he walked in he almost laughed. Owen was seated comfortably on their padded bench, a book in his hand and his feet up as though he'd been relaxing.

"Oh, hey. Any coconuts?"

"I saw one, but it was too high."

"Oh well."

"Yeah. I didn't bring a tool along to help me reach it. Hey, any idea when our next mission will be?"

"No," Owen said, perking up at the opportunity to probe. "Why?"

"I'm just eager to get back to it. The second and third missions were so insane. It gets you pumped, right?"

Owen looked confused, an expression he was good at. "I guess so."

"Which was your favorite?"

"Of the two we . . . ?"

"Of all of them."

His hesitation told Cam most of what he needed to know. Owen didn't correct him. His new roommate didn't know if Cam knew there'd been a first mission before he arrived, and he wasn't sure whether he should acknowledge it. Siena was telling the truth.

Owen finally recovered. "The pirates was my favorite. Being on the scuba team was awesome! Did you see me shoot through the hole in the door?"

"Yeah," Cam said. "You were . . . awesome."

Hours later, Owen was off spearfishing in the lagoon, and Cam flipped open Ari's diary, looking for information. He discovered that the notebook was more than a titillating account of his encounter with Jules. There were details about doctor visits and training exercises, meals, and even bickering among Deathwing members. It was a record of their service in the organization. Valuable. Dangerous. It had been meant to be used for strategy notes, but Ari was a voracious writer. Cam had written very little—it felt too much like an assignment from one of his college courses, and he'd be damned if he was going to spend his last year of life doing homework.

"Knock, knock," Wally called from the doorway, and Cam slapped the notebook shut.

"Yeah? What?"

"Doctor visit."

"Now?"

"No. Fifteen minutes. Saddle up."

They gathered at the beach. Same routine. Boat, helicopter, and blindfolds the entire time, until they were in the gli club. This time, Zara beat him handily at Ping-Pong, and he couldn't score even a point on Donnie. They were getting better, Cam thought. *Faster, stronger, more focused.*

There was a buffet with fresh fruit, bread, soft ripened cheeses, and a pepper pot stew for those waiting. Tegan and Owen went first.

Cam sat beside Zara while Wally and Donnie played pool. She ate mango with a toothpick, then rolled the toothpick around with her tongue so that it danced back and forth across her lips like a thorn on rose petals.

Cam pointed at the door to the exam rooms. "The last time these guys did a scan of my tumor, it looked like it was getting smaller," he lied.

"That's odd," Zara grumbled. "They haven't done a scan of me the entire time I've been here."

"Weird. You'd think that would be the first thing they'd do." He watched Zara frown and persisted. "What do they usually test with you, then?"

"Speed. Strength. TS-9 stuff. I have the fastest reaction time of anyone on the team, you know."

"They didn't test mine."

"You're not enhanced, so why bother? No offense."

"None taken. You're right. That's probably why they're actually working on the thing that's killing me. In your situation they're clearly focused on the drug they're killing you with instead." Cam whistled, waiting for her to think about it. He didn't have to wait long.

"Your checkup was short last time, wasn't it?"

"Yeah, but the scan machine was amazing. It's in another room. Takes an image in real time. I don't know why they don't do it for you."

Zara sat bolt upright now and had scooted to the edge of her seat. *I've got her,* Cam thought.

"Did they say you might be getting better or that it's even possible?"

"They don't say much. But sometimes I wonder if they misdiagnosed me. You know. Mistakes happen."

Zara sat back. Her dark brow wrinkled into a sort of Z shape so that Cam could see her thinking. They sat for a time, the click of the pool balls, smacking hard or kissing lightly, the only sound.

"I didn't feel sick at all when I was diagnosed," she said suddenly.

Cam nodded. "What about now?"

"Just light headaches so far. The primary TS-9 symptom. And my stomach isn't right."

"Your stomach?"

She rolled her eyes. "Bloating."

"I can't tell."

"Thanks. But I can."

"That's it?"

"My pee is dark yellow. Beyond yellow. More like orange. And my hair . . ."

Cam glanced at her short, dark locks. "It looks normal, except that you took a knife to it."

"Not that hair." She frowned. "I had to shave my upper lip the other day, my legs are going crazy, and it's not like you can get a good waxing around here."

"Did your own doctor diagnose you?"

"No."

"Did a specialist nobody knew fly in and do it?"

Just then, Tegan and Owen were led back through the doors by the tight-lipped woman who had examined Cam on their last visit.

"Zara and Donald. You're next."

Wally snickered. "Calling Donald Duck."

Donnie shot him a look and slapped his pool cue on the table. Zara stood and headed for the door, but she cast Cam a backward glance. He shrugged.

Tegan looked pale. Cam asked him to play some pool, but he declined. Cam asked again, winking to try to get him away from Owen, who was circling the food table. Finally, he understood and grabbed the rack. Cam whispered to him as he lined up the balls, alternating solids and stripes.

"You look like crap."

"Only because that's how I feel."

"What's going on?"

"Headaches, man."

"Did you ask them for something to deal with them?"

"They don't want to mix anything with the TS."

"Maybe you should stop taking it."

"It's keeping me going, they said. I'd be worse off without it."

"But . . ."

Tegan turned irritated eyes toward him, and Cam could see that he'd been crying. "Look, they're the doctors. Not me. And not you!"

It wasn't the right time, Cam decided. Maybe it would never be.

When it was Cam's turn, he went in with Wally, and they were taken to separate rooms. This time, Cam was closely escorted through the door with the stretchy-faced woman at his shoulder, and she closed it behind her with a telltale click.

They locked me in this time, he thought as he hopped up on the padded, paper-covered exam table.

"I'm ready," Cam said simply.

"Ready for what?"

"For the TS-9. Or is the TS-10 ready?"

"TS-10?" She glanced up at a mirror on the wall.

The mirror was large and set into the wall, not hung. The reflection was strangely dark. *One-way*, Cam thought. *Somebody's watching this.*

"Ward just said—" Cam pretended to catch himself. "Or maybe I wasn't supposed to say anything."

She flashed a smile without showing her teeth. "We're always hoping for a new, better medication. It's normal to wonder. TS-9 is what we have."

"I'd like some."

"I don't think so," she said a little too quickly.

"We were told it's voluntary when we're ready, because we're dying anyway, right? Ward says that all the time. I'd hate to tell him you're not on the same page."

She nodded carefully. "It's your decision, yes, in consultation with your doctor."

"My doctor is *you*, right?"

"Yes."

"And here we are consulting."

She took a deep breath and forced another smile. "Well, let's check you out then, shall we?"

She was not happy—he could tell—but she took out a checklist and began to administer tests. She took blood pressure and a blood sample again, shined a light in his eyes and ears, and she asked him a series of questions: whether he felt persistent headaches, nausea, vomiting, mood swings, emotional instability, memory loss, seizures, lowered alertness, changes in vision, hearing loss, fatigue, weakness, difficulties in speech or swallowing, decreased coordination, fever, uncoordinated movement, paralysis of the face, drooping eyelids, eye movements, confusion, disorientation. His answers were universally "no."

In between each question, he pestered her, asking her to check his vision, his hearing, his reaction time. He pointed to the machines that Jules had described and asked how they worked, then sat down at them whether she asked him to or not. She glanced up at the mirror at times, but gamely took him through the tests. She even administered the time-consuming memory test after he repeatedly asked to take it.

At the end, he pasted on a grim expression. "So my symptoms must be bad. I probably need some TS pronto, huh?"

"I'd say definitely no."

"Come on, you can be honest with me, doc. Everyone else is taking it."

"Every patient is different."

"But I must be getting worse."

She hesitated. "Not appreciably."

"Appreciably?"

"Noticeably."

"So I'm not getting worse?"

Her eyes flitted to the mirror and back to Cam.

"No," she admitted.

"So no TS?"

"As your doctor, I don't recommend it at this time."

Cam did his best to look disappointed, and to further sell his act he hesitated before accepting her advice with a sad nod. When she finally led him from the room, keeping a hand on his shoulder to make certain he didn't walk the wrong direction, he even mumbled dejectedly to himself. "Everyone else is so much stronger and faster than me. I can't even win a game of Ping-Pong."

The door closed behind him, and he stood in the room with his teammates again, trying not to let his expression give away what he was feeling. Honestly, he didn't know whether to be happy or horrified. He'd confirmed what Siena had told him.

I'm not dying!

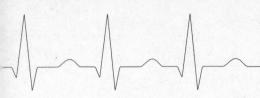

CAM'S PLAYLIST

28. THE ENDLESS NOTHING 🔊
by Necromoor

*"I was your thunder, you were my lightning,
in the storm before this endless nothing."*

Ward caught Cam as the others made their way back to their condos and walked him over to the lagoon.

"The doctor said you were asking a lot of questions, Cam?"

Cam shrugged. "I have a lot of questions."

"I'd like to think I make myself available for questions," Ward said. "Anything I can help you with?"

Sure, Cam thought. *What's the best way to stalk and kill a wild boar? How about a runaway girl? Or maybe I should ask: am I really dying?*

"No," Cam said instead. "I think the doc answered them all."

"I just wish you had come to me first." Ward didn't persist, and Cam decided he probably already knew what Cam had asked, and what the doctor had answered. Ward flexed his bulging shoulders and rolled his thick neck, a habit he had when he was frustrated.

Pilot sauntered over and joined them. "Our next mission is coming up, Cam," he said. "And I've got a special assignment for you."

"Really? What's that?"

"Individual training. I'll pick you up in the boat tomorrow morning."

Cam nodded. "Is that where Jules went?"

"Cam, you know Jules was released from her commitment. She told us she told you."

"Oh. I thought maybe it was a secret," Cam said quickly.

"It is. We don't want a flood of requests. Everybody wants to go home at some point during their year, but we can't do it for everybody. She was a special case. And yes, she shouldn't have told you. Have you told anyone?"

"No."

"Good. Training is what we've told everyone else. It should feel like when Ari was working on the yacht or Wally was off hang gliding. Only for her it will be a longer period of time. Eventually, her absence here won't matter."

Pilot pitched the falsehood so easily that Cam was almost impressed. *It should be harder to lie*, Cam thought.

Ward slapped a strong hand on Cam's shoulder. He seemed to want to say something, but Pilot gave him a sharp look. Instead he just patted Cam on the back. It was supposed to be reassuring. It wasn't.

Cam didn't know how to get in touch with Siena, so he simply folded the note and placed it beneath the condo.

> *I'm ready to go NOW.*
> *What do we need?*

It was a dark afternoon that felt later than it was. Rain clouds writhed on the horizon like a nest of snakes. It would be a beautiful and treacherous night, Cam thought. Jungle rain could be romantic under the canopy, dripping and drizzling from leaf to leaf, winding its way to the ground where it soaked into the loam. Wind would rumble through the treetops, but it was divided and conquered by the thick foliage by the time it slunk to the ground, reduced to aimless breezes. And lightning had such a generous selection of tall targets that it never looked for humans to strike. But the open beach afforded no such protections. Cam watched the sea for a time. The storm was coming fast, and its gusts would rattle the condos. The waves would roll up the beach and make them wonder if they should huddle in the bunker or even climb the bluff—no small feat in a storm and more difficult for the unenhanced. The structures held off the rain perfectly well, but Cam had once made the mistake of trotting from one to another in a downpour, and he'd arrived as soaked as if he'd swum there across the lagoon.

It was not a good night to flee.

It was also not a good night to be cooped up with Owen, who, though he wouldn't admit it, was deathly afraid of lightning.

"Cribbage?" Owen offered.

Cam was secretly flipping through Ari's diary up in his bunk. "I think I'd rather trim my nails," Cam said.

"Okay."

Cam peeked down over the edge of the bed. Owen looked hurt. He dealt a version of solitaire that Tegan had taught him. He was shuffling the deck of cards with one hand. Cam watched as one card flew free and Owen snatched it out of the air before it fell back to the desk.

"Wow," Cam exclaimed.

"Yeah, they upped our dosage on this visit," Owen explained.

"It made you faster?"

"And stronger." Owen shoved one hand under the solid wood desk and lifted the entire thing a few inches off the floor. He smiled. "You should see what Donnie can do. But Ward says it's the *focus* that's most enhanced." Owen took four cards and threw them up. He stabbed at each, pinching three of four between his fingers.

Not perfect, but impressive. It was clear he couldn't focus completely with the storm clouds rolling in.

"Do you think we ought to head up to the bunker?"

"Yes. Definitely. Go ahead."

Owen frowned and continued his game.

He doesn't want to be here, Cam thought, *and yet he won't leave.*

The first lightning strike lit up the ocean outside of their doorway a few minutes later. Its jagged bolts dove into the whitecaps that crisscrossed the water, joining sea and sky in a web of white. Owen pulled the door closed and looked up at him anxiously.

"Go," Cam repeated. "Unless you're supposed to stay here with me for some reason."

He shouldn't have said it, he thought, but he couldn't help himself. He was pissed. They were teammates. They even had the same tattoos. Yet Owen was watching him on behalf of their handlers. His loyalties lay elsewhere. If Siena showed up in the storm, they'd have to kick his ass and tie him to a bunk. But after seeing him catch the tumbling card with a flick of his hand, he wondered if they could.

"I was assigned to this condo," Owen said stubbornly.

"By our fearless leader."

"He's more like a coach."

Cam watched Owen work the cards as thunder echoed across the water. He was quick and strong on the TS-9. But he wasn't a natural athlete like Donnie. In fact, Cam could tell that, without it, Owen had probably been painfully average. "Did you play sports before?"

Owen sat the cards down. "Yeah. In fact, I got to the semifinals of our neighborhood's Fourth of July pickle ball tournament."

Cam waited for more, unintentionally betraying the fact that he was unimpressed by Owen's big pickle ball triumph.

"It's a pretty big neighborhood."

"Any team sports?"

"I almost made the high school basketball team."

He got cut, Cam thought as Owen explained the unfairness of the team's selection of the ten players who were not him. *That kind of thing sticks with a guy.*

"... and so, if it wasn't for that, I would have made it."

He's on a team here. An enhanced team. He hung around with Donnie, the top athlete, and he sucked up to the coach. Cam recalled how excited Owen was to make the scuba squad.

Suddenly, the condo lit up, and a split second later, thunder shook it violently. Their lights flickered. When Cam looked again, Owen was gripping the desk with both hands, the cards forgotten and scattered across its surface like escaped mice.

"Bunker?" Cam suggested.

Owen nodded, and they both went to the door. Cam threw it wide.

"Holy crap!"

He caught himself before he stepped out into the surf. The waves lapped against the wood steps that led up to the hut. Their condo was the last in line, and the bunker was at the far end. Between them, the surf came and went at irregular intervals, sometimes ankle-deep, sometimes waist-high.

"We can't run through that," Cam said. "We could get knocked down and dragged out by a big one."

The beach lit up again, and then there was no question of leaving the condo. Owen's arms were wrapped tight around the pole holding up his bunk. Cam slid back inside and pulled the door closed.

"Is this thing anchored firmly enough to withstand a storm surge?"

Owen looked up at him, miserable. "It's been here since before I got here."

"Ever have waves like this?"

"No."

"Where the hell is Coach Ward now? Why didn't someone come get us or blow a horn or something?"

A thin sheet of water snuck in beneath the loose-fitting wood door and slithered across the floor like a hungry tongue licking at their feet.

"Oh god, we're screwed!" Owen whimpered.

"Up onto the bunk!"

Shaken by Cam's shout, Owen scrambled up the ladder onto his bed almost without letting go of the pole. Soon, the water began to rise steadily. It pumped in under the door in rhythm with the thump of the waves against the thin east wall of the condo. The tide and the waves were conspiring, and when the water was knee-high, Cam climbed atop his own bed.

"What do we do?" Owen asked.

"We see how high it rises. Maybe it won't get much higher. If it makes it up to the window, we abandon ship. I don't want to have to dive underwater to get out."

Another wave slammed into the wall, shaking their beds. The window had been impossible to see through since the rain began to fall, and so Cam couldn't see them coming. But he could feel each one as it hit the condo. The force of their impact varied, and it was agonizing waiting to see if the next one would tear up the condo and sweep them away. Then their light went out. Another wave hit, and the condo groaned under the weight of the ocean pressing against it. A loud cracking sound signaled a beam giving way somewhere underneath.

Siena! Cam thought. She wouldn't have been under the hut, he thought, would she? She couldn't.

When the next wave hit, the condo rotated, torn loose on one side.

"We've got to make a run for it," Cam said.

"You mean a swim for it."

"Come on!" In the dark it was difficult to tell what Owen was doing, but it was clear to Cam as he lowered himself into the water that his new roommate wasn't "coming on."

"Where are you?" Cam called.

"The lightning will hit the tallest thing on the beach," Owen called down from the bunk. "And that will be us if we go out there!"

"Lightning takes at least two minutes to recharge. And we climb the bluff in less than that during our runs." It was a lie. Cam had no idea how long it took for an electrical charge to build in the atmosphere. But it was a lie Cam was willing to tell to get Owen out of the doomed condo. If the waves ripped it free of its anchors, it would be sucked out to sea or battered against the bluff. Either way, Cam didn't want to be inside when it happened. "As soon as we hear the next strike, we're going!"

Cam waited. Another wave pounded the wall. He held his breath, but it wasn't a large one. Finally, an ear-splitting crack shot through the darkness. Cam reached up and found Owen's hand.

"Go!"

Owen leaped down. Cam unlatched the door, and it swung open in the water. But it was he who hesitated.

"My music!" he gasped, and he struggled back inside to find his headphones and player, leaving Owen clinging to the doorjamb. Cam nabbed the player from the desk and fought back through the water to the door.

"It's been almost a minute," Owen whined when Cam returned.

"No!" Cam said. "It's only been thirty seconds. I've been counting. We still have a ninety-second window. Plenty of time if we go now!" It was another lie, but a necessary one.

They were fortunate—the waves outside were receding as they exited, and they were able to stumble down into thigh-high water. It pulled at them as they fought through up the beach, and Cam knew that the ocean would throw a new one at their backs in moments.

"The rope!" Cam pointed in the direction the bluff seemed to lie—a patch of darker darkness in the rainy and moonless night. His soccer legs churned through the water, but progress was painfully slow. It was like every childhood nightmare Cam had ever had of running through the dark in wet sand with a huge monster about to pounce from behind. Only this time, someone was with him. He was still holding Owen's arm, he realized. Only now Owen was dragging him, his enhanced legs plowing water and pumping through the sand. He wondered if Owen's fear of the next lightning strike was driving him almost as hard as the TS-9. It didn't matter. He was a lifeline, and Cam clung to him.

Then they were out of the surf, high enough on the beach that the next few small waves didn't reach them. The rope was nearly impossible to find in the dark, however. They felt their way along, wet hands grasping blindly at rocks and thorny foliage until Owen suddenly lifted him from the sand. Cam didn't have hold of the rope himself. Owen hoisted him up with one arm hooked under his armpit. The next wave crashed into Cam's legs. It would have crushed him against the bluff and yanked him out to sea, but Owen held him just high enough that it merely shook them on the rope.

"You have to grab on!" Owen yelled over the wind. "I can't hold you *and* climb."

It was an amazing feat of strength to support him at all, Cam thought as he grabbed for the rope. His hand closed around it just as another wave higher than the last took him from behind. The wall of water slammed both of them against the bluff. The thick brush cushioned the blow enough that it didn't crack his head open, but he lost his grip on the rope. Instead, he clung to Owen's waist. To his surprise, his roommate was climbing, pulling them both upward even as the water sucked at them like a cold, hungry demon's wet mouth. It retreated without claiming its prize and left them dangling in the darkness.

"Try again!" Owen gasped, supporting them both until Cam located the rope once more.

His hands were wet and slick, and it was all he could do to hold on. Owen climbed a little and then lowered a leg for Cam to grip and helped pull him up, repeating the method again and again until they were safely above the surge of the surf. They found a ledge where they could rest and pressed themselves against the hill. Lightning struck again, and Owen held Cam tight, like a boy hugging his older brother after seeing the shadow of a boogeyman. Cam wondered if Owen had a brother and decided that he probably did.

"I can climb now," Cam said, though he wasn't certain. He

wanted to keep Owen moving. Being paralyzed with fear halfway up a cliff in the rain was precarious, and even a guy on TS-9 would tire eventually, he thought. *Or would he?*

The others were already at the temporary shelter in the jungle, which was little more than a tarp with stacked wood walls to keep the rain and large animals out. A cheer went up when he and Owen stumbled in. There were no dry towels, but a fire was already crackling beneath the smoke hole. They'd all made it to the shelter before the waves hit.

"Why didn't you come when the storm began?" Zara asked.

Cam flopped down and rolled his exhausted head toward her. "I wouldn't go, and Owen wouldn't go without me."

"So you were stupid and he was loyal?"

Cam was too tired to argue. Besides, he hadn't thought of it that way. She wasn't wrong.

Owen interrupted. "It was Cam's idea to make a run for it, or I'd be out to sea somewhere by now."

"Yeah, but you practically carried me up the rope when the waves hit us," Cam replied.

They shared a relieved laugh. Wally joked that they'd each done their best to get the other killed.

"That's teamwork for you," Owen added.

And suddenly Cam understood him. Owen simply wanted to make the team. That was his simple dream. To be a starter. As much as Calliope wanted to perform and Ari wanted to drive, Owen wanted to be picked first at recess. And perhaps Owen wasn't so much spying as making sure Cam was doing okay, he thought. Concern and suspicion were sister emotions easily mistaken for one another. In the end, he was maybe just a kid who was scared of lightning and trying to do everything his coach asked of him.

Cam put his knuckles up for a fist bump. Owen smiled and tapped them.

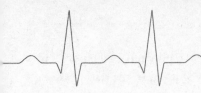

"Can't wait for you to change, but I can hope."

Cam awoke to a presence again, someone kneeling over him as he lay on the ground. It was not yet dawn, but the storm had passed. Under the tarp, under the jungle canopy, under the residual gray clouds, and without the sun there was almost no light, but Cam knew it was Siena before she spoke.

"Yes or no?" she whispered, her voice so soft he might have thought it a dream.

"Yes," he said.

She led him out of the shelter and through the forest. Siena was better in the dark than he was, and soon they came to a small pool. Cam heard splattering water. He knew the place. He'd seen it in daylight. The stream ran down a sheer bank and into the pool, which then overflowed and disappeared over the bluff. In the light, a person could stand beneath the cascading water thigh-deep in the pool and look over the sea. Cam felt the vastness of it out in the darkness beyond his sight. They stood uncomfortably close so that they could whisper and yet still be heard above the plummeting stream.

"The waterfall?" Cam said.

"Yes. We can talk here."

He came right to the point. "I confirmed it. I'm not getting sicker."

"It would have been quicker and easier if you'd just trusted me from the beginning."

"Like you trusted me from the beginning, Miss Vague Love Notes?"

It was dark, but Siena's hesitation betrayed her blush. Perhaps she smiled. Perhaps not.

"They weren't *love* notes," she said finally.

"I want to thank you," Cam said. Without eye contact, some other gesture was necessary to lend the appropriate level of sincerity to his expression of gratitude. He lifted a hand in the darkness to touch her arm. But she was closer than he thought, and his hand found her hip on its way up instead. Rather than grope his way up her body, he let it linger there. She hadn't expected it. He felt her pull away slightly, but not enough to dislodge him.

"It's a bit early to thank me. I could be getting you killed."

"I might not have a chance later."

"I guess you're welcome," she said. She bit off the last word to eliminate any sentiment her tone might otherwise have hinted.

There was silence between them then. In the darkness, the patter of the waterfall surrounded them, and the mist it sent up made Cam shiver. His hand was still on her hip.

"The water is cold here," Siena said, as though reading his thoughts, or perhaps she could *feel* him trembling in the dark. It was one of those empty phrases meant to save her from emotional exchange. Small talk.

"This is where you showered, isn't it?" The thought of standing in a shower with her stirred him. He suddenly wondered what she might look like with her long tangled hair brushed smooth, and without the tattered rags she wore.

"I'm jealous of your warm shower," she said. "But that hasn't been the worst. It took me two weeks just to get up the nerve to steal shoes. The big-eyed girl and the pale one left theirs out on the steps every night. But it took me a long time to sneak down to their hut and take a pair. I thought they were the height of luxury. I'll never take shoes for granted again."

"That was brave of you."

"I left tracks from a dead monkey's feet so they'd think a monkey took them. Not the smartest two."

"I never heard about the missing shoes."

"That was before we met."

Cam smiled in the dark. It was a schoolgirlish thing to say. It made him feel like they were a couple, in a strange way, especially while his hand was still on her hip. *And we might die today*, he thought. He pulled her close and kissed her.

Cam was surprised by the stench of her breath. It made him wince, and he immediately felt bad. It wasn't her fault—she'd been living in the jungle, and who knew what she'd been eating. Raw fish? Bugs maybe? And a few bites of poultry.

She pulled away. "Oh my god!"

"What?"

"I . . . I haven't had a toothbrush for months."

"No. You're fine," Cam lied. "I just didn't know if that was the right thing to do. This is a weird time for me. For both of us. I'm sorry."

"It's okay," she said. She still hadn't let go. "We can keep hugging."

Cam took her in his arms, and the waterfall's spray shrouded them so that they were the warm center of its cool mist cocoon.

"I was a totally normal girl, before," Siena whispered. "I wore tasteful makeup and went out on Friday nights. In real life, in the world of toothpaste, I would have kissed you back."

"What do we do now?" Cam asked. He liked holding her and didn't want it to end. *But everything ends.*

"The storm's over," she said. "And the bunker is unmanned."

Cam took a breath. "We obtain supplies?"

"Yes. Then we sneak off in Pilot's boat after they come ashore. There has to be a village along the shore within fifty miles. We can do ten miles a night and hide the boat each day."

"What if he comes in the kayak? You and I aren't paddling to Florida."

"He won't bring the kayak after this disaster. He and Ward will come in a fast inflatable. We're lucky they got caught away when the storm hit. We've got a window of opportunity here."

Cam's clothes were still soaked, but there were dry sets in the bunker.

They located the northernmost rope down to the beach in the darkness. It was an easier climb than the center rope he and Owen had ascended. They felt their way to the flat wall of the bunker and let themselves in. The lights flickered on inside. Cam could hear its generator still humming. They'd have been safe from the storm inside. There were watermarks at eye level on the door where high waves or spray had hit and some flooding in the main hall. Otherwise, everything seemed intact.

"Food first," Siena said, heading straight for the pantry. "Then fresh clothes. Is there a gun in here anywhere?"

"I don't think so, but we could check Ward's office."

Siena gathered canned fruit and dried meats in a backpack that Cam found, while greedily stuffing fresh food into her mouth— leftover roast pork and bread. She gulped down three cans of fruit juice. Cam found a canteen and filled it with water. There were matches and knives in the kitchen. Cam wrapped a butcher knife in a cloth and wound duct tape around it to create a makeshift sheath. Siena grabbed a metal bowl. It could be used as a frying pan if they needed to cook or to boil water, she said, something Cam hadn't thought of.

Ward's office was next. It was locked, but the bunker's interior doors were cheap. Two kicks, and the jamb splintered. There was no gun, which didn't surprise him. He'd never seen Ward carry one, and the Deathwing philosophy didn't lend itself to lethal weapons. Siena, however, spotted Ward's machete hanging from a belt on a hook behind the door and helped herself, strapping it around her narrow waist. She had to cinch it up past its last hole.

The room was less an office than a place for Ward to stash his personal items during training. There were no files. No computer. No communications equipment either. Ward and Pilot carried radios on them, but there was nothing anyone could use to call the outside world. Clearly, they didn't want recruits finding records or contacting anyone.

"Blankets," Siena said. "If Pilot goes airborne to find us while we're floating the coast we might have to dive into the jungle."

"Do you know where we're going?"

"South."

They'd gone south to find the *Harsh Mistress* in the next cove, Cam recalled. But they'd cruised half a day beyond that in a big, speedy yacht before hitting the pirate outpost. It might be a long trip.

The blankets were in the utility closet. Cam opened the doors and pulled out two. There were new toothbrushes and paste. He hesitated, and then selected soap and shampoo. He handed them to Siena.

"You miss this stuff, right?" he said.

"I'd love some shampoo," she admitted. She took them while Cam pulled a first aid kit and pretended to see if there was anything else they needed.

"Want one of these?" he said as casually as possible, pointing to a toothbrush.

Siena's hand shot up to cover her mouth.

"Was it that bad?"

Cam bit his tongue. For all the care he'd taken, he'd still failed to approach it delicately enough. He shrugged and shook his head in a last-ditch effort to make it not a big deal.

"You're the one worried about it. I didn't even notice."

She went to the nearby sink. A small round mirror hung over it. She hadn't seemed to care about her appearance, until she saw herself in the cheap plastic-rimmed mirror under the dim fluorescent light of the bunker with Cam standing by. She touched her hair and tentatively opened her mouth. Tears welled in her green eyes. They dripped into the sink as though from a leaky faucet. Red-faced, she took the brush, paste, and some floss, and she scrubbed her mouth so hard that her teeth bled.

They gathered as much as they could in backpacks they took from the equipment room.

"How are we doing on time?" Cam asked.

"I wasted too much of it being a baby. Now that the water is calm, they'll be on their way here. Every minute we're in this building doubles our risk."

"Time to go then?"

"One last thing."

She hurried to the training room and threw open a cabinet that Cam knew well. Inside were ten live darts, enough for one mission.

"Five each," she said, and they packed them away.

It was still predawn, but the clouds were lifting, and the tan sand of the beach was now visible at the dim level of an old sepia tone photograph. The sea was as black on one side as the bluff's wall of foliage on the other, and the background music of surf provided a loud and steady *swish-thump* rhythm, punctuated by occasional sharp animal sounds from the jungle.

They wouldn't hear the boat engine until it was close, Cam thought, or see it until it pulled up on the sand. "Where do we hide?"

"There." Siena led him down the beach.

His condo was gone. The note he'd left for her, gone. Three condos had survived. Two were livable. The third was still anchored, but was bent so severely that the floor was nearly diagonal.

Four snapped posts jutted up from the sand where Jules and Calliope had lived, like the legs of a flipped table. The remains of Zara's place were heaped against the bluff—it had been flattened, and its pieces were piled up so that it looked as though someone had just emptied an assembly-required do-it-yourself hut from its box.

Cam's and Owen's condo had simply been erased. No posts. Even the dip in the sand where Siena had hidden was scoured away clean. Cam stared at the empty beach. He had to concentrate to even remember what it looked like with the hut on it. Siena pulled him to the bluff, where she lifted the foliage away. There was a depression in the raw dirt, and Cam saw that it had been dug away. With no pile of sand on the beach, it was clear that she had carted the dirt away a few full pockets at a time. The hiding place was near the southern rope, the same rope Owen had pulled him up onto to save him from the hungry sea, the same hungry sea that would have claimed him had Donnie not swum after him in the riptide during scuba training.

"I can't go without them," Cam said.

"What?"

"I have to give the rest of my team the chance to come with us."

"You mean tell them we're going? No chance. They'll know good and well within an hour of our departure, okay? Two if we're lucky."

"If you have questions about why I need to do this, you have every right to ask."

"Yeah, I have a question. Are you out of your damned mind?!"

Cam sighed. "That's not a question about why." He wasn't surprised at her reaction. He'd realized she wouldn't agree at the same moment he'd realized he had to do it.

"These people hunted me, Cam. H-u-n-t-e-d."

"They've saved my life more than once, even Donnie."

202 ⅃⅃⅃⅃- Royce Scott Buckingham _____

"Cam, you can go to them. I can't physically stop you—I'm not enhanced anymore. But now that I have supplies, I also won't need to wait for you. As soon as Ward and Pilot go up the ropes to the jungle camp to find all of you, I'm leaving."

Cam grabbed the rope and began to climb as Siena swore loudly and slid behind her curtain of foliage.

The sky was growing light in the east, out over the ocean, and Cam's hands were raw from the rope. He made it to camp to find Zara hunched by the morning fire. She grinned.

"Morning, stranger. I wondered where you'd gotten off to."

"We need to wake up the guys."

Zara looked around. "Wow. I *am* the only girl left."

No, you're not, Cam thought.

She smirked. "Don't tell anyone I slept with five guys last night."

Cam didn't wait for her to help. He shook Wally and Owen until they stirred. He didn't brave laying hands on Donnie, but instead went to a metal pole and began to bang it with the butcher knife.

They rose, grumpy and complaining. Wally's red hair stuck up as though he had a Mohawk. Tegan sat holding his head and wincing at the light of the fire.

"Wingman?" Donnie glared. A biting fly landed on his bare chest. He snapped his hand up to catch it by one wing between his fingers without looking. He crushed the wing and tossed the maimed creature toward the fire, where it spiraled downward into the flame and popped. "What the hell are you doing?"

"I have something to tell all of you," he said gravely, sheathing the knife.

Donnie shrugged. The others waited, blurry-eyed with sleep and equally unmoved.

"What?" Wally said when he hesitated. "You had a spooky nightmare? Dreamed you were dying?"

"I dreamed I wasn't."

"That's a nice dream, Cam," Owen said sleepily. "But not worth rousting everyone for."

"You slacks should be getting up anyway," Zara said. "The storm has passed. We should go check the damage."

"Listen," Cam said. "I'm *not* dying. Maybe none of us are."

There was silence for a moment, then Donnie spoke. "Tell me this isn't what you woke us up for."

Cam took a deep breath. He couldn't tell them about Siena—he owed them, but he owed her too.

"During my last visit to the lab, the doc said I wasn't deteriorating," he said.

His announcement was greeted with what he considered an appropriate period of silent surprise. *I have their attention*, he thought.

"What the hell does that mean?" Donnie seemed both intensely interested and annoyed. "Don't screw with us."

"Did they use the 'r' word?" Zara asked.

"Remission" was a word they'd been taught to forget. There was too much false hope in it, Ward said. Even the mention of it had them holding their breath. It was what they wanted to hear, and it would be a simpler explanation than what he believed was happening, but it wasn't the truth.

"Not exactly," Cam said.

They let out a collective groan.

Donnie rolled his eyes. "So you'll last longer than some of us. Congratulations."

"I don't think I was ever sick," Cam tried. "And I think it's the TS that's killing you."

Zara's face was hard, the way she steeled it when she felt vulnerable. "This isn't new info, Cam. It's the TS or the glio. If you're trying to make yourself feel better because you're struggling along unenhanced, fine. But don't expect us to cheer just because your tumor took a month off from killing you. We'd rather go out rock stars."

"I don't feel like a rock star," Tegan said. His eyes were mashed shut, wincing against pain, and Cam realized he was having one of his TS headaches.

"Maybe you're not sick either. At least maybe you weren't until they gave you the TS. Maybe they're lying."

Zara screwed up her face. Wally shook his head. Donnie stood up and pointed right at Cam's chest.

"Listen, we've got an entire team of doctors with their own private lab—not to mention helicopters and million-dollar yachts—giving us complex medical diagnoses on a biweekly basis. While, on the other hand, we've got one desperate former athlete in denial feeding us a wild-ass conspiracy theory. You'll pardon us if we don't believe you."

A figure threw open the entrance to the shelter, and morning light streamed in. They all turned, surprised.

"Believe me then," Siena said.

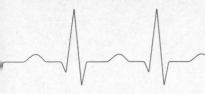

"Boom-boom goes the drum."

Donnie looked as though he'd seen a ghost.

"You know me," Siena said. It was more statement than question. She watched Donnie, Owen, and Tegan carefully, with her hand on the machete, poised to flee or defend herself.

Still holding his head, Tegan said nothing, while Owen grimaced like he'd just swallowed a spider. But Cam had to give Donnie credit. He suppressed his shock enough to at least respond.

"You're the runner who went over the bluff with Peter," he said carefully.

She nodded.

"But you're alive."

"The fact that I survived the fall isn't what's important," she said. "I survived their diagnosis."

"Who are you?" It was Zara.

"She's from last year's class," Cam said.

"Last year's class?"

"TS-8."

Cam hurriedly explained, cobbling together Siena's information with his own and some from Ari's notebook. It was difficult. Much of what he said was speculation, and some of it didn't fit when he tried to put it into words. But they all listened—a girl appearing out of the Amazon jungle like magic had earned their attention. However, they began to look confused as Cam rushed and stumbled through his theory.

Tegan looked more ill than before, while Donnie and Owen gritted their teeth. They'd hunted her—their first test when they arrived—and Siena kept a wary eye on them, honoring Cam's plea that she give them a chance, but clearly not trusting them.

Finally, Zara interrupted. "If they're experimenting on us, why aren't you on TS?"

Cam was surprised when Siena answered for him.

"He's the rat they don't inject. Every experiment has one. We had someone like that. He escaped with me, only he didn't get away. I was enhanced. He wasn't." Her eyes flitted elsewhere, blinking against tears, and Cam could see that she'd been friends with him, whoever he was. Maybe more than friends.

"We don't have all of the answers," Cam said. "But I know they're lying to us."

"Maybe for our own good," Donnie argued. "You ever think of that?"

Siena fidgeted. "Cam, we don't have time for this. I'm leaving. Ask them the question."

Cam drew himself up. He'd made his best case. He'd summoned all of the authority he possessed and spent the entirety of his credibility appealing to the team with which he'd sweated and bled for months. It had to count for something.

"Will you go with us?" he said.

No one moved.

"Step forward now if you will," he added.

Donnie didn't budge. Taking his cue from Donnie, Owen didn't either. Wally and Zara looked at each other and shook their heads. Tegan just hugged his knees, nonresponsive as well.

"None of you is concerned about what we've discovered?"

"Concern isn't enough, Cam," Zara said. She sounded torn, but not ready to commit.

Donnie crossed his arms. "I'm not going to throw away the opportunity to be a superhero for the last year of my life just because some freaked-out girl isolated herself in the woods for a few months and thinks the organization is out to get her. Ward told us she was trying to compromise the mission when he sent us to find her. And from what I'm hearing now, he's right."

Cam groaned. "I know something's wrong. Come on, we're in this together. We're teammates. We're friends."

"Last I checked, you were fresh out of friends."

Cam looked around. Donnie was right. Ari was gone. Calliope, gone. Jules, gone. He was isolated, unenhanced, the weak link at best. There was an uncomfortable silence.

It was Owen who finally spoke. "I think Cam's got a point," he said tentatively.

Cam was shocked. So was Donnie, who glared at his minion for breaking solidarity, as though Owen had betrayed him by speaking at all.

"Some of this stuff *doesn't* make sense," Owen continued.

Donnie interrupted. "Dude, we're supposed to be a united front. You spend one night with this guy and now you're in bed with him, or what?"

"I just have concerns too. And as soon as Ward gets back I'm going to ask him a few choice questions." Owen glanced at Cam for support.

But talking to Ward wasn't what Cam had in mind, and it was Cam's turn to fail to respond. His own silence hung in the air as heavily as the group's had when he'd asked for their allegiance.

"We're done here, Cam," Siena whispered.

She was right, he saw. He backed out of the shelter beside her, leaving Owen with a hurt look, and they dove into the thick foliage, headed for the southern rope.

Siena reached the cliff edge first and urged Cam to hurry so that they could climb down and slip into her hiding place before the others came. But they were too late.

"Boat!" She pointed to a Zodiac skipping across the waves, toward the beach. Two occupants. Ward and Pilot, no doubt. "We're too late. Let's go back and . . ."

"Oh no . . ." Cam directed her attention to the bluff's short rope on the north side of the compound. Donnie and Owen were already descending to meet Ward.

Siena stared. "They'll tell him about you. And about me."

Cam could see Siena recalculating, her expression slumping as she realized that her escape was ruined.

"I'm sorry," Cam said. It sounded lame—mere words were such an insignificant gesture in the face of shattered hope.

"I could have done this without you," she said, as much to herself as to Cam. "The supplies were unguarded. You were all up on the bluff. Ward and Pilot would have left the boat on the beach to come up and find you. I'm so stupid."

"You're not stupid. You care."

"About you? I don't even know you."

"You believed I was a good person. And I believe my teammates are. They joined because they wanted to do good. We all did."

"I just want to go home now. If I'm not dying, I want to live."

"Maybe they'll let us go, give us a new home and fake identity."

Siena gave him a sharp look that accused him of naïveté. "You really believe that?"

"My teammates who died took the risks voluntarily. I've never seen them kill anyone."

Donnie and Owen were on the beach. Cam marveled at how quickly they'd shimmied down the rope. Their strides were long and powerful. The extra TS was pumping through their veins, amplifying their systems beyond what nature intended. He imagined it blowing their brains like cheap speakers.

They met Ward at the surf as he and Pilot pulled the Zodiac ashore. They yelled over the crash of the waves, and Cam found himself leaning out over the precipice, straining to hear. Their voices were maddeningly near audible.

If Ward and Pilot were surprised when they saw the storm's devastation, they didn't show it. They afforded the condos no more than a glance. *They consider them replaceable*, he thought. The bunker was intact, an ugly square brick dropped in the sand against the otherwise beautiful russet and green bluff. Cam watched carefully as Ward addressed Donnie, the presumptive spokesman of the two recruits, asking him quick questions. He saw Donnie point at the south rope. They were discussing him, and probably Siena too. Cam ducked, crouching in the brush. Finally, Ward turned to Owen.

Owen spoke, and Cam could see Ward's expression grow sad and resigned, even from a distance. Owen was asking questions, the difficult ones, Cam's questions, accusing questions—not at all in line with the team philosophy. Pilot looked on, grim-faced. Finally, he motioned Ward aside. Ward hesitated, and then debated with him for a moment, but, in the end, he stepped out of the way.

Cam heard a muffled pop, and Owen's questions ended abruptly. Owen looked down, confused, and then collapsed.

With impressive and unexpected quickness, Donnie caught Owen before he fell. *Enhanced reaction time*, Cam thought. From the distance, he couldn't tell exactly what had happened, but when Pilot turned to Donnie, Owen's limp form hung between them like a five-foot shield. In the moment that Pilot hesitated, Donnie threw Owen at him, his augmented strength allowing him to fling the heavy body as though it was no more than an inflatable dummy. Pilot lurched backward, his heel striking the Zodiac's pontoon. Owen's body hit him in the chest. Pilot tilted, overbalanced. His arms pinwheeled for a moment, and then he flopped back into the boat.

Owen wasn't moving. He lay in the surf, flopping over as a wave pushed him up onto the sand.

"They darted him!" Cam exclaimed.

Donnie was running. Ward ran after him, but Donnie flew across the sand at inhuman speed. *Enhanced speed*, Cam thought. Ward broke off the pursuit, while Pilot clambered out of the boat and pulled out his hand radio.

"South rope!" Cam yelled to Donnie. "Here! Up here!"

"More boats," Siena said.

A chill ran through Cam as two more Zodiacs whipped around the southern point. They bore men in dark clothing. Pilot had radioed them, clearly. For an instant, Cam wondered if they'd been lurking on the other side of the point throughout the training, waiting every day to be called in case of emergency, in case of too many questions.

"Run, Donnie!" Cam yelled from the top of the rope. He found himself cheering for the boy he'd thought he hated.

Donnie raced past the empty site of Cam's old condo, well ahead of Pilot, who had taken up the pursuit. Donnie leaped for the rope and caught it on the fly ten or twelve feet off the ground. He was climbing hand-over-hand while Pilot was still stumbling up the beach through the heavy sand. Pilot stopped and scanned the bluff. *He's looking for the rest of the team*, Cam thought. *He wonders if we're all watching this.* Cam wondered too.

Donnie ascended so fast that it looked like he was jogging up the side of the cliff. Cam reached out to him, and, when he arrived, took his hand and helped him up.

"What happened?" Cam asked.

Donnie didn't answer, but simply stood staring down at the beach, wide-eyed as the other two boats pulled up.

Cam was suddenly angry. He got in his teammate's face, despite that Donnie was bigger and enhanced. "Why'd they dart Owen? Why'd you throw him in the water and leave him?"

Finally, Donnie turned toward him, and Cam saw that his lip was quivering. "They didn't dart him," Donnie stammered. "They shot him. He's dead."

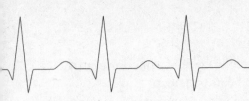

CAM'S PLAYLIST

31. NO WAY! 🔊
   by Go Fish

32. TREADING WATER
   by The Blind Leading the Blind

33. THIS LITTLE PIGGY
   by Squeaky Wheel

"Don't wanna, ain't gonna. Humma-humma-humma."

Siena's machete came down on the rope, snapping it neatly. It tumbled and twisted down to the beach. Below, the men from the other boats were huddling with Ward and Pilot. Several of them carried rifles, though they were not pointing them up at the bluff. Yet.

"We need to go," Siena said to Cam. "Is he coming?"

"Donnie, are you coming?" Cam asked.

Donnie nodded, and they started off through the underbrush. They reached the second rope quickly, and Siena cut it. The men below had fanned out. Cam counted the rifles. Four of them. Plus Pilot's gun, apparently a pistol.

Zara's head popped out of the foliage down the bluff above the short third rope. She spotted them and silently mouthed the words, "What the hell?"

Cam pointed down at a man in dark clothing who stood at the base of her rope. He waved up to her with a friendly smile and began to climb.

"Cut the rope," Cam mouthed back, making a sawing motion. Then he realized she only had a small needle-nosed knife. She bent to work on it, exposed. Cam saw one of the men on the beach kneel to aim his rifle up at her.

"No!"

The log that flew from the jungle was three feet long and as thick as a man's head—a chunk of heavy fruitwood from the shelter, stripped of its limbs. It tumbled out into space end over end, descending in a lazy arc. The man was preoccupied, sighting in on Zara. He never saw it coming. The log struck him in the shoulder with a loud crack, and he went down, curling in the fetal position. Another man ran to him, but instead of helping, scooped up the gun from the sand and took aim at Zara again. But he was too wary of flying logs. His eye flitted away from the gun sight as he zeroed in, and his first shot whanged off the rocks just below Zara's hands.

Cam was surprised to see her smile. Then he saw that she'd finished cutting the knot. The man who'd been climbing saw too. He stopped and began to climb back down. It was a strange sight, Cam thought, because as he descended he simply kept accelerating. He still held the rope, but the rope no longer hung from the bluff. Instead, it descended with him, limp in his hands, and they hit the beach together at a speed that made Cam wince. He managed to land feet first, but his legs crumpled beneath him. Cam had seen plenty of soccer injuries. The man would never walk right again. Both of his knees were ruined.

But there were more men and more guns, and there was no more time to stand in the open atop the bluff. Zara glanced at him, and he motioned her back to the shelter. She didn't even pause to nod, but simply dove back into the trees.

Cam and Siena hustled Donnie through the foliage and into the shelter, where the rest of the team stood, grim-faced. Wally was groaning over and over, as though someone had put his voice on repeat.

"This is so messed up. So messed up. Soooo messed up."

Donnie's head hung, and he swung it back and forth in disbelief. Zara was panting, a grin of satisfaction still tugging at the corners of her lush lips. Tegan held his head. Cam stood waiting. After a moment, he realized that they were all staring at him.

"What do we do now, Wingman?" Zara asked.

When he couldn't answer, Siena whispered in his ear. "Into the jungle. They'll be up here in minutes."

"You tell them," Cam said.

"It's your team now, Cam. You're the leader."

He saw that she was right. They were waiting for him to give orders. They didn't look to Zara or Donnie. Cam had been correct, not them. And none of them knew Siena. They would only follow Cameron "Wingman" Cody.

"Sooo messed up," Wally groaned.

And if Cam didn't lead them away from the compound immediately, Wally would be correct.

"Into the jungle!" Cam ordered.

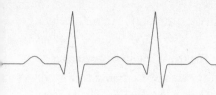

CAM'S PLAYLIST

32. TREADING WATER 🔊
by The Blind Leading the Blind

33. THIS LITTLE PIGGY
by Squeaky Wheel

34. FLY
by The Dread

"Sink or swim? Not really a choice."

At first, the territory they navigated was familiar—the training ground where they'd dodged paintballs with Ward and Pilot. The forest was still freshly drenched from the storm, and they were soon miserably soaked from pushing through the wet brush. They moved quickly, but couldn't run. The terrain didn't allow it. Siena pointed out places where she'd hidden as they passed.

Donnie had retreated into himself, muttering, "I was wrong, so wrong. I'm such a jerk."

Cam let him stew. He was a jerk, and he had been wrong.

Past the training fields, the brush thickened, and there were no paths. They found themselves crawling through thorn-riddled bushes and climbing trees only to find that they needed to double back. It was slow going, and Cam was among the slowest of them.

Unenhanced, he and Siena—and Tegan, with his headaches—struggled to keep up. Siena felt certain they were being followed. It was only a matter of how closely. If they reached something resembling civilization, it was clear that all six of them would immediately break the unbreakable rule. Ward and Pilot wouldn't let that happen. Cam wondered for a moment what would happen if they promised to stay hidden, like Jules had. *Too late for that.* She'd made her deal before things had gone to hell. *Good for her.* Of course, if they were nowhere near civilization, the organization could simply let them wander in the jungle until a panther ate them.

"Sinkhole!" Wally announced.

Cam caught up with the group and stood at its edge. He marveled again at the deep pit with its motionless blue floor—a bizarre emptiness carved out of the forest. It seemed so long ago that he'd crash-landed in the massive kapok on its rim and first met their philosophical personal trainer. Ward had been quick to help and instruct and guide, but Cam recalled that the swing of the machete had made his first impression. It was strangely comforting to glance over and see that Siena had taken it from him.

They stood reverent on the rim, catching their breath after their flight through the forest, feeling insignificant in the presence of the spectacular oddity of nature whose rare combination of tranquility and grandiosity might have conjured a belief in a higher power, had Tegan not suddenly vomited into it.

The wet splatter of his last meal twenty feet below ruined it for Wally.

"Man, did you have to chuck in the pristine water?" Wally complained.

"I'm sorry." Tegan coughed as he sank to a knee. Cam's big teammate held his head with both hands, his thick fingers gripping his wavy brown hair tightly. His face contorted, and he yanked two large hunks loose, as though they were snakes burrowing into his head that he was trying to pull out.

Cam knelt beside him and put a hand on his back, and he looked up. His eyes were cloudy, distant.

"Hey, hey. Take it easy," Cam tried.

"I threw the log," Tegan whispered.

"I figured that was you," Cam said gently.

"Women don't usually pay attention to the big fella."

He was talking about Zara, wondering if he'd impressed her. He didn't seem to realize that she was standing directly behind him.

"I think she noticed you." Cam winked.

Tegan's lips curled into a half-grin, half-grimace, almost smiling, but his mouth wouldn't quite allow it.

"We need to keep moving, buddy." Cam tried to help lift him up. Tegan teetered on his knee and then sat down heavily on his rump.

"He's delirious," Siena said. "It's from the TS. How long has he been on it?"

"The longest of anyone," Zara said.

"And they upped the dosage recently," Cam added. "Does that make it worse?"

Siena shrugged. "He seems really sick."

"But what does it mean?"

"I don't know!" she snapped.

Wally kicked the trunk of a nearby tree. "You're the one telling us what's supposedly happening to our brains."

"I don't know exactly how it works. It's bad, okay? I started to get the headaches, but not like this. I stopped taking the stuff."

Tegan reached out. He took Cam's arm and pulled him down to his level. Even in his condition he was strong.

"I did my best," he said. His gaze was vacant now, his eyes swimming loose under lids that flickered up and down as his face contorted with the agony in his head.

"I know you did," Cam said. He gave him a mannish hug—heads apart, one-armed, with a quick back pat.

But Tegan clung to him, squeezing him close. "My head hurts, Dad."

Cam's heart leaped into his throat. He fought back tears as the rest of the team looked on in stunned silence. *Handle this, Cameron,* he told himself. He smoothed Tegan's torn hair. "I'm proud of you, son," he said. "Very proud. You've done well."

Tegan held him for a time. When Cam finally pulled away, the big guy looked at him, curious. There was a flicker of recognition.

"You can go now," he said.

He slumped, and Cam arranged him so that his back rested against the giant kapok tree. Then Cam rose and faced his team. They waited for him to make a decision.

"We have to leave him here."

Wally burst out in a series of muffled profanities, and Zara looked like she wanted to say something, but they didn't argue. They knew he was right, and moments later they were making their way around the sinkhole without their big teammate.

Soon they had reached the far side. Zara was the first to look back across the hole. She hissed a warning.

"Gun!"

She motioned with her elbow in the direction of the threat, just as she'd been taught in training, and they turned to see even as they dove for cover. A man stood over Tegan's reclining body, holding a rifle. The team scrambled behind an uprooted tree that had toppled onto its side like a fallen giant at the edge of the sinkhole, everyone except for Siena. Unenhanced, she reacted slowly and was still in the open when the man trained the rifle on her.

"Freeze!" he yelled in English. He glanced at a radio hanging loosely at his waist. It was clear he wanted to call for help, but he wouldn't take his hands off the gun.

Siena froze. She couldn't outrun a bullet. Cam swore and stood.

"That's right," the man said when he saw Cam stand. "The rest of you come on out too. There doesn't need to be any more trouble."

Cam moved in front of Siena. But he didn't join her. Instead, he replaced her and pushed her toward the dead tree.

"Stay there!" the man barked at Siena, but he kept the gun on Cam.

"I'm still here," Cam said, buying enough time for Siena to find cover. "I'm all you need to negotiate. Let's start with the basics. We don't even know what you want."

"I'm tasked with bringing you in safely. There's clearly been a terrible misunderstanding."

"Safely with a gun?"

"But we're told you're strong, highly trained, and dangerous, which you proved back at the beach. We've got two men down."

"Why'd you shoot Gordon?" Cam yelled, testing him to see if he knew their names.

"Gordon attacked your trainer's supervisor."

Supervisor? Cam thought. The hierarchy between Pilot and Ward had never been clear, but it was now.

"He's lying," Donnie hissed. "Owen didn't move."

"What's your name, son?" the man called.

"Tegan," Cam said. "And if I was over there, I'd grab you so my friends could get away."

"But you're not over here," the man said.

Cam's heart quickened as he saw Tegan stir. His huge teammate rolled over slowly and wrapped his thick arms around the man's legs.

"Hey!" the man yelped. He struggled, and then brought the gun down on Tegan's arm. Tegan held on with everything he had left. His great strength had waned, but he was able to wrench himself sideways and roll over the man's knees. The man went down, and the gun went off, but it was pointed at the soft loam of the jungle floor and made only a muffled *whump*. Man and recruit rolled over once, and then ran out of earth and were falling. Twenty feet later, they hit the water together with a splash not unlike Tegan's vomit.

The man bobbed up, gasping for air. The gun was gone. So was Tegan. The team edged out from behind the tree.

"Careful," Cam warned. "Be ready to take cover if others show up."

The man floundered, staring up at them. Cam could see him reaching for the radio at his waist. It was gone too.

"Are others coming this way soon?" Cam called out. "The truth, or we'll sink you." He motioned to Wally, who wrenched a stone the size of a cantaloupe from the forest floor.

The man hesitated. "Yes," he said.

"Then we'll leave you for them to save."

He looked around. "Wait! How do I get out?"

"Your buddies," Cam replied.

The man looked distressed. He surveyed the smooth rock walls. "I'm not a good swimmer!" he cried.

"We'll leave you the rope ladder," Cam said.

He turned to see that Zara had already cut it. It tumbled down into the blue, where it writhed under the surface like a fleeing snake and sank. The man struggled, trying to pull off his heavy boots, but the laces were soaked, and each time he reached for them, his head went under.

Cam reached for his own rope.

"We don't have time, Cam," Siena said. "There probably *are* more of them coming soon."

Cam frowned deeply.

Siena put a hand on his arm. "If he's telling the truth, he'll be okay. And it will delay the others."

"He wrote his own fate," Zara said.

"And if no one comes soon?" Cam shook his head disapprovingly at her. She met his gaze with her unblinking stare-down eyes as she returned the blade with which she'd cut the rope to its sheath. He didn't have time to confront her about it, and so he simply led them away from the edge of the hole, back into the jungle.

"If you lied, you're screwed, buddy!" Wally shouted at the man as they turned to go, and he threw the stone. It hit the water so close to him that it sprayed his face, and then, just like all other things unlucky enough to fall into a lost and isolated hole, it tumbled into the depths and disappeared.

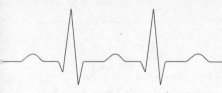

"Wee, wee, wee, where's the way home?"

"So where are we going, Cam?" Zara asked.

"The lab."

The surprise among the group was universal, but Siena's expression was the most distressed.

"Are you joking?" she spat.

"It's the only place we know that isn't jungle. And they must have ground transportation, or at least communication with the outside world."

"Right," Wally sneered. "Are we going to fly there? I'm enhanced, but I haven't grown wings yet."

"I don't think it's that far."

"How can you say that? We flew in the chopper for an hour to get there."

Cam pulled Ari's journal from his pocket. "Remember how Gwen was good with directions? That was her thing, right? And she kept time in her head by counting. She told Ari that, after a few helicopter trips to the doc, she started counting how long it took. She also could see light through the blindfold every time she faced the sun. When the light came at regular intervals every few minutes, she surmised that she was . . ."

". . . flying in circles," Zara finished for him. "Smart girl."

"Yes, she was," Cam said sadly. "Presumably Pilot circled so we wouldn't realize how close the facility was. Gwen counted the total time and subtracted the time we went in circles. The flight time turned out to be less than five minutes, by her estimation. She also determined from the sun that when we weren't circling, the chopper was headed generally west. Inland."

They listened with fixed stares, as intently as if Ward were briefing them, their enhanced concentration both welcome and a bit unnerving.

"We know lift-off was at the clearing south of the compound at least three miles by boat," Cam continued. "And the cruising speed of a helicopter is probably somewhere around one hundred and twenty miles per hour."

"How do you know that?" Wally asked.

"The instrument panel. That's what it said just before I got dumped here."

"Wow. You remember that?"

"Yeah," Cam said, shrugging. "And if we travel for five minutes in the chopper at one hundred twenty, that would only be about ten miles."

"Through the jungle," Siena pointed out.

"I didn't say they were easy miles."

"And when we get there? Then what?" Zara asked.

"I don't know. I'm working on it." It seemed to placate them. After his impressive analysis of the location, they cut him some slack on his lack of further planning. They would have time to think about it while they traveled. Cam was grateful. He didn't have all of the answers. *I'm a wingman, not a leader, like Ari*, he thought. Pilot had even said so when he was recruited.

Zara pointed at Siena. "How come you haven't tried walking out before?"

"The jungle sucks," she said. "I don't care how many enlightening programs they show on the eco channel, it's dangerous, dirty, and creepy, with vicious animals and bugs the size of your hand. Even the plants will grab, cut, and poison you."

"Not a nature buff, I see," Zara said.

"Besides, we could wander around out here lost until we died."

"We can't go back," Cam said. "Now would be a good time to tell us why you didn't hike out of here. Obviously, you stuck around for a reason."

"I wanted to go by boat. It seemed a better option."

"Why is that better than through the jungle?"

Siena looked indignant, but she finally rolled her eyes and explained.

"Look, I had to wade across a river, and I heard this splash. I got spooked, so I backed out and went up a tree. I stayed up there for like twenty minutes, until I thought I was being stupid and came down. But when I put one foot on the ground, this huge alligator lunged out of the water. If I hadn't still been enhanced, it probably would have eaten me. I spent the entire night in that tree."

She looked embarrassed. *But anyone would have been frightened*, Cam thought. Then he remembered his bladder's reaction when he'd thought he was being eaten by a shark. Her expression had the same shame in it, maybe more. *She shit herself*, he realized.

"They don't have alligators here," Cam said, trying to turn the discussion clinical. "It must have been a caiman."

Wally laughed. "Those little things they have at the aquarium?"

"Caimans are in the alligator family. They can get big."

"How big?" Wally demanded.

"I don't know," Siena said, irritated. "Big enough. Bigger than me. And I was in the water with the damned thing."

"Nine to fourteen feet," Cam said. "But they can reach sixteen."

"How do you know all this stuff?" Wally said, shaking his head.

"I'm detail oriented, I guess. I remember that tidbit from one of those nature programs Siena doesn't care about."

"So you got scared?" Zara said to Siena. "That's why you stuck around camp?"

"Yeah, I got scared. Okay? Don't you? It doesn't matter now anyway. I didn't get a boat."

"No," Cam said. "We didn't. So we move on. Just tell us when we get to the river where you met your reptilian friend."

The group started off again, measuring its progress through the thick jungle understory in yards instead of miles. They still needed to put more distance between themselves and the compound before they could stop for a real rest. Cam listened for the thump of helicopter blades. He didn't hear them, but they avoided open spaces just in case and worked their way through Siena's hated patches of thorny brush with only her machete to blaze a trail for them. It made the going even slower.

Finally, they ascended a small rise from which they could see several hundred yards behind them and parked themselves beside a stream, exhausted. At least Cam was exhausted, and from the look of it, Siena was too. His enhanced teammates seemed to catch their breaths quickly, and they waited dutifully for Cam and Siena to rest.

"Cam," Siena said privately, "I've got some more bad news that needs to be dealt with immediately, now that we have a moment."

"Great. Just when everything was looking so cheery." Cam steeled himself. "Go ahead."

"They're tracking us."

"That's not news."

"No. I mean they're *really* tracking us. By satellite."

"But we've been staying under the canopy."

"They implanted GPS devices in my team. I'm willing to bet they did it with you too."

"Implanted?"

"Subcutaneous. You know what that means?"

"Under the skin."

"Did they insert anything into you during your medical checks?"

Cam shook his head, but his hand drifted up to his rump where he'd taken the monstrous shot. There was still a vague lump there that he'd thought was just scar tissue. He began to get a queasy feeling.

"Zara," he asked, "did the doctors implant anything during your medical visits?"

She looked at him quizzically, but her hand immediately went to her own immaculate rump.

"No need to answer that," Cam said, and he turned back to talk to Siena alone again. "So they know exactly where we are?"

"Probably. And which direction we're going, and who is left. It's the way they kept track of us in TS-8."

"Lovely. How are we supposed to—?"

"They need to be removed," she interrupted, and she pulled up her sleeve to show him a hideously ragged white and red scar on her shoulder. "You're lucky," she said. "I didn't have a knife."

Cam didn't want to imagine what she'd used to get it out. He drew his butcher knife. It would work, but Zara carried one too, and hers was sharper. "How big? The size of a watch battery?"

"Smaller. Mine was BB-sized."

"You're sure about this. I don't want to slice into Wally's butt and be wrong."

"I'm not sure about anything. But we should cut somebody and find out."

Cam glanced about for likely candidates, someone who wouldn't complain about getting their butt cut open, especially if nothing was found. *Not Zara. Not Donnie. Definitely not Wally. And Siena no longer had a*

GPS in her. When his team stared back at him, his choice became clear.

"I'll do it," he finally said to Siena. "Use Zara's knife, but you do it. I don't want her carving me up. And don't go deep enough to hit muscle. I have to be able to walk."

Siena shook her head. "I almost passed out when I tore myself up. I'm not doing it again."

Cam grimaced. "Zara then?"

"Afraid so."

He called them all together and explained the situation. They were serious and didn't laugh, as he'd thought they might. They were all nervous that they *would* find something in his rump and that they'd be next. Worse, that more men were coming with guns and knew exactly where they were.

Cam knelt and lowered his pants while Zara stood behind him with the knife. He asked her to try to pinch it out first. It didn't work, but when she felt around she did confirm that something solid was imbedded in his flesh. She split open the skin with a quick incision.

"Ugh! Warn me, eh?"

"I didn't want you to clench."

"That's gonna leave a mark," Wally said, but no one laughed.

"Pity," Zara added, shamelessly examining him. "It's such a cute butt."

Cam grimaced as he felt her fingers groping. Then she gave him a swat. "Done!"

She held up the object she'd removed. It was a flat disk the circumference of a pencil lead, smaller around than a BB and made of metal and plastic—obviously a computer chip. It had tiny sharp hooks jutting from its surface to keep it in place. "One injectable tracking device," she announced.

Cam blew his long hair out of his eyes, concerned. "This means we have to hurry," he said. "Line up, everyone."

Zara did the duty. She'd already done it once, and there was no time to waste arguing. Soon everyone from the team was bleeding, and Cam had four chips in his hand.

"Should we smash them?" Wally asked.

"No," Cam said. "We should use them."

"How?"

"Bring me a stick of wood," he said. "We'll attach them to it and toss the wood in a stream. The water will take them downstream. They'll think we're following the river."

Zara shook her head. "Back to where we came from? The stream empties in the bay near the compound. That won't slow them for long. We should go back to the sinkhole and dump them all in there. They'll think we committed mass suicide."

"Like Jim Jones," Cam mumbled to himself.

"It would take them days to fish out bodies that aren't there."

"Too risky," Cam said. "They already found us there once, and Tegan's tracker is still taking them there. Plus we'd be giving up the small lead we have on them."

A bird squawked loudly at them from above, sending them all scrambling for cover. "Shut up, bird!" Wally barked, and he threw a chunk of rotten wood up at it.

Cam considered the bird. Its white wings and body contrasted dramatically with its black head, and webbed feet that looked like they'd rather be in the water clung to a branch. A smallish beak belied its big voice. *Some type of gull*, Cam thought—a South American cousin to the sort that frequented the docks back home on Bellingham Bay and fought for scraps behind the waterfront restaurants.

"Siena," Cam said, "do we have any food in the pack a sea gull might like?"

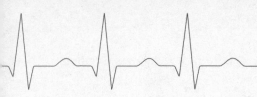

CAM'S PLAYLIST

34. FLY 🔊
by The Dread

35. TELL ON YOU
,by Drummer Boy

36. MIGHTY MIGHTY
by Hydroplane

"Catch that updraft. Flyyy . . ."

Minutes later, the gull flew off with four tracking devices in its belly. Cam didn't simply bury the computer chips in a cracker. When the gull fluttered down to the food, he'd had Zara leap on it. She squatted a few feet from the bait, and then launched herself like a trapdoor spider, grabbing the gull by one foot with a single hand. She was so lightning fast and precise that Cam was relieved he'd never have to fight his way past her on a beach again. After the bird was secured, he'd stuffed the tiny chips into its mouth one by one and followed them with a nibble of cracker to make sure they went down. Then they had chased the madly squawking thing off.

It would serve. Gulls moved about. It wouldn't remain in the trees for long. In fact, it had likely only made a quick stop at the river on its way to or from the coast or the sinkhole. Cam couldn't smile—their circumstance was too perilous—but the image of men in boats circling a sea gull with guns drawn made him want to.

Afterward, they hiked for an hour more, setting out at a forty-five-degree angle from their previous path, in case someone was mapping the direction of their progress. Cam's enhanced teammates continued to pace themselves for him and Siena. He was grateful for that. The jungle terrain was alternately easier and more difficult, depending upon the density of the understory. Once, they sent Wally up a tree to see how far he could see. He saw the ocean behind them, but only green ahead. Siena recognized the area. It was the farthest she'd come on her own. The dull brown river that horrified her crept through the trees, ignoring its banks. They walked with it, but soon it was all around them. Cam could see the tension in her expression. She jumped at every sound, and kept her lower lip pinched firmly between her teeth.

They were navigating a low swampy area when Donnie dropped back to slog through the knee-deep water alongside him.

"Cam, I have something to say," he mumbled, which was notable, because Donnie had said almost nothing since Owen had gotten shot, the same way he'd shut up for a time after Ari had been named team leader for mission one.

"Sure," Cam said.

"What do you want me to do?"

"What do you mean?"

"I mean, what's my assignment? I feel useless."

"We don't have assignments."

"I think we should. Not that it's my decision. You're leader now. I concede that."

"I'm not your leader. You don't need to concede anything."

"But I was so wrong about it all. I don't even trust my own instincts anymore." He grabbed Cam by the shoulders in a way that might have been horribly aggressive but was more likely a product of not realizing how much his strength had increased. Cam winced—it was like having each arm caught in a five-fingered vise.

"Oww," he said evenly.

Donnie let go and took a deep breath. "Sorry. I'm lost here, Cam," he said. "I need you to tell me what to do."

"We're all lost, Donnie. But every one of us signed up for this. We were all wrong together. We bought into it." Cam surprised himself by speaking slowly and gently. He felt like he was talking Donnie off a ledge. "We still don't even know what this is, right? Were those pirates really pirates? Who was the politician we framed? All we know is that somehow things got royally screwed up."

Donnie stared blankly. "So what do I do?"

Cam sighed. "Security," he said finally. "You're my muscle."

Just then, Wally splashed through the mud toward them. "We're still being followed!"

Cam whipped around. "Where?"

"Maybe one hundred yards back. Solo dude."

"How do you know? I can't see twenty *feet*."

"I heard him crashing through the brush. Listen."

Everyone froze and listened, their concentration absolute. Donnie and Zara exchanged a look. They heard it too. Cam strained. He heard nothing. Siena couldn't confirm it either. But Cam didn't doubt the senses of his enhanced teammates.

"You can tell for sure it's just one guy?" Cam asked the group.

"Yep," Zara answered. Donnie nodded too.

"Gun?"

"No way to know," Donnie said. "We need to assume so." Having squared his role with Cam, Donnie fell into soldier mode. *Ari was right*, Cam thought. The guy was an a-hole, but he was someone you wanted on your team in a fight.

"Should we move along?" Wally asked.

Cam held his fist up for silence, studying their surroundings. "Maybe we can use this guy," he said. "I want to know more about what's going on. I say we jump him. All in?"

They nodded. Cam took the pack from Siena and passed out darts. "Just one, and only if he's armed. Don't stick him twice." He shot Zara a look. She frowned, but it was clear she got the message.

A kapok loomed in the river, large enough for their purposes. Cam doffed his pack and stashed it among the roots that poked above the water, hiding it just enough that it would be noticed, but not so much that it looked like it was meant to be seen. He sent Wally up. There were few low-hanging branches, but Wally was able to shimmy up using infrequent handholds. At times, he hauled himself upward with one arm or even leaped from one hold to the next. There was a crook in the branches fifteen feet up where he ducked out of the line of sight, but he left a shoe tantalizingly exposed. The rest of them took up positions along the shore fifteen feet away. It would be a long dart throw. He assigned Donnie to take the first shot. Then they waited.

The man crept through the water, wary, no more than five feet from where Zara knelt, still as a statue. Cam had chosen the ruse well. The kapok demanded attention as soon as it came into view, and the corner of the pack caught the man's eye—a symmetrical, artificial object so out of place in a natural world. Wally shifted, making a faint scraping sound as a final enticement, and the man bit entirely. He kept his eyes up and eased past Zara without a glance. Had Cam known he would pass so close, he'd have given Zara the shot. Donnie was farther away. But the orders were already set.

This man was older than the last, with thinning hair. Like the first tracker, he didn't grab for his radio. To talk would make noise, and he had the drop on Wally if he remained quiet. He knew they were dangerous—as the other had said, they'd proven as much at the beach—and he clung to his gun.

Cam wondered about the drowning man's fate—a man could only tread water fully clothed for so long before he sank. This pursuer was too close behind them to have stopped to pull him out. He'd either missed his comrade or had seen him but not helped. Either thought was grim.

The hunter took aim, but shooting Wally in the foot didn't seem to satisfy him. He waited for Wally to move, standing among grasses so high they obscured him almost entirely. Cam could see

Donnie's frustrated expression. His throw was iffy. But patience was not his greatest attribute. He took the shot. His arm whipped forward, and the dart flew. Its delicate flight clipped the grass, tilting its shaft. The tip hit the man's arm at an angle and barely pierced the thick fabric of his heavy shirt. He looked down, startled, like a picnicker who'd been stung by a hornet. The dart hung in the material for a moment, then dropped to the forest floor, its load only partially discharged.

The barrel of the gun drooped, then fell from his limp arm and splashed into the mud, but he didn't go down. Zara cocked her dart to her ear.

"No!" Cam shouted. "No second dart!" He couldn't be sure another wouldn't kill the man.

The man took off running, thrashing through the water. He was hindered by the loss of use of one arm and thrown off-balance.

"Get his radio!" Cam yelled.

Zara caught him easily, before he could reach for his radio with his working arm. She threw herself around his neck and rode him to the ground like a rodeo steer. The man had a knife, but no chance to pull it, and Zara was already beating him senseless when Cam arrived to stop her.

"Enough! We need him conscious."

Siena brought the rope, and they tied him. Then Cam sat with him. He was balding and had narrow eyes. Caucasian, but his tan told Cam he'd been in the area for some time. His khaki shirt was new. The rifle was a Bushmaster AR-15, something Wally recognized and quickly claimed. Cam had heard of it. It looked military, but the AR-15 was one of the most common civilian assault rifles in the United States. Something easily purchased through any gun store. In fact, it was the type of gun used by a famous Washington, D.C., serial murderer to snipe innocent people.

Cam lifted their beaten captive's chin. "We have some questions," he said.

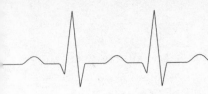

"I'm the one who is gonna tell on you."

Cam helped the man into a sitting position. "Let's start with a name. I know you'll probably make one up, but it gives me something to call you besides asshole."

"Gary," the man offered.

"All right, Gary. I need you to tell me some things. You know we're serious, right?"

The man who called himself Gary felt his head where Zara had slammed it into the muck repeatedly. "I'll talk. Just keep her away from me."

"Should have thought of that before you came after us!" Wally snapped at him.

"Who sent you?" Donnie growled.

"And why are you trying to kill us?!" Zara interrupted.

"I'm just getting paid. That's all. I've got no animosity toward you."

Wally pointed the rifle between his eyes. "Yeah? Well, how do you like me now?!"

Cam put a hand up to ease the barrel of the gun away, and he motioned his teammates back.

"How many more of you are on our tail?" he asked in a calm voice, though he didn't feel any calmer than the rest of them.

"Just me and the one you put in the killing jar. But I expect he's dead by now."

"You didn't help him? Good god, why?"

"I didn't know him. I get paid to find you, not help the competition. If I stopped to fish him out, I might have lost you."

Cam was shaken. He hadn't meant to kill the man.

Zara stepped in. "There were eight, plus Pilot and Ward. Four are out, by my count. I know you've been in radio contact. Where are the rest of them?"

"Back in the boats. Probably gone by now."

"Stay here," Cam said, and he pushed the bound man into the mud like a turtle on its back. "We need to discuss what to do with you."

The team gathered a few yards away, just out of earshot.

"He's lying," Zara said. "No English-speaking guy gets hired off the street and flown to South America. If they wanted thugs, they could have hired some local dirtbags."

"I agree," Siena said. "Thugs don't use the word 'animosity.'"

"He's with the organization."

Cam nodded. Ranuel the teenage pirate had been hired off the street. Gary was no Ranuel.

"We should off him," Zara said.

Cam frowned. "Are we killing now?" he asked. "Did we switch from good kids to executioners when I wasn't looking?"

"Being a good girl hasn't really worked out for me." Zara stroked the edge of her knife with a thumb.

"So are we like them?"

Donnie shook his head. "We're faster and stronger."

"That's right, we're *better*," Cam said. He didn't want to argue with his teammates, but his voice carried a tone of challenge. *Killing should never be the first choice*, he thought. *Then again, what if it's the only choice?*

Siena spoke. "We've gotten exactly nothing useful from this guy. He's delayed us for ten minutes. They might be tracking him. And if we let him go, they'll just put another gun in his hands and he'll come after us again."

Cam frowned and blew his long, wispy hair out of his eyes in frustration. It was too long, he thought absently. Siena was right, of course, as she always was. But she hadn't proposed the death penalty. She'd left the decision to him, their team leader.

"All right," Cam said. "I have an idea. . . ."

The black caiman sunned itself on the far bank. It was, perhaps, even larger than Siena had claimed—ten to fifteen feet by Cam's rough and admittedly amateur estimate. The Amazon jungle's top predator made no attempt to hide. Indeed, it appeared to be dozing confidently, its massive tail dipped in the river as though feeling for disturbances in the water. The wide, slow bend where Siena had first seen the massive creature provided a natural home, and, as Cam had guessed, the caiman had seen no reason to leave it.

Gary lay facedown in the dirt, tied up with Siena's rope, his head on the shore and his legs submerged in the shallows up to his thighs. Cam spoke to him from farther up on the bank.

"Do you know what a black caiman is?" Cam asked.

Gary strained to lift his head from the dirt and nodded.

"Good," Cam said, "because not everyone does. Wally thought they were those miniature reptiles at the zoo. But they're not only found at the zoo. And they're not really miniature, are they?"

Gary didn't answer—he was too busy trying to pull his feet out of the water.

"I read somewhere that one of mankind's greatest fears is getting eaten alive by another animal," Cam continued. "It's instinctual. Visceral. Goes back to our caveman days. It's in our blood, so to speak. Is that one of your fears, Gary?"

Gary lay silent. Cam could see him thinking, but it was difficult to read his emotion. *Concern? Fright? Anger? Some of each?*

"If you're not scared, we can simply leave you here on the shore. They'll find you eventually, assuming they care more about you than you cared about your teammate. Unless, of course, the local wildlife takes an interest in you first."

The questioning was taking too long. They'd already wasted time tying him up. Cam had hoped it would be worth it, but he couldn't wait much longer. He motioned Zara forward. She drew her knife and sliced a rent in Gary's pants while Cam talked.

"You know how, in the movies, the hero always tricks his captors by delaying them while help comes. Well, you're not a hero, Gary, and this isn't the movies."

Another shallow slash from Zara's knife and Gary began to leak blood into the river.

Cam spoke loudly to Siena. "Do caimans smell blood in the water?"

Siena shrugged. "I don't know."

"She doesn't know, Gary."

Gary squirmed. "I work security for them, okay?"

Cam and Siena looked at each other.

"Pull me out. I'll talk."

"You're talking fine from there. Keep going. What is security?"

"We're brought in if the experiments abscond."

We're the "experiments," Cam thought. It was an ugly word to use for real human beings.

"What's 'abscond'?" Wally asked.

"Run away," Siena said.

"Are there other security personnel following us now?" Cam said.

Gary spat mud out of his mouth. "They think you're working your way back to the ocean, for some reason."

"The bird," Zara whispered into Cam's ear.

"Are they tracking you, Gary?"

"No. But they know generally where I am. I told them I was following a fresh lead. You left a pretty obvious trail."

"What were they doing last time you checked in?"

"Still looking for you. And scrubbing the site."

"Scrubbing?"

"Making sure there is no evidence that you were there."

"Why did they turn on us?"

"They said you turned on them."

"Why are you supposed to kill us?"

"They didn't tell me why!"

Gary's tacit admission that he was assigned to scrub them—to kill and not capture them—made Cam's heart skip a beat. It also made him angry. Cam kicked at the water, splashing in the shallows.

"Not helpful, Gary! Did they say anything at all? Go ahead, I'm listening. So is the caiman, maybe."

Gary had to squirm to rotate so that he could see the reptile. It remained motionless on the shore, so still it could have been dead, but Gary did not look reassured. He took a deep breath.

"I heard a guy say somebody was gonna blow the operation. Reveal it, or something like that."

Jules, Cam thought. *Good old bigmouth Jules.* Either her e-mail to her sister or her appearance in Scotland had set something off.

There was a splash upriver behind Gary.

He yelped and twisted. "What was that?!"

Wally chuckled to himself and picked up another rock.

"Pull me out!" Gary pleaded.

"What happens to us now?"

He twisted in his bonds, looking for the caiman. "Is it in the water?"

"Calm down. That's your flight instinct interrupting our

productive conversation. Ward taught us to ignore that. You can too. I only have a few more questions." Cam had to cross his arms to show he wasn't about to let him up yet. "What happens to us, Gary?"

He hesitated, but answered. "It's a total program scrap."

Eyes flitted among the team members. Cam exchanged a grim look with each of them in turn, Siena first, and then the others. "They" were the program. And "scrap" didn't need to be defined. They'd been written off like a bad investment. "Sold and taken as a tax loss," Cam's dad might have said.

"Let me up," Gary pleaded, squirming to see what was behind him. "I've told you the truth. Leave me tied if you have to, but get me out of the water!"

"One more question, Gary. Where is the medical center?"

Gary stopped thrashing. He stared at Cam. When he didn't answer, Wally hurled his second rock, thumping the caiman in the haunch. It stirred, its huge eyes blinking open.

"I'd like an answer, Gary."

The splash was bigger this time. Gary wrenched himself sideways and spun. By the time he turned, the shoreline was empty, a large smear in the mud the only evidence that the caiman had ever rested on the far bank.

"Oh god . . ."

Cam waited. Gary pulled up his legs. But his feet were still in the water. They quivered from the effort, making telltale rings in the slow river.

"We're going there with or without your help," Cam said.

The caiman's wake appeared on the surface of the water ten yards away, a rippled V pointing directly at Gary's dangling feet.

"I'll help you!" Gary insisted.

"I asked for the location."

Gary spluttered, trying to talk faster than his mouth could form words, searching for the right thing to say, anything that might save him.

"It's close. Maybe two miles. I don't know a path, but it's southwest. I've got a compass in my shirt pocket, and—"

The caiman exploded from the water. But Donnie was ready. As it surfaced, he leaped forward and yanked Gary away from its snapping jaws. It might have chased them up the bank, but Wally ran in from the side and set one foot on its head, leaping from it like a springboard.

"Yee-haw!" Wally yelled. He landed and spun, dancing out of the path of the angry reptile's mouth and clapping his hands in a juvenile taunt. "Here caimy, caimy!"

Cam shook his head. The monstrous animal was tracking Wally's ridiculous dance. It was stupid and dangerous, but there was no controlling Wally, and it allowed Donnie the chance to drag Gary into the trees. Donnie managed it with one hand, his incredible strength on full display.

Cam plucked Gary's compass from his pocket. "Southwest of here two miles, you say?"

Zara didn't look convinced. "He knows where we're going now. If they find him, he'll tell them where we are."

"No, I won't," Gary said.

"Shut up," Zara said. "We can't leave him here alive now, Cam."

Cam felt his stomach turn, and he wanted to smack his own head. She was right. They gathered away from Gary again, even Wally, who had led the caiman on a merry chase before tossing a few more rocks at its head to drive it back into the water.

A good leader listens to his team, Cam thought.

"I'm taking suggestions on what to do with Gary. We're not going to have another unilateral decision, like we did at the sinkhole." He didn't look at Zara, but they all knew he meant her. She didn't need to be called out.

Zara spoke first. "If you want a consensus, let's just vote."

"Leave him on the bank for the caiman," Wally said.

"That's cruel," Cam pointed out.

"Circle of life, man. A caiman's gotta eat."

"We can put him in a tree," Siena said. "They might find him eventually."

"Might not."

"Donnie?" Cam asked

"Whatever your order is, I'll carry it out."

"I want your input. I've got two for leaving him tied and alive and two for . . . not."

Donnie's jaw and fists were clenched, and he breathed heavily. When he spoke, it was with ferocious conviction. "Like I said, my vote is whatever yours is, Cam."

The TS was giving Donnie frightening focus. Everything about him was intense—his stares, his speech, even his small movements.

"All right then."

Cam spoke to Gary as his stronger teammates hung him by his armpits in a tree, out of reach of the caiman.

"We're leaving you here."

"I won't tell them where you're going," Gary promised.

"No, you won't." Cam drew a dart and plunged it into Gary's thigh. It would knock him out for several hours, more than they'd need, Cam hoped.

Zara poked his body to ensure that he was unconscious. "With the partial dose he already had, that might kill him," she said.

"Might not," Cam replied.

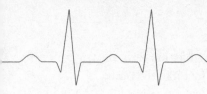

36. MIGHTY MIGHTY 🔊
by Hydroplane

37. LACE UP
by Game Day

38. LET YOU GO
by Raven Dark

"We're young, strong, and burn half as long.
Whoaaa, mighty, mighty!"

They surveyed the clear-cut field from a nearby rise. The trees ended abruptly at the south end, where space for two buildings had been carved from the dense jungle. It looked like a missing piece from a forest jigsaw puzzle. The buildings were a mishmash of corrugated metal and vertical planks, some of which were water-stained a dark hue at the bottom and crumbling, obviously rotten. The roofs were dense thatch.

"They're shacks," Wally said.

"Pretty big for shacks," Zara observed.

"Maybe they're old farm buildings. Slaughterhouses or something?"

"In the middle of a swamp?"

Cam studied the grounds. "No roads in or out."

Siena pointed. "That outbuilding has modern electrical lines running from it. Generator, I'll bet. Just like the bunker."

Cam studied the grounds for a time, scanning for . . . "There it is!" he said, pointing to a gravel pathway. "Do you remember the crunching when we walked in for our doctor visits?" Cam remembered it well. They'd been herded blindfolded from the helicopter to the examination rooms. Touch and sound were enhanced when sight was not handy to gather information.

Zara directed their attention to an open space where the ground was flat, bare, and worn. "Helicopter pad?" she suggested.

Donnie stared. "And there's stucco beneath the planks."

"How can you tell?"

"You can see it between the cracks."

"*I* can't." Cam let out a chuckle.

"What are you laughing at?" Donnie said.

Cam realized that it was the first time he'd laughed at being inferior. "I'm just feeling like a blind man with a Seeing Eye dog."

"Anyone see communications equipment?" Siena asked.

"There can't be phone lines out here, but there are trees tall enough to be cell towers."

"Guards?"

"None visible."

"Cameras . . . ?"

They circled the complex. The more they examined it and the closer they approached, the more obvious it became that it was a modern facility in disguise. It seemed primarily meant to fool anyone who might fly over.

"What good is it to go in there when there's no transportation out?" Donnie asked.

Siena supplied multiple answers. "Phone. Radio. Internet. Map to the nearest village."

"And diagnostic information," Cam said. "The results of all those tests we've been taking."

"You're drawn to it," Zara said.

"Like a fly to the flame," Wally said.

"I think that's a moth," Zara said. "Something else attracts flies."

"You know what I mean," he snorted.

"I think this qualifies either way," Cam said. "There's some serious bullshit going on in there."

"I don't see any extra activity," Siena said. "They don't know we're here. But we've only got a couple of hours until 'Gary' wakes up and tells them where we went, assuming they find him."

Zara shook her head. "We should have fed him to the caiman."

They assumed cameras and made their approach away from the front and rear doors. Wally handed the rifle off to Zara and went solo, flattening against the side of the building and scanning for hidden lenses. Soon he was peeking around the corner at the front entry. He signaled that he'd spotted two cameras, one each at the front and rear entrances—the minimum necessary to cover the facility. He scurried back to the group, sprinting across the open ground and then army-crawling unnecessarily through the brush.

"There *is* a guard," he panted, and he took his gun back from Zara.

"Where?"

"Alcove by the front door. On a smoke break."

Cam wrinkled his brow. "Take him out? Or do we avoid the risk he'll raise the alarm and move on?"

"We came this far," Wally said.

Siena nodded. So did Donnie.

Zara shrugged. "You know my vote."

"Is he on camera?"

"Nope. He's inside the alcove."

They circled, crouching low. When they faced the front entrance the guard was visible. He lounged in a cheap plastic lawn chair, cigarette hanging from his lips. It was difficult to tell if he had a cell phone or radio, but his gun was visible. AR-15. Wally pointed to the camera mounted above the alcove.

Cam turned to Zara. "Can you get close enough to disarm him?"

"Sure," she said. "I can wander up like I was just strolling by and ask him for a cigarette, and then karate chop him like on TV."

Cam rolled his eyes. "Okay, I get it. Not a good plan. Can you hit him from here, Wally?"

"Easy," Wally said. He checked the magazine and flipped off the safety. "Where do you want it?"

"Trigger hand?"

"He'll run inside."

"Leg first then?"

"Sure. Then I'll do his trigger hand."

"Really? You think you can do that?"

Zara lowered herself next to Wally. "Let me point out that if you hit him in the head, he will neither go for help nor shoot back," she said. "And if he has a cell phone . . ."

Cam frowned. She was right. "Any sign of a cell phone, Wally, and you do what you need to do," he said.

"Done," Wally said, and raised the butt of the AR-15 to his shoulder.

Cam thought that his teammate would have to take his time, but Wally swung the gun up and fired in one smooth motion, his hands strong and steady. There was a loud pop, but no echoing crack or *pow* that might be heard for miles around. The noise was not a high risk. Security cameras were not typically designed to pick up sound. Cam saw the man's leg jerk sideways, and a dark splotch appeared on the wall behind him—blood in a Rorschach pattern. It looked like a sea gull to Cam. Wally squeezed off two more shots before Cam could stop him. The first took off a finger on his right hand. The second punched a hole dead center in his left palm. The guard went over in his chair and curled into a ball. There was no brave teeth-gritting or courageous return fire, no

Herculean effort to crawl for the door. Just an awkward and painful-looking tuck into the fetal position.

Zara and Donnie were on him in seconds. There was some risk—they had to cross the camera's field of view. However, with an exterior guard on duty, there was less chance eyes would be on the camera—it would likely be recording, not monitoring. Cam arrived at the alcove as his teammates were checking the door and frisking the guard for keys.

"He's bleeding," Cam observed.

"That happens when you shoot someone," Wally said.

"He's bleeding *a lot.*"

Wally examined his handiwork. "He's just lucky I aimed to the left of his weenie."

"He's bleeding too much," Cam persisted.

"You must have clipped the femoral artery," Zara said.

"Meaning what?" Wally asked.

"He'll bleed out quickly and die."

"We didn't want him killed," Cam said, exasperated. "We just wanted you to shoot him in the leg."

"I *did* shoot him in the leg."

"To incapacitate him."

"I am not familiar with the incapacitation region of the leg. You said 'leg,' so I hit a leg."

The man moaned and pawed at the air, confused. He hardly registered their presence.

"First aid," Cam ordered.

"What do you want us to do, put a tourniquet on his thigh?" Donnie said.

"Can't be done." It was Zara. "You can't cut off blood flow to the entire leg."

"We decided to shoot him to disable him," Donnie said. "The fact that he might die is the risk we took."

Cam knelt beside the man. "We took the risk *for* him. That's not fair."

"Are you hearing yourself?" Zara said. "How fair have they been to us? What sort of risks have they been treating us to, eh?"

The guard was sweating like a pig, but he had a kind face that reminded Cam a bit of his favorite professor. The loss of blood had clouded his eyes, and he stared past them into the distance. His skin was cold and clammy. Ari had explained the symptoms of circulatory shock once during training, and the man had all of them.

"I feel responsible," Cam said. "Isn't there anything we can do?"

Siena held up a key ring. "He needs a doctor."

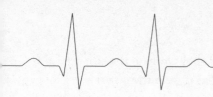

"Na-na-na-na. Na-na-na-na. Goaaaaaal!"

Donnie kicked open the door to the gli club, where a little man in a lab coat with large round glasses whirled to stare at them. He stood across the room with a coffeepot and cup, frozen mid-pour. He glanced at the guard dripping blood and gasped.

Wally leveled the AR-15 at him. "Are you a doctor?"

They dragged the guard up onto the pool table. The doctor was one of a skeleton crew in the facility. There was a supervisor and two lab docs. This one was not in charge. Zara kept the knife at his back, and he didn't try anything. He was familiar with her reaction time. He had an accent. European, though Cam wasn't sure what it was exactly. Russian, maybe, or some neighboring region thereof. The man didn't ask why they'd shot the guard or what the team wanted, which told Cam that he understood they were on the run. He did seem confused about why they wanted to help the guard.

"How do we save him?" Cam asked.

"There's massive blood loss. First we stop it, then a transfusion."

"You have blood?"

"No. We must have a donor. Fly him out, maybe."

"You're *not* calling in a helicopter. Work on stopping the bleeding for now."

Cam sent Donnie and Wally to secure the other staff. "Search them and lock them in a room with no communications gear. Don't shoot them."

"Yes, sir," Donnie said.

"Please don't call me 'sir,'" Cam replied.

Wally gave him a faux salute. "Yes, Your Excellency."

They took the rifle and the doctor's keys and left the room.

"Face it," Siena said. "You're their 'sir.'"

"I'm not calling you 'sir,'" Zara said, and she gave him a sly grin. "Unless you can make me."

The doctor was finishing up the sutures. It was a rushed job—ugly hamburger work meant to save a life, not a leg. The man's finger could not be saved, and the damage from the hole in his hand would have to wait for assessment. The doctor only cleaned it and wrapped it.

"I have done what I can," he said. "Without blood he still dies."

"Then he dies," Zara said.

"No. That's unacceptable." Cam took a deep breath. "Doctor, do you know who I am?"

The doctor stared at him through his thick glasses. "9K. The soccer player."

9K? Cam thought. It was the name on the survey forms he'd filled out, not Cam or even Cameron. *That's who I am to these scientists. Subject 9K.*

"Then I'll bet you know my blood type too, right?"

The transfusion was done in an exam room. Wally came back

to check in during the procedure and confirmed that the other doctor and lab technician had been secured. Donnie was guarding them. Wally swore when Cam told him about the transfusion, calling it "idiotic," among other things. But as the blood began to flow, Cam felt certain they were doing the right thing.

Zara lay on the table next to the man, her muscular arm extended and pierced with a sizable needle. Cam was the wrong blood type, the doctor had said. Zara was type O, compatible with anyone, a "universal donor," the doc called it. She'd debated, but Cam told her that it was always right to save a life, when it was in your power.

"That's what I thought when I joined," she said.

The process would take one to four hours, according to the doc. Enough time to investigate the facility. Wally and his gun stayed to keep tabs on Zara, while Cam and Siena went to poke around. The doctor had not been helpful regarding transportation. They used the helicopter exclusively, he said, and Pilot flew them, which wouldn't do at all. The nearest village was forty miles south. Too far to walk through the jungle, and much of the land in between was flooded swamp—a caiman haven, among other problems.

Cam headed straight to the observation room behind the one-way mirror, where he'd seen the lab techs working with his team's blood. The gurney was gone. There was a refrigerator with vials neatly labeled 9A through 9K. There were more samples of some subjects than others. 9C had only one. *Peter*, Cam thought. On the next shelf were the 8s, A through J. The 7s were also A through J. The 6s were A through I. The 5s A through J again.

"They have a team every year," Cam said.

Siena wrinkled her nose. "Unless . . ."

"What?"

"Unless not every team lasts an entire year. They told us they were working on extending the life of the TS, and we were supposed to have a full year. But if we were the longest-lasting batches, that means previous teams got less time."

Cam could see Siena thinking. Then her lip curled into a snarl.

"I didn't feel sick at all before I was diagnosed by their specialist. It was only after they began 'treating' me that I started having glioblastoma symptoms."

Cam put a hand on her shoulder, and she allowed it to stay.

"It was all a lie, Cam. They made me feel sick. They induced the symptoms to match their phony diagnosis. Then they offered me the bait, and I snatched it out of desperation."

When Cam didn't disagree she squeezed her eyes shut so hard that she looked like a child wishing away monsters in the night. In a way, she was.

"I was a good girl. I was smart and responsible and nice. I did everything I was asked to do. Why me? Why us?"

"Maybe that's why," Cam said. "We're not sick. We're pure subjects. I'll bet they already tested this drug on diseased and third-world subjects long ago."

There was a heavy door with a huge lever handle. Cam went to it and listened. There was no sound, but it was cold to the touch. He pulled, and it opened into a refrigerated locker room with rows of large drawers. Cam could see his breath. The gurney he recognized was parked at the end of the room.

Siena was already drifting through the rows. She selected the nearest drawer handle.

"Don't," Cam said.

"There are unpleasant truths that we came here to uncover, Cam. We gain nothing by ignoring them." With that, she drew open the drawer.

Cam almost threw up. Calliope's face was even whiter than it had been in life. She wore a rubber cap, and her long red hair was gone. But it was clearly her. She lay still with her eyes disturbingly wide open. Death was supposed to be peaceful, but her permanent stare didn't make her seem at peace to Cam. In fact, she looked a lot like the door guard in shock.

"They had her body sent here," Cam said, tracing a finger up to the label above the drawer. It read 9E. He glanced about. The other drawers were also labeled—9A, 9B, 9C, 9D . . . all the way through 9K. He gasped. "It's us!"

Siena shut Calliope's drawer and walked down the row. "8F. That's me." She yanked it open. Thankfully, it was vacant.

Cam couldn't do it, so Siena opened the next two, 9I and 9J.

"That's my friend Ari, and this one is Gwen," Cam said, tight-lipped. Then she reached drawer 9K. She slid it open and Cam stuck his head into the empty space. He wondered if the dead felt claustrophobia. "I'm looking into my own tomb," he said.

"Cam . . ."

"Yeah?"

"I need you to see something here. I don't want you to, but you *need* to."

Cam turned. Siena had drawer 9H slightly open. "I'm so sorry," she said, and she pulled it wider so that he could see inside.

Cam staggered backward. "No. Nuh-nuh-no! That's not fair!"

Jules was more recognizable than Calliope without her hair. Her oversized eyes and smallish chin were distinctive. She too wore a cap over her shaved head. Worse, there was a clear incision where they'd removed a portion of her skull, presumably to study the effects of TS on her brain.

Cam didn't even realize Siena was hugging him until she caressed his hair. She pulled him gently away and pushed all the drawers shut with her foot, seemingly out of respect for the privacy of the dead. Then they stood together, and she shared her warmth in the cold room.

After a while, she whispered to him, "Your teammate Owen isn't here yet. Even if they're not looking for us here, they'll be bringing his body soon. They won't want him to rot. We should prepare for company."

"I need to sit for a minute," Cam said, and he hoisted himself up onto the gurney. She nodded and stepped away.

The rows of drawers didn't end with the 9 series. Just like the vials of blood, there were 8s and 7s and 6s too. *It's a morgue*, Cam thought. *We're all in the morgue. We're just too naïve to know we're already dead.*

The scream was faint through two heavy doors and around two corners, but they heard it.

"That's Wally," Cam said, jumping up. "Something's wrong."

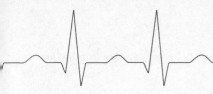

CAM'S PLAYLIST

38. LET YOU GO 🔊
   by Raven Dark

39. ANGRY YOUNG WOMAN
   by Calli

40. ME ON STEROIDS
   by Addictionopolis

"Let me let you go."

Cam knew it was bad, because Donnie was in the room and had the doctor pinned against the wall by the neck. Wally paced, unable to say anything comprehensible through his profanity and the blows he dealt his own head with his open hand.

"What's going on here?"

"He's killing her, Cam," Donnie said.

"I didn't know!" Wally yelled.

"Wally killed who . . . ?"

"No. The doc! This doc. He took three pints of blood out of her."

"What?!"

"I didn't know how much was too much!" Wally wailed.

The doctor gargled through Donnie's choke hold.

"No!" Donnie growled. "Don't even try to speak. I will rip your throat out."

Cam turned to Zara. She was as pale as Calliope. He leaped to her side, grabbing her arm. She was barely able to turn her head.

Donnie rammed the man against the wall by the neck, so strong that the doctor's entire body rattled with the impact.

"Wait! I need to talk to that man," Cam said.

"Cam, it's too late to talk," Zara whispered. "Just do . . ." She couldn't finish. She was fading.

"We might save her," Cam said. But the look in the doctor's eyes told him he was wrong. "What happened?"

"A bad reaction to the procedure," the man said. "Allergic reaction maybe."

"You took three pints?"

"A medically safe amount if—"

"Put it back!" Cam said ridiculously.

"I cannot do that. They would both die."

"I don't give a shit about him! Save her!"

Cam glanced at the guard. His tongue lolled from his mouth. He didn't look any better than Zara. Cam shot an accusing glare back at the doc. But he only stared at his own feet. It was clear he wouldn't be saving anybody.

Cam knelt beside her. Her chest stopped moving up and down. No breath whooshed from her lips. *An absence of life.* Her year was over. No more extreme experiences. No more kicking ass. She lay still. Except for her slightly open eyes, she might have simply been asleep. *A normal girl dreaming of getting married and picking out dishes,* Cam thought. *A girl who wanted to kiss me.* But there would be no more kissing. She was dead. Cam kissed her anyway, lightly on the mouth, like a gentleman, but long enough to mean something—a wedding kiss. Nobody protested. Indeed, nobody said a word. Afterward, he reached out and shut her eyes for her, and she looked peaceful.

Someone was kneeling beside him. Siena. "Cam, he killed her on purpose."

"I did not," the doctor insisted.

"He did, Cam. You know he did."

Cam hesitated. "I need to think about this." But he couldn't think. The idea that Zara was gone was scrambling his thoughts.

"I need time. I just need to . . ."

"That's right," the doctor said. "We need to talk this through. I can explain. You see, the procedure was compromised when . . ."

Cam felt the anger rising inside him, like bile about to erupt from his throat. "It's too late to talk," he growled. He motioned to Donnie.

Donnie's arm lashed out quicker than Cam could follow, and when it recoiled it held a pink, bleeding object. The man's tongue. Siena quickly stuck him with a dart to cut off his horrible gargling scream.

Cam turned in place, lost. "We were saving a life. Why would a doctor do that?" It was an absent question perhaps directed at his teammates, perhaps himself, or at the god he'd abandoned, or at nobody.

Donnie wiped his bloody hands on a towel. "We try to do something good and a doctor screws us over? Sound familiar?"

"And I recommended she do it," Cam groaned. "I served her up."

"I didn't see this one coming either, Cam," Siena said, looking through the man's pockets. "None of us did."

"I had the gun on him the whole time," Wally groaned.

"If you didn't, he would have killed you too and then ambushed the rest of us." She held up four syringes the doctor had filled with inky fluid. "Look familiar?"

"He knew we were trained not to kill," Donnie growled. "But that's going to change."

"I've failed you all as leader," Cam said, remembering something that Ari had told him. "I need to be brilliant *before* half the team is dead." He might have slumped onto the floor then in despair, but Donnie grabbed him by the arms.

"We're still onboard, Cam."

Wally nodded. "You got us all the way to here. Otherwise, we'd all be dead on the beach with Owen."

Cam turned to Siena for support.

"You need to stay sharp," she said. "Don't puss out on me."

Cam didn't know whether to laugh or cry. She could have said a million things, he thought, but that was the one that reached him.

"We need to round up the other staff," he said.

The others were in an observation room, where Donnie had locked them, a doc and the supervisor. Cam got his first look at them through the one-way mirror. They knew they were being watched, and so they sat, behaving themselves. The underling doc was one of the men he'd seen when he'd stumbled into the lab during his medical visit. The supervisor was Indian—India Indian, not Native American.

Cam entered.

The supervisor stood and smiled. His teeth were very white. "Hello, Cameron."

Cam did not smile. "Hello, Dr. Singh."

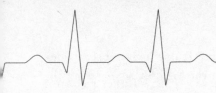

"Like the day I watched them put my dog down."

"I know that's not your real name," Cam said.

"Names are unimportant. But so long as we are using them for reference, where is Dr. Talis?"

"Unconscious."

"And my guard?"

"Dead."

"We need to talk, you and I. This treatment of my staff will not do at all."

"You're killing us. We know you are."

Dr. Singh shook his head as though Cam didn't understand. "Some few subjects die in the process. But we are changing life for all of humanity, Cameron. Our species is about to evolve dramatically through science, through medicine. And we are so very close.

Any group could be the breakthrough. It might have been yours. We had great hope for you, but then the big boy began to get the headaches."

"Those 'subjects' were *people*—Jules, Ari, Owen, Calliope, Tegan, Zara."

"A privileged few. You were told you would sacrifice. You agreed."

"We were told we were dying."

"Everyone is dying. Most live long and ordinary lives of nothingness in debilitating fear of it. We give our subjects a year to be exceptional with little fear of death. We free them. It is a gift."

Suddenly, Cam realized why Dr. Singh smiled when he spoke to patients about their deaths. They were curiosities to him, a hill of ants to a schoolyard boy with a magnifying glass, perhaps a dissected frog. He'd heard of doctors who began to feel omniscient when they presided over mortality. "God complex," they called it.

Cam shook his head. "There's a flaw in your logic, doc. I'm not enhanced. I didn't get my gift. And now I'm pissed." He motioned Donnie and Wally forward to tie them up.

They began to bind their captives to two examination tables.

"I have a personal question," Cam said. "And it's going to bug me forever if I don't ask. Why did you pick me?"

Dr. Singh spoke clinically, as though dictating an autopsy. "You seemed a team player. You were not supposed to lead. Donald was chosen for his loyalty. He is supposed to lead." Singh turned to Donnie. "Donald, would you like to resume your rightful position?"

Donnie stopped tying him, and, for a moment, Cam wondered whether he might take Dr. Singh up on it. Then he spoke.

"Do you want me to kill him, Cam?"

For the first time, Dr. Singh's smile disappeared. Cam let the question hang, purposefully not answering.

"I don't think you're even curing sick people," Cam said. "Siena, what are the best-selling drugs in the world?"

Siena gave a halfhearted chuckle. "Viagra? Botox? Rogaine?"

"Vanity drugs. You're not developing treatments, you want *enhancement.*"

"That's why they sought healthy subjects," Siena said, seeing where Cam was going.

"Right. They researched us. They chose us. Two geniuses, three superior athletes, a huge strong guy, a musical prodigy, and a couple perfectly healthy college kids."

"And me," Wally said.

Cam smiled. "Yeah, well, I've got no explanation for you, buddy."

Siena glared at Dr. Singh. "I'll bet when they sell it at ten grand a pill, the rich will not only be financially superior . . ."

". . . they'll be physically superior too," Cam finished.

Singh protested. "No. Untrue. It would be available at a price any median-income family could afford as soon as the patent expired and generics were made."

Donnie fidgeted. "My question still stands," he reminded Cam.

Cam pointed at Dr. Singh. "He's killed innocent people. There's an entire refrigerated room full of them in back. He's a serial killer."

"That carries the death penalty where I come from," Donnie said.

"No. No. We have a good purpose," Singh insisted.

Donnie took him by the neck, while Wally kept the AR-15 trained on his wide-eyed assistant.

Singh spoke faster now, serious and unsmiling. "Innocent people died building the Golden Gate Bridge, the pyramids. And we do something far more significant here, something evolution would have taken centuries to achieve, something it has stopped doing. We will physically improve mankind."

Cam shook his head. "No, you won't."

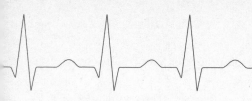

CAM'S PLAYLIST

40. ME ON STEROIDS 🔊
   by Addictionopolis

41. INCONTINENTAL
   by The Steam Punks

42. WE'RE ALONE TOGETHER
   by The Flat Earth Society

"My better self is on the shelf.
I'll get me down when I need my help."

Helicopter blades thumped in the distance. Wally heard them first, a full thirty seconds before Cam did. They'd only had an hour between the time they'd talked with Dr. Singh and the chopper's approach, not as much time as Cam would have liked. Their preparations were rushed. He hoped they'd be enough. He'd raided the offices while his teammates prepped, looking for phones, computers, and information. There were computers, but they were password protected, and hacking into sophisticated systems was something for ridiculous spy fiction, not real life. He searched for written records instead. There were a few handwritten notes. He cursed the doctors' penmanship, but he was able to make out most of their observations. Much of it meant nothing to him, but there were enough tidbits to piece together some answers.

At the sound of the chopper, Cam joined Wally at a window overlooking the landing zone.

"If they're carrying passengers, you can be sure they know we're here."

The helicopter circled lazily. They were scanning the grounds. Cam was glad he hadn't posted Wally on the roof.

"If they come out with guns, shoot them," Cam said.

Siena arrived and squatted beside them, her foot tapping rapidly. "Donnie is in place at the front door. I'll handle the rear entry as soon as we see what we're dealing with."

"It's not good," Wally said. "Full boat. With rifles."

"Can you handle them?"

"Sure. Why not? We took this place." He flipped off the safety of the AR-15.

Cam could see in the windows now. They were lined with grim faces. Siena bit her lip, which made her look more like a little girl than Cam had seen before. *She's scared,* he realized. Her breath whistled through her teeth as the chopper hovered close to the ground.

She scolded Wally. "You think beating up a few soft doctors proves anything? It looks like they've sent an entire army."

"Wally's enhanced," Cam said. He patted his sniper teammate on the back to lend support. "It's a good test. A clinical study, if you like. This is what you were designed for, right man?"

"Right-o."

As the helicopter skids bumped the ground Siena flashed him an ambiguous look and took a deep breath. Then she touched Cam on the shoulder and darted off. Cam watched her go. She leaped down the stairs, taking them three and four at a time. She was gone too suddenly for his liking, and, considering the manpower and hardware descending upon them, Cam wondered if he would ever see her again.

He stayed with Wally, where he could see the entire field. The window was cracked open, not unusual in the Amazonian heat, but Wally kept his rifle and head down. He didn't want to attract their attention at the outset. They'd be watching the doors initially. Donnie and Siena would make certain of that.

Pilot was flying the bird. Cam could see his glasses and headphones. When he set it down, the doors jerked open, and men poured out. Things happened so fast that it was difficult to tell whether they were company men or hired mercenaries. Either way, they were equipped to kill; AR-15s for the lot of them, along with Kevlar and helmets. Two ran for the building, one each circled left and right, and the final two dropped to the ground to prone out and cover the others.

The wait was excruciating. Wally knelt with the rifle, not yet poking it out. Then Cam heard a door open and close. *Donnie*, he thought. Just enough to get their attention. Their heads all turned toward the front of the building at once.

And Wally shot them.

The runners were first. He took them in their feet. *Whap-whap.* They each took one more step and then crumpled to the ground like action figures dropped by their child owner. Wally tilted the barrel and put one each through the four shoulders of the prone men. Because they were already on the ground, it was hard to even tell that they'd been hit. The men on the wings sensed something amiss. One stopped in his tracks. That's when Siena threw open the back door. Both whirled and pointed their weapons, exposing their sides, and Wally put bullets in their hips, just below their Kevlar vests.

Wally never hesitated or adjusted his sights. He simply moved the barrel of the gun from man to man, squeezing one or two rounds per target as he went, disposing of them in quick succession. When he had finished, he returned to each man and put another bullet in his functioning extremities, until none had use of his arms or legs. Then he pulled the rifle inside, whistling a happy tune.

Cam didn't laugh. He felt sick. Six men lay writhing, and it had taken less than ten seconds. He stared at Wally. If they were looking for enhanced soldiers, the experiment was clearly a success.

"What?" Wally said.

"Good job," Cam said. He could think of nothing else to say.

"One more coming out!" It was Siena's voice.

Cam and Wally peeked out the window, careful not to linger in case the next man had pinpointed the origin of the gunfire. But he wasn't packing. He strode from the helicopter, walking without haste directly toward the facility. He was built like a weight lifter, but moved like a panther, his broad shoulders relaxed. He carried no gun, but wore a knife at his belt.

"Ward," Wally breathed.

"What the hell is he doing?" Cam said.

"Should I shoot him?"

"No." Cam said it instinctively. He was still horrified by the carnage Wally had left lying around the field. And he knew Ward, which made it difficult to give the order to shoot. It had been so much easier with men they didn't know. *Another reason they used numbers to identify us*, he thought. Dr. Singh had said names weren't important. *Because names humanize the subjects and make it harder for the staff to kill them.*

"What do we do with him?" Wally asked.

Cam glanced at the helicopter. Pilot still wasn't taking off, but he'd maneuvered the chopper's tail toward them so that Wally had no clear shot at him. Ward was holding up the universal sign for parlay.

"Let him come," Cam said.

Ward stopped twenty yards from the window and looked up, close enough that there was no chance he could get away or attack without being shot. Cam noted that Ward had figured out where the shots were coming from, while the others hadn't.

"Who's in there?" the team's personal trainer called out.

Cam's plan didn't require that he lie to Ward. He kept out of the sight line, in case there were men in the woods, and he talked through the open window.

"It's Cam."

"Cam, are you in charge in there, or just a spokesperson?"

"It's pretty much all on me at this point," Cam said. "So, what can I help you with?"

Ward laughed. It was almost as disturbing as Wally's inappropriate mirth in awkward situations. "How many of you are left?"

"Lots."

"No. Not a lot. I know that. Five, maybe four. Is that Wally up there with you?"

Wally whispered to Cam, "How'd he know?"

"You're the monkey shooter, remember? Most accurate on the team, if I recall."

"Oh yeah." Wally brightened like a boy whose parent had just told him he was the best actor in the school play.

Ward waved. "Let's chat, Cam. This is getting out of control."

"No kidding. But it's a bit late to talk, I'd say."

"It's never too late to talk. Talking is your most powerful tool, and usually the first option, remember?"

"I remember. But all of the lies have seriously dampened my faith in your catchphrases and buzzwords."

"I have not been dishonest with you, Cam. I'm just your trainer, and I trained you to the best of my ability. Anything I said, you can rely on."

"Why should we believe you?"

Ward glanced over his shoulder at the helicopter. The blades were still spinning in case Pilot had to make a hasty exit. It was loud enough that, when he spoke, only Wally and Cam could hear him.

"Because I was a TS-1."

Wally's orange eyebrows leaped into dual arches. He looked at Cam, but Cam didn't have a response. He was just as shocked. *Another lie?* He didn't think so.

"Any chance you'll come down here and talk to me?" Ward called up.

"No," Cam replied. "You come in here."

"I was afraid you'd say that." Ward frowned. He took his knife from his belt and dropped it on the ground. "All right. Here I come. Hold your fire."

Wally turned to Cam and whispered. "Should I hold my fire?"

"Not necessarily."

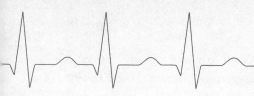

41. INCONTINENTAL 🔊

by The Steam Punks

42. WE'RE ALONE TOGETHER

by The Flat Earth Society

"I been to Paraguay, Uruguay, far away.
Doesn't matter anyway. Incontinental!"

Donnie let Ward in through the front door, and Wally greeted him in the hallway with the muzzle of the AR-15. They brought him to Cam in the gli club with his hands bound in front of him.

"Siena!" Ward looked genuinely surprised when he saw her. "You've survived all this time. Wow. I'm proud of you."

"Hello, Ward," she said evenly.

"Where shall we start, Cam?" he said, plopping down in a huge easy chair.

Donnie, Siena, Wally, and Cam stood in a semicircle around him. A small security monitor sat on the Ping-Pong table nearby, its screen quartered like a comic book page with views of the front and back doors, the field to the south, and the forest to the north.

"Tell us about TS-1," Cam said.

Ward kicked one leg over his other knee, settling comfortably into the chair as though about to recite "'Twas the Night Before Christmas" to his grandkids.

"Well, I didn't die, clearly. My teammates went quickly. Three months. There were only five of us back then. There were urinary tract problems, the headaches, and the most horrible acne. It was a cluster from the word 'go.' But one guy got stronger, a lot stronger. That was enough. I was the baseline, like you, but they gave me placebos.

"When my last teammate began to die, I figured I wasn't going home either. But I didn't want to kick the bucket any more than you, and they were going to continue the program with or without me. They came for me, and I couldn't fight them, so I decided to find some good in it all. I'd noticed something wrong with their methods—my fellow recruits and I had no purpose. It wasn't enough for us to sit around in a lab playing Ping-Pong and getting our vertical leaps measured. We had no goals. We were bored. We underachieved. We atrophied. I told them my theory. I convinced them that real-life situations were the ultimate testing ground. Then I volunteered to design the program for them. I would give them real performance measures. And I would make sure that every recruit was given an incredible experience, something significant in exchange for their life."

"Ari's yacht," Cam said.

"And Wally's hang glider. Tegan's scuba diving."

Cam was surprised. He hadn't guessed that one. "The soccer match was for me," he said.

"In part."

"You gave us bucket list things because your employers were killing us," Siena muttered.

Ward wrinkled his nose at the characterization. "Things you might not have had the resources or opportunity to *ever* do on your own. Oddly, though, the most common dream was to do something good for the world. So I proposed missions using three criteria: (I) to do something good for mankind; (2) to satisfy one or more recruit's wish; and (3) to advance the cause of the organization. You truly did great things. Your session almost didn't get going because our idiot doctors got themselves kidnapped. But we worked that right into the program, and you fixed it! Everyone was very impressed, by the way. Then you ensured that a corrupt, unpredictable man would never hold a high position in this country's government. Frankly, you're the best class since TS-5 saved an entire nation from civil war."

"Whoa," Wally exclaimed. "An entire nation?"

"Small country. Long story."

Donnie watched the monitor. The helicopter was still in the field, but it was possible Pilot had radioed out. "If you're trying to delay us while more soldiers come, we will not hesitate to kill you," he warned Ward.

"I know. But I can assure you nobody is coming. I shouldn't be telling you this, but we're fresh out of men. Pilot will have to fly out to regroup. It's not as easy as you might think to find reliable employees willing to risk their life. Risk their life, maybe. Reliable, maybe. But both together is tough."

"We killed people," Cam said. He knew he should have been furious, but he was unable to rid his voice of guilt. *Guess there's still some of that nice guy in here*, he thought.

"It doesn't matter," Ward said. "They like the program. You're the stars of their research. But if I can't fix this issue, they'll go back to a contained experiment. No beach houses for the next group. No bucket lists."

"Who are 'they'?" Cam asked suddenly.

"Stockholders. Managers. Foreign investors. A small council monitors this program through several layers of anonymity. I don't know them. They don't even know each other."

"Names aren't important," Cam said to himself. "You don't care about us. Only the TS matters."

"I don't give a flying fig about the TS! Don't you understand?

I'm the one person who does care about you!" Ward's lip quivered, his expression somewhere between angry and hurt.

He is a Boy Scout, Cam thought, convinced more by the fact that Ward didn't swear than anything he'd said.

Cam changed the subject. "How much do you think this facility is worth to them?"

"I don't know. The research alone is worth millions."

"Not if we burn it down," Cam said. He turned to his teammates. "Okay folks, this'll be our third mission, the last good thing we do before we graduate. Let's finish what we started here."

Donnie didn't move to join him. "I have one more thing I need to do."

"What's that?" Cam asked.

"I'm going to go 'talk' to the guy in the helicopter."

"Why?"

"Because he shot Owen."

Siena nodded. "Pilot won't wait for Ward forever. And we can't let him fly out and regroup."

Cam thought for a moment. "Ward, we're gonna need your shirt and pants."

They stripped Ward and tied him to the pool table. Donnie looked up as he pulled on Ward's clothes. Cam saw pain in his face, physical pain against which he was waging a mighty battle. Donnie was getting the headaches, Cam realized, the bad ones.

But Donnie refused to show weakness. He gritted his teeth against it. "I hope you'll forgive me for being a little intense at times," he said, struggling for words. "It's just . . . it's how I perform best." He extended his strong hand, and Cam grasped it tightly.

"I'm just glad you're on my team," Cam said.

It was enough.

"Wally, you with us?"

Wally laughed. "Dude, I love to fly."

Cam slouched as Donnie walked him out into the field. The chopper was still turned away in case of gunfire. Donnie marched Cam and Wally ahead of him, prisoner style, keeping his own face concealed behind Wally's red head. With his build and Ward's clothes, Donnie looked just like their personal trainer. Halfway across the field, he even gave one of Ward's hand signals. The chopper blades still rotated so that the bird was ready to lift off, but the trio was able to approach within fifty yards before Pilot realized it wasn't Ward and fired up the engines.

They broke and ran across the uneven ground. Donnie and Wally were amazingly fast, but running was one thing Cam could do just as well, and he flew with them, unenhanced, through the grass, past the wounded or dying mercenaries. Perhaps one day everyone would be enhanced, Cam thought. Then he wouldn't be fast anymore. But he also wondered what the point of having enhanced athletes or soldiers would be if their opponents were enhanced too.

Pilot wasn't enhanced. He hadn't recognized Donnie soon enough, and he didn't react quickly enough. Wally and Donnie leaped onto the chopper's skids before he was clear. Cam thought he could hear Wally howling maniacally, or it might have just been the whine of the engine. Cam jumped too. And he fell short.

"No!" But his voice was lost in the thumping of the blades.

He stood quickly. It was too late. The helicopter rose beyond his reach. It struggled with the weight of the two boys hanging on one side, but Pilot began to level it.

Cam stood and pulled out a length of chain with a heavy padlock tied to each end. A crude bolo, the same weapon with which Zara had taken him down his first day. Three quick swings, and he let it loose, throwing it as high as he could. It struck the rotors atop the cabin and disappeared into their invisible circle, whipping around and around with the blades, its padlocks hammering the cabin with a machine gun cadence.

Up went the chopper, climbing into the sky. Donnie stood on the left skid and kicked out the window, while Wally wrenched the door from its hinges and Cam's chains beat the rotors to hell. They continued to rise until the only thing Cam could see was the trajectory of the fading chopper as it banked in a lazy arc and descended into the jungle canopy. The sound of the impact was distant, a muffled *whump* not unlike the bullet of an AR-15 hitting the loam of the forest floor. If there was a fireball, he didn't see it. Didn't want to.

Cam squeezed his eyes shut. Moments later, he felt a hand on his back. *Siena.*

"Can I hold you?" she whispered in his ear.

"Yes."

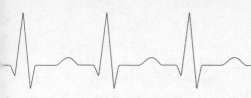

42. WE'RE ALONE TOGETHER 🔊

by The Flat Earth Society

"No such thing as alone when I think of you."

Cam and Siena worked their way down the steep hill to the ocean-front clearing a few miles southeast of the TS-9 compound. Trees had been cleared in a circle fifty yards inland to create a helicopter landing zone, and a small bunkhouse was hidden in the foliage nearby. The Zodiac was pulled up onto the shore and hidden in brush as well. *Our ticket to civilization.* There was no beach. The forest spilled directly into the water, eroding heavily, its green trees doing battle with the blue sea, and losing.

Two hours earlier, Dr. Singh's assistant technician had furnished them with the location the landing site. Not at first, but Singh's death had convinced him. Cam hadn't needed to ask or even participate—he'd simply walked out of the room and left his unsmiling doctor with Donnie. When he'd returned, Singh was gone, and his helper was more cooperative.

The techie was good for more than just directions. Hacking computer passwords might have been something people only did in the movies, but getting someone to cough one up was entirely possible, and the panicked man had given it up so fast that Siena hadn't even had time to threaten him.

With the help of a printer with a scanner, Ari's diary was quickly turned into a computer file. Cam omitted the pages with Jules's personal details. There was no general access to the Internet, but there was an e-mail function of sorts, and Cam knew his friend Mason's address.

Their message included the diary, doctor's notes, incriminating protocols, and instructions to Mason to forward the information anonymously to the USDA and every other drug regulation agency and media outlet he and Siena could think of. Cam had no way to know if they would take it seriously, but Siena convinced him it was worth a try. Multiple watchdog organizations were to receive copies too, along with the governments of Suriname and Brazil, who could find the facility within a few hours, long before the organization could arrive and scrub the site. The e-mail was sent with photos they took on a camera they found in storage. Cam included one of himself so Mason would know it was all legit. He signed the message simply: "Deathwing."

The tech doc was a good talker. He would spill everything when the government arrived. They left him alive. Singh and the other doc, Siena's killer, had been a tougher call, and Cam had agonized over it. But Donnie had saved him the moral dilemma. "I knew you couldn't do it, pal," he'd said after it was done. "And I know you don't approve. But just think of it this way: they're killing a lot of people. With them gone, we're a lot of lives in the plus column."

And Ward . . . Cam still wasn't sure whether he was good, bad, or somewhere in between. They gave him the benefit of the doubt and left him for the authorities to sort out. He'd have some explaining to do, Cam thought. *The picture of him and the tech sitting in front of row after row of open drawers with teenage bodies is going to require all of his communication skills.*

They left Ward locked in Cam's drawer, and the assistant in Siena's. Cam worried that they might get claustrophobic, but not for very long.

As they readied the Zodiac for their trip along the coast to find the nearest village or town, Cam took inventory of their packs. He still had his headphones and player, and Siena still had the diamonds. The jewels would serve them well when they reached civilization. Siena had been right about that too.

He looked up to find her staring at him. He clicked the PLAY button, and "We're Alone Together" drifted up faintly from the earbuds in his hand.

"Are you still having headaches?" he asked her.

"Not so much anymore."

"Now that you're off of it, maybe you'll survive."

"Cross fingers." She paused, thoughtful. "I'm going to miss it, though. The enhancement I mean."

"You don't need it. I like you normal."

She smiled.

But Cam frowned. "I've always been just some normal guy. I never got to be special."

"True," Siena said, nodding. "You're just some nice, normal guy who fought his way through the Amazon jungle and saved me from a murderous international corporation, unenhanced."

Cam laughed.

"And you kissed a dead girl," Siena added.

"Why on earth would you bring that up right now?"

"Because I'm alive. . . ."

Cam smiled. He slid one earbud into her ear and one into his own, and then they kissed. A lot.

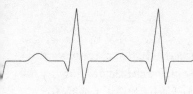

EPILOGUE

The Western Washington University campus looked just the way Cam had left it—green and dripping from rain, with students scurrying past on their way to calculus, the gym, and the student union building. He stared out from beneath his hoodie. A month of facial hair obscured his jawline, and even kids he knew walked past without giving him a second glance. They laughed and chattered about their futures as though he had never existed at all. *The world just went on without me.*

Mason's dorm sat at the far south end of campus.

Cam had thought, had hoped, there would be stories about the organization in the news. Big stories. A huge pharmaceutical corporation crashing down as a result of his e-mails to Mason containing the details of the TS operation. There weren't. Clearly, his friend had thought it was a hoax and hadn't sent them on.

But he would remedy that. Cam grinned. His appearance was going to be quite a surprise to Mason. He had debated visiting his family first, but their shock would be greater, and he wasn't ready for the emotional turmoil. His childhood friend was a good test run.

The benefit of a quiet dorm was that it was quiet. When Cam stepped into the Buchanan Towers lobby he saw only a boy in sunglasses and a girl with a book in her face, and they looked away as quickly as he did. *Serious academic types*, Cam thought.

Cam took the elevator to the fifth floor and knocked at Mason's room. No answer. He didn't hesitate; the technique Ward had taught him to force a door had him inside in less than a minute.

The room was classic Mason—spotless, organized, practically symmetrical—with one notable exception: the Stratego board was sitting out with only four pieces on it. Cam looked closer. The blue Spy and blue Scout stood together in the lake at the center of the field. Two red Bomb pieces sat in the far corner squares. And when Cam tried to move the Spy, he found it was glued to the board. All the pieces were. It was odd, but then Cam's game-loving buddy was an odd guy.

It was no use. Mason was out. Cam slid from the room and closed the door. When he turned, a girl was standing at her door across the hall staring at him.

"Have you seen Mason?" he said quickly.

"No."

"Okay." Cam started to walk off.

"Not for like a week," she added.

Cam stopped. "What?"

"Yeah, he kinda disappeared. Must have gone home or something."

"In the middle of the term?"

She shrugged and closed her door. Cam spun, suddenly alert. He eyed the elevator, then ducked back into Mason's room. Mason's wrinkled shirts hung on a three-foot-long wooden dowel in the closet. He dumped them, removed the dowel, and ran for the stairs.

Cam descended rapidly, checking over the rail at each landing, and when he reached the second floor, he climbed through a window and dropped to the ground outside.

The ridiculous sunglasses should have been a dead giveaway. No college student in rainy Bellingham would wear sunglasses during fall term. Cam circled the building, returning to the front entrance, where he peeked inside. Sunglasses boy was gone. *Probably up the elevator.* The girl who'd been hiding behind the book was still there, but she was watching the stairwell intently, not the front door. Cam eased it open and snuck up behind her.

The dowel made a loud *crack* when it hit the side of her head, and she went down hard. Cam didn't make the same mistake Donnie had made with him on the beach his first day. He was on her instantly, the wood pressed against her larynx, keeping her quiet.

"You know who I am?"

"Yeth," she hissed.

"Then you know how dangerous I am." He pressed the dowel against her throat hard, until her eyes bulged, then he let up. She didn't have to answer. He could see that she got the point. "Funny how every minute becomes more precious when you only have a finite number of them left. You still don't want to go early. Now I'm going to let you talk, but if you scream or lie you're done. Are you the only one here?" he said, baiting her.

"Two"—she gasped—"of us."

Cam nodded. She'd passed the first test; she wasn't lying. "Where's my friend?"

"We don't know."

Cam pressed on the dowel."

"We don't know!" She wheezed with an accent he couldn't place.

"Where are you from?"

"Sydney."

Cam recoiled, surprised, releasing the pressure on her throat. "Australia?"

"You think your site was the only one?"

Cam's head spun. She was a recruit. He'd realized that. She'd been sent to find a defector the way his own team had hunted Siena. He'd realized that too. *But she's from an entirely separate operation.*

Cam almost didn't blame her. She was clearly new, not yet well trained, and had been dropped into a foreign country for her first mission. *I'm her first mission.* There would be eight more. Some of them would be looking for Mason. *And Siena,* Cam realized. Others might be visiting Jules's sister.

He heard chatter outside. Someone was coming. Students. Cam wrangled the girl into a nearby broom closet and broke off the door handle.

God bless Mason, Cam thought. His brilliant friend had sensed trouble and fled, but he'd left Cam a clue from their childhood. Stratego. He'd put the pieces in the wrong places, something only Cam would understand. Cam was the blue Spy, clearly. Mason was the blue Scout—he'd been a Boy Scout in middle school. Besides, the Scout was the vulnerable piece in Stratego, and it could run. The red Bomb pieces were the two recruits waiting in the lobby. The other player. *The enemy.*

He walked out of the Buchanan Towers dormitory as three students walked in. When the girl in the closet heard them, she started screaming, "Assault!"

And he fled.

The enormity of it all began to sink in as he hurried across the Western Washington University soccer field. The company was here. The company was in South America. The company was in Australia. *They're everywhere.*

He felt stupid and horrible for getting Mason involved. If the Stratego board was correct, Mason would be on the lake cowering in an empty cabin at the scout camp, which was closed off-season. Cam would find him there, then go after Siena.

We'll run, he thought.

Cam was a good runner, and he had a feeling he might be running for the rest of his life.

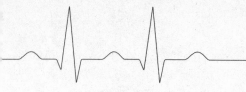

ACKNOWLEDGMENTS

I'd like to thank my editor, Brendan Deneen, for working with me on this project. Here's to the first of several. May it sell, entertain, inspire, and sit proudly on our shelves, generally in that order. And my best to Mike Kuciak for making the introduction.